Red Stag

Red Stag

A Novel

GUY DE LA VALDÈNE

LYONS PRESS
Guilford, Connecticut
An imprint of Globe Pequot Press

THERE ARE TOO MANY PEOPLE TO THANK IN THE MAKING OF THIS BOOK SO I SHALL ONLY NAME THREE: COLLEEN DALY, COLLEEN DALY, COLLEEN DALY

First Lyons Press paperback edition 2011

Lyons Press is an imprint of Globe Pequot Press.

Library of Congress Cataloging-in-Publication Data

De la ValdËne, Guy.
Red stag : a novel / Guy de la Valdène. — 1st Lyons Press paperback ed.
p. cm.
ISBN 978-1-59228-627-0
1. Young men—Fiction. 2. Administration of estates—Fiction.
3. Illegitimate children—Fiction. 4. Deer hunting—Fiction.
5. Normandy (France)—Fiction. I. Title.
PS3604.E1287R43 2011
813'.6—dc22

2010050811

Printed in the United States of America

10 9 8 7 6 5 4 3 2 1

THERESE,

FOREVER

I sit here
On the perfect end
Of a star

watching light
pour itself towards
        me.

The light pours
Itself through
A small hole
In the sky.

I am not very happy,
But I can see
How things are
        faraway.

"Star Hole," Richard Brautigan

Prologue

The first time I set eyes on Vincent I was standing in the snow next to my father, trembling under the authority of a loaded shotgun. I remember that it had been a perfect night for poaching, January cold and windless. A full moon had whitewashed the thin layer of fog that lingered above the feeder creeks. Above, the sky was clear; below, the ground hard. Deer had moved down from the forest to glean the wheat fields on Count Robert de Costebelle's estate. Buyers in Paris waited in the wings, ready to pay cash for a carcass in good condition.

I recall my father cursing and I remember wanting to hit him for being so old and hardheaded and most of all for getting us caught. A small gnarly terrier scurried between my feet, uprooting pockets of snow in a fit of agitation. Vincent stood next to his uncle, Serge Lebuison, gamekeeper of Merlecourt. The year was 1958. I was eighteen years old.

My name is Jean-Christophe Artaban—Ragondin for short. I am a retired poacher living in a small village in the Pyrénées. For centuries, within certain social circles, the precise taking of illegal game was considered an art, but to the landowners of the region I was born to, the occupation that shaped my life was deemed dishonorable. As a boy, long before Vincent and I became friends, instead of shooting marbles or playing foosball with my classmates, I escaped to nearby rivers and learned the skills required to trap nutria, spear carp, and tickle trout, just like my father and his father before him. Decreed by the blood of my forebears, poaching was my destiny.

I learned the imperative particulars of patience and stealth at a young age, and, since my teeth were long and yellow, my father nicknamed me Ragondin: the water rat, a wily creature, brown and slick with oversized dentures and a pelt that was once worth something. I wished he had nicknamed me Wolf or Hawk, but he didn't, and I have been known as Ragondin ever since.

My father was a fervent Communist who had coveted the game on Count Robert de Costebelle's land for forty years. He believed that nature's crop was not the perquisite of the rich but belonged to the people, particularly to those in need. A few days before I met Vincent, my father uncovered evidence of deer feeding on winter wheat in a field next to the woods adjoining the castle. He made plans to ambush them, and at dusk the next day we set out—my father, his two brothers, and me. Together we waited for darkness, in my uncle's Simca station wagon, eating cheese, smoking, and drinking red wine straight from the bottle. When it was dark and time to hunt, one of my uncles passed around a bottle of Calvados. I remember tilting my head back and feeling the familiar heat of fermented apples rush down my throat and settle in my stomach.

That night, instead of stalking the herd on foot as we usually did, my father, who was drunk, chose to chase the deer at high speed behind the car lights while his eldest brother held a gun out the window. All we managed to do was relocate hectares of snow and urge the herd into a frenzied retreat. The next day, in a foul mood and fighting a hangover, my father insisted we try again. This time the car was filled with unease and cigarette smoke but no wine or brandy. What we didn't know was that Étienne Verdier, the count's farmer, had called the gamekeeper and reported the previous night's disturbance.

At dusk, Serge Lebuison, faithfully followed by his nephew Vincent, and Jules, their small wirehaired terrier, had staked out the corner of the woodlot that offered the best view over the wheat field. A man with an unpredictable temper, Serge carried a twelve-gauge shotgun loaded with buckshot on a sling over his shoulder. It was common knowledge that once hidden the gamekeeper would not move, regardless of how cold and uncomfortable he grew to be, and except for the small cloud of breath that rose from his lips he resembled a burr on the bark of the tree that hid him.

The hinds stepped into the field first, tentative and feminine under a pale moon rising. The stag, a big-bodied animal with an uneven rack, emerged from the woods a few minutes later, and walked stiff legged to the does. Silhouetted against the landscape the buck stood listening, ready to bolt, watching his hinds glide quietly over the snow. My uncles remained in the car while my father and I approached on foot from the far side of the woods. We were not expecting trouble. The snow sifted down through the branches and fell on our shoulders. Yielding to our weight, it packed comfortably under our feet. My father, a big man in poor health from a life of excess, plodded along, wheezing. He used his shotgun to push snow-burdened limbs out of his way. I followed, furious because of the noise he was making. A wood pigeon scrambled out of a tree in a clatter of wings just as we reached the edge of the woodlot. I caught a glimpse of the stag a long way out of shotgun range. Sensing our presence, it raised its head. The hinds, closer to us, stood their ground, ears cupped, tails twitching. My father signaled me with his free hand not to move and, in a crouch with his gun at the ready, eased his big body toward the herd. The stag angled swiftly toward the tree line.

Just then the beam of a flashlight found us and we heard the gamekeeper yell to stop what we were doing and to drop the shotgun. His words ricocheted through the woods. Father cursed, Jules barked, and I felt my heart jump into my throat. My father hesitated a moment before he released his hold on the gun. Serge walked out from behind a pine tree, flashlight and shotgun steady in each hand. Jules ran in tight circles, barking, a rake of hackles stiff up his back. Vincent stumbled over a branch, righted himself, and stood looking awkward, cold, and fifteen years old.

The sweat on my father's cheeks had turned to frost. His eyes were hidden under thick white eyebrows and the jagged scar that split the left side of his forehead had turned purple. Serge let out a snort. "Jérôme Artaban," he said in a tone of derision. The gamekeeper then trained his flashlight on me. "Your father's an imbecile, the first rule in your line of work is not to get caught. Everything else is secondary."

Back in those days I looked younger than my age and was rachitic from a battle with tuberculosis. I stood bent over with hunched shoulders, as if someone had pushed a hand into the middle of my chest. Vincent picked up the shotgun and stared down, bewildered, at my snot-rimmed nose.

I had heard about the German bastard living at the castle but didn't expect him to be so young, nor so vulnerable. It was too dark to see his eyes, which I had been told were different from anyone else's in the village. But I could tell that, unlike me, his face was thin, almost delicate, and his cap hid a head of curly brown hair.

Serge asked about our accomplices. When he didn't get an answer he told his nephew to shoot in the air. Vincent looked puzzled and self-conscious. He stared at the gun in his hands and then at Jules, the terrier, for help.

"It'll bring the others," Serge said.

The shotgun was a single-barrel, sixteen-gauge, that had been custom built to break in two at the breach and fit inside a pair of trousers. It was a gun built for use in close quarters. The shell inside the barrel was filled with buckshot. Vincent shouldered the stock and pulled the trigger. The noise echoed through the woods sending a dozen birds rushing out of the canopy of trees. Cold, shocking night air slipped inside my shirt. When the sound of wings quieted Serge ordered us on the ground with our hands behind our necks. He rested the muzzle of his shotgun on my father's backside and turned off the flashlight.

"Don't even fart," he said.

To this day, I've never met a tougher gamekeeper than Serge Lebuison. His temper hovered millimeters from madness. That night, I suspect, he took pleasure in tormenting my father by having him lie face down in the snow. Serge hated poachers.

I heard the engine first and turning my head toward the sound, caught a glimpse of headlights. The Simca skirted the woods and angled toward us, the lights bouncing erratically over the field. Serge signaled our position with his flashlight and then turned it off. I chose that instant to jump to my feet and run.

Serge must have told Vincent to chase after me because almost immediately I sensed him behind me in the underbrush. A coiled spring unwound in my legs and I ran as fast as I ever had, zigzagging through the trees with my hands held in front of my face, praying that I would stay on my feet.

When the sound of a shotgun rang out sudden and loud I stopped and looked back, shivering, unsure what to do. Moonlight fell through the branches and glanced off the falling snow. A car engine raced and then rattled to a stall. I wanted to run but fear and silence immobilized me. A dog barked in the distant courtyard of the Verdier farm.

Serge's voice was loud, even though by then I had

put a hundred meters between us. He was shouting at my father and uncles.

Vincent had also halted at the sound of the gun. I knew I should wait for him to move first but I jumped in a panic and took off running. Dread pushed me from one tree to the next and I could not shake it even though I knew, from having chased game myself, that my terror was palpable, that it had an odor, that it made Vincent feel stronger than he was, invincible. When his long legs caught up with mine it felt as if he were stepping in each one of my footprints, making the chase last longer than necessary. Then I felt his hand on my collar and he yanked me to the ground, where I lay on my back, choking. Vincent Lebuison stood over me and when I looked up he kicked me in the stomach. I wrapped my arms around my face and brought my knees up to my chin.

"I didn't mean that," he said, reaching a hand down to me. But I didn't trust him and pulled away, guarding my head with my forearms. I begged him to let me go. My body shook with cold and the apprehension of going to prison. I could see my wrists poking out of the sleeves of my jacket. Vincent looked over his shoulder as if he expected to see Serge and said he didn't have a choice, that he had to take me in.

I told him that my father and I would go to jail. That there would be no one left to tend to my mother. This was a lie, since she had run off when I was six years old to join a carnival where she learned to swallow swords and other such implements for a living.

Vincent shook his head. He leaned over, picked up a dead branch and threw it at me. I couldn't stop my lips from trembling. "I'm taking you to Serge," he said in a loud angry voice. He stepped closer.

I shielded myself against the expected blow. When it didn't come I looked up through the crook of my elbow. "My mother will starve," I begged.

Vincent almost kicked me again, not because he wanted to but because it was expected of him. I recognized the weakness and struggled to my feet. "You owe me, Artaban!" I heard him shout as I disappeared into the darkness. The tone of his voice was tinged with loathing at his own compassion.

I ran into Vincent Lebuison at the bistro in the village later that spring. He was sitting at the zinc-covered bar drinking beer and lemonade and seemed pleased to see me. He waved me over and shook my hand. As I sat on the stool next to his he told me that the moment they arrived home that night, his uncle had pushed him up against the front door and told him he had been conned, that I was eighteen years old and had received a three-month suspended sentence the year before for poaching, that the next time I was apprehended I was going to jail.

I ordered a brandy and paid for Vincent's drink. My father and uncles had spent a month behind bars and the week after being released my father was stopped for drunk driving. The police discovered a dead doe in the trunk of his car. It had been there since the night of the day after he'd been released from jail.

"He died in prison of a heart attack a few weeks later," I said, swallowing my drink. Vincent lowered his head and said he was sorry.

"Don't be," I laughed. "Every Monday morning since I was ten years old he'd smack me across the face like the Arabs do to their wives before leaving on a trip. 'That's in case you're thinking about misbehaving while I'm gone,' he'd say, and then go about his business."

From that day on I made every effort to repay Vincent for letting me escape. I loaned him copies of my books and nude magazines, bought him drinks, and repeated stories my father had bragged to me of poaching and fishing the various estates in the valley. We started seeing more of each other and after I swore I would never trespass again on the Count's estate Vincent invited me to his home, the old paper mill, when Serge wasn't there.

Vincent never made me feel guilty for the trouble he got into for letting me go, and I never brought up his lineage. I realize now how unfit we both were for the world that surrounded us and how we had unconsciously substituted the animals of the forests and the fishes in the rivers for our families. Each of us came to recognize that particular form of loneliness in the other. Serge must also have sensed something because other than grumbling that I was a bad influence he never stopped us from seeing each other. In time we became inseparable friends.

On the first night of the millennium, remnants of the tremendous blizzard that tore through northern France the day after Christmas claimed the Pyrénées and tumbled down the mountainsides, chilling the village in which I live. The wind that followed was thin and bitter—nothing like the full-bodied storms of my native region—and for the first time since I retired here a year ago I wanted a dog at the end of the bed to warm my feet.

I packed a sandwich in the pocket of my hunting jacket the next morning and followed a game trail a thousand meters up the steep slope behind my house until I reached the meadow that saddles the snow-capped peaks closest to the village. There I witnessed a spectacle long since disappeared in Normandy: a pair of golden eagles soaring, long wings cupping and releasing the wind, yellow talons tangling in midair like old men shaking hands. Icy clouds sailed past the raptors in shreds. I smoked and watched and flapped my arms and closed my eyes. All my life I've wanted to fly and for an hour that morning I was the monarch of the sky. When I looked through the binoculars Vincent had given me for Christmas I saw sheep in the valley, sunlight fanning across the mountain slopes, and the silhouettes of eagles dancing.

In the mountains, the angle of the sun rising and falling is abrupt and unforgiving. Soon there were shadows on my shadow, and the wind, in its endless quest for resolution, blew keenly down the passes. There was snow in the forecast. When I reached the bottom of the mountain I was cold and my bones felt brittle. But, rather than dwelling on my physical shortcomings I applied the inevitability of age to a growing number of excuses for stopping at the village bistro. Before I went home, Michel, the bartender, made a provincial remark about the cloud cover and permanent drizzle of my beloved Normandy: "The chamber pot of France," he declared it.

I live in a one-bedroom house on the outskirts of a small village in the heart of the eastern Pyrénées, thirty kilometers from the Spanish border. In the summer the slopes of the Pic du Canigou are coated in flowering heather. Patches of creeping azaleas mingle with wild rhododendrons and bearberries. The emerald-colored pastures in front of my house are laced with blue gentians, and the perfume of the Mediterranean Sea soars from Perpignan, exciting the village girls who secretly meet on warm nights in the meadows and dance in their nightgowns with their hands in the air.

Last winter, before I was completely reconciled with the idea of retirement, I dug a pit across a game trail leading to the Gorges de la Fou and covered it with pine branches. The next night it snowed and a male izard, or Pyrenean chamois, fell in and broke its front legs. I marinated the meat in red wine and then cooked it for an entire day as I was used to doing with the wild boars of Normandy. But though I had separated the sheep from its nuts, I couldn't cook the rut out of its meat.

Today, I regret leaving the rich lands of my youth and entertain the thought of going home. I think of soft gray clouds, curtains of rain, and Calvados brandy. My mouth waters for yellow butter and soft cheeses that feel like a woman's lips. In the mountains the cheese is hard like the bones of the goat that provides it.

Maria de Maillol, the widow who comes once a week to clean my modest house, knocks and then enters. She removes her wooden *sabots* at the door and slips her feet into a pair of sneakers without laces. In her youth Maria was a flamenco dancer. Now, the handsome angles of her aging face challenge those of the mountains we live in. Maria and I are lovers.

She wants to know why I am not outside, but am instead sitting inside an armchair with a blanket around my shoulders. "Small men like you don't get sick," she says. "It's the big ones like your friend who fall over and die."

I wrap an arm around her generous waist and tell her that the wind and femmes fatales like her torment me. She shakes her head and tells me to blame myself. "That's because we both have attitudes. It's your own fault. You are mystified by our strength," she exclaims and moves a long black braid of hair over her right shoulder.

She walks behind me. I can't hear her tennis shoes. She tightens the sheets on my bed and rattles things in the kitchen. Then she pauses, hoping that I will honor my promise to tell her Vincent's story. His visit, which ended the week before Christmas, had spiked her curiosity. His eyes still trouble her.

"My head is full of wind," I say instead.

She clucks, pours boiling water into a mug over fresh lemon juice and honey. "To draw out your fever," she says, adding brandy.

"I don't mind fevers," I say, recalling a time I smoked opium every day for a week with a friend who had smuggled a fistful back from Cambodia.

"Your promise, then," she said.

I close my eyes and see Vincent's face as a young man, a slender face veiled in melancholy, unkempt brown hair, and eyes colored by good and evil. It may seem odd to hold onto the memory of a few weeks plucked out of a lifetime, but in this case the unthinkable compels the mind not to forget. I am a romantic, and an aging romantic must be forgiven exaggerations. I have no qualms about replacing ambiguous details with convincing ones, but the events that turn this story need no prodding or embellishment. As the current of history blends with half a century of memories, what has endured is a tale of forbidden love, of murder and revenge, and the saga of the great red stag. I ask Maria if she would like to sit down next to me. I tell her that I will have to start Vincent's story years before I knew him. She nods and smiles and retrieves from the kitchen a platter of sliced Serrano ham, country bread, a bottle of Rioja, and two glasses. "For later," she says. "When we are hungry."

Vincent was five years old in 1949, when he and his mother moved to the castle from her family's farm on the outskirts of the village of Merlecourt. She was to be the countess's maid and Vincent a playmate to the count's two children.

Vincent held his mother's hand as they made their way across the cobblestones of the village square. She carried a brown suitcase and he a sheet filled with clothes. They passed the small grocery store, the carved oak doors that guarded the entrance to the stone church, and the bakery, where the smell of warm dough stretched across the street to greet them.

They passed through the estate's wrought-iron gates and walked along a gravel avenue lined with trees in the shadows of the heavy, green canopy. In the underbrush, the brambles grew high and opened into tunnels and caves deep enough to hide in. Vincent was startled by a man in a brown corduroy jacket hurrying away from them behind a thicket, his head tilted forward as though he were tracking something on the ground.

His mother told him not to worry, that it was only his uncle Serge. But the man Vincent had just seen seemed different, darker, more suspect than the uncle he knew.

She teased him and with her dark eyes wide told him that Serge could turn himself into a werewolf. Vincent would have bolted back to the farm they had just left had it not meant returning to the torments inflicted by his mother's older sister. The memory of his aunt hitting him on the top of the head with a metal ruler while twisting his ear until he knelt on the stone floor, and then instructing him to pray for forgiveness, frightened him more than all the werewolves in the world.

After Vincent and his mother reached the crossroads leading to the castle Marie Lebuison stopped to let her son catch his breath. At first he refused to look up because he had heard that châteaux were really dungeons where men wearing masks hung children by their thumbs. The shaded avenue, the elusive figure of his uncle, and his imagination had only reinforced those fears. He tightened his grip on his mother's hand and kept his eyes on the ground. Marie set her suitcase down and raised his stubborn chin.

Vincent expected to see turrets and pillories and purple-headed crows, but instead he was greeted by manicured lawns that unfurled like emerald carpets between rows of the most enormous oak trees imaginable. The morning sun lit a succession of sunken gardens gleaming with red and yellow flowers, topiaries, marble statues speckled with lichen, flowing fountains, and a pair of wondrous white swans floating on a distant moat.

At the end of the avenue was a stone bridge that led to a deep gravel courtyard with lawns on both sides and more trees. Two children standing on the bridge turned and waved. Roland and Nicole.

He glanced in their direction but turned back to the fairy-tale castle. To a five-year-old boy whose bedroom had been nothing more elaborate than a converted cattle stall, the château was magical—a prism of glass and stones. Narrow chimneys rose out of a black slate roof, flanked by rose-colored facades painted by sunlight. Tall wooden French doors on either side of the castle stood open and Vincent could see through them to another lawn and beyond that to fields and pastures that stretched to the river Eure.

The moment Vincent and his mother reached the bridge, Roland introduced himself and handed him a lint-coated nougat. The young master was heavy, fair-skinned, with light brown freckles and wild red hair. His shorts were torn and his shoes caked with mud. Vincent instinctively bowed his head.

The girl was thin with long auburn hair. She stepped forward and kissed him on the cheek. The day before, the Countess de Costebelle had hired Vincent's mother when she found out that the twenty-two-year-old sister of Merlecourt's gamekeeper had a son who was born on the same day, month, and year as her daughter. Nicole stared into Vincent's eyes, introduced herself and clapped her hands. Vincent had never been kissed by a girl before.

The countess greeted them in the foyer of the castle where she had been sorting through bundles of flowers wrapped in newspapers on the marble floor. Choosing those that pleased her she wove them into graceful bouquets inside bright crystal vases. She smiled as she placed a long cool finger on Vincent's cheek and welcomed him into her home. The countess who had once been a ballet dancer, had pale blond hair, hollow cheeks, and the wintry complexion of someone raised in the English mist. She spoke fluent French and collected jade figurines that matched the color of her eyes. Her fingernails were pink, like the petals of a rose.

Later that night, after Vincent and his mother moved into their quarters in the attic of the north wing of the castle, Marie Lebuison came to her son's room and listened to his prayers. When he asked her if they were living in a magical place, she whispered "Abracadabra," and kissed him goodnight.

At the door she turned and told him he should respect Roland and Nicole. He would learn from them. "They are everything we are not," she said.

Vincent's room on the fourth floor of the castle was simply furnished with a bed and a chair and a table for his homework. And although the ceiling was low and the castle's water pipes rumbled during the night, he loved it. When he was given the leftover clown print wallpaper from Nicole's room, he forgot he had ever lived on a farm.

After classes in the village he would either play with Roland or work in the castle's underground kitchen. Built below the water level of the moat, there were dark rooms for roots and tubers, the walk-in iceboxes, the pantries for grains and preserves, and a large dining room area with adjoining bathrooms for the staff. The kitchen proper, which was as big as a flatbed truck, had deep double sinks at each end, a tremendous butcher-block table and a cast-iron, wood-burning stove. In those days before the accident one meal inevitably followed the next, an abundance of food that to a farm boy raised on lard and potatoes and his grandmother's traditional Sunday chicken-in-the-pot seemed unimaginable. Vincent worked for eight years under the tutelage of Chef Gaston, a big man from Burgundy who cooked soufflés as light as air and drank four liters of red wine a day.

Seven domestics worked inside the castle: a maid on each floor, the chef and sous-chef, a laundress, and François, who served as majordomo and butler. Though some of the staff lived in the village and others in the annex to the stables, everyone ate the chef 's food. Vincent dined with Roland and Nicole twice a week and the rest of the time took his meals downstairs with his mother and the help. The underground conversations invariably centered on Robert de Costebelle, his family, politics, and the staff's sex life.

Vincent's relationship with his mother changed when they moved to the castle. On the family farm they had been mother and son, parent and child, but once settled in the castle they became independent of each other and behaved more like brother and sister. She would be petulant and coquettish one minute, morose and irritable the next. To Vincent it was all part of a complicated game that he didn't understand but never questioned because he loved her. When he was seven years old she explained to him how children were made. And when he asked if he could touch her breasts, she opened her blouse.

Chapter 1

The heavy rains that fell on Normandy in the summer of 1963 swelled the rivers of the valley and spilled into the adjoining pastures, drowning the grass and herding the cattle to higher ground where, lowing mournfully, they huddled en masse under the shadows of trees, chewing their cud and shitting down each other's legs. Deep furrows disfigured the plowed fields where the cultivators had surrendered to the weather and listed, lamentably, in the mud. When the waters finally receded, the sun scarred the earth and molded the tractor troughs into unyielding ruts that braided the dirt roads feeding the valley of Merlecourt.

In those days the Saturday night dances that took place in the villages of the department coincided with the emergence of spring lilies and continued through the stormy heat of summer until the uncertainty of fall discouraged attendance, which, in turn, dampened the enthusiasm of those merchants who underwrote them. The last dance of the year was scheduled for the second Saturday in October.

Vincent and Ragondin had made plans to meet at the mill at dusk on the day of the dance, bicycle to the village and, once in the bistro, partake in the festivities and engage farm girls in conversation. Later, after they had danced and the musicians had retired, they would lead their partners on a romantic stroll along the banks of the river Eure. The back end of this plan was plainly wishful thinking. Each weekend they would return home forlorn, sometimes drunk and always empty-hearted, only to commence, with the optimism of youth, making plans for the dance at the end of the following week.

Women looked upon Ragondin as entertaining and capable of quoting from the many books he had read, but they also knew him to be lascivious, an idiot savant with a mouth filled with obscenities. Although intrigued by his wit, not a single girl in the village envisioned him as a boyfriend, much less a husband. It didn't help that Ragondin looked like a ragamuffin, an unkempt puppet whom someone with a sense of empirical humor had stepped on. Even at his most charming he couldn't resist administering unwelcome caresses to the backsides of the girls he was trying to seduce. His actions were more impulsive than lecherous, because what Ragondin found most amusing was what was revealed in the surprised expressions on the faces of the girls he pinched. Although his conduct had over the years prompted open- and closed-fisted blows to his head from girls, boys, and older people, his behavior was viewed by Vincent as a reaction to rejection, rather than as the gratuitous pleasure of coercing tender flesh.

Vincent, on the other hand, was without question the most polite and handsome young man in the region. But, he too was shunned by the village girls, some of whom would later in life question why they had not allowed themselves the pleasures of an obliging memory. Those who had listened to him as a young boy, fascinated by his stories of hawks and bats and toad-eating foxes, were now attracted to fashion and the lives of movie actors, and since Vincent knew nothing about clothes or the cinema he was labeled a boor. However, almost all of the girls in the village would have forgiven Vincent his lack of social acumen had they not been forbidden by their parents to fraternize with a bastard.

It became apparent to both Ragondin and Vincent that for them to muster the courage required to confront these predictable rejections they had better swallow as many cognacs—beers, in Vincent's case—as it took to stretch their imaginations and loosen their tongues.

Physically, they had both matured since the night of their first meeting in the wheat field behind the Verdier farm four years earlier. Ragondin, to counter a receding hairline, sported, in a gesture of ill-mannered rebellion, a long, sparse mustache that curled over his lip and into his mouth. He had graduated with acceptable grades from vocational school three years earlier and since then had worked for the only farrier in the valley. His arms were disproportionately muscular from beating iron and his teeth, as Vincent would often tease, had grown in size from those of a water rat to those of a mule.

For his part, Vincent's legs were powerful from playing soccer for his boarding school team and now, working full-time on the estate of Robert de Costebelle, he was strong from pitching hay and cutting firewood. He liked the smooth feel of an ash ax handle, the sudden transfer of weight to his shoulders, and the impact of metal in his wrists; most of all he loved the warm exhaustion that spread upward from his loins at the end of the day.

Vincent was taller than most men in the valley and if it hadn't been for a forgivable look of uncertainty in his eyes, he would have appeared untamed and wild; a man who might have, given the choice, lived in a wooden hut in the middle of a dark forest. As it was, though, beneath his good looks, Vincent's face seemed to Ragondin overwhelmed by the burdens of his past.

The night of the dance, Ragondin rode to the mill on his bicycle from his aunt's apartment where he lived on the outskirts of Dreux. It was early, when he left the noise and disillusionment of the suburbs behind him. The light on the narrow road that wandered through the countryside was tempered with a gray luminosity particular to bottoms and hollows at dusk, a soft light that loses definition as it nears the earth, in this instance a valley with a river at its feet and a hardwood forest rising to the east.

Vincent lived with Serge and Jules in the ell of a converted paper mill that had been built three hundred years earlier at the junction of two rivers. For centuries, one river had supplied the mill with running water while the second river now produced just enough electricity to light the living quarters. The cob walls of the mill were covered with ivy that fanned upward from the flint-stone foundation to an overhanging thatched roof. The house had no telephone or refrigerator; perishables were stored on blocks of ice in an outside larder built under the lower limbs of a Douglas fir next to the kitchen. A stand of birch trees buttressed the rear of the building, providing shade in the summer and a windbreak in winter.

Ragondin reached the mill on his bicycle, in bad temper for losing his job earlier that morning. His employer's wife had propositioned him as he drove her to the market in Dreux the day before, taking off the scarf that hid her short blond hair and inquiring if he found her desirable. Until then, Mme Leblanc, a heavy-set thirty-six-year-old woman from Alsace-Lorraine, with cavernous nostrils and pale blue eyes, had not said a hundred words to Ragondin in the three years he had worked for her husband. Surprised that she was not only a coquette but also a forceful one, he hesitated before answering; honesty not being an option, he told her that she looked lovely.

Ragondin had waited across the street from Mme Leblanc's beauty salon at his favorite bistro/restaurant for two hours, reading *Le Figaro*. Edith Piaf had died in Paris earlier in the week, and Jean Cocteau, had had just enough time to make a statement to the press extolling the voice and soul of the Little Sparrow of France, before succumbing himself. That morning in Dreux the front page of every newspaper mourned the loss of both the heart and the mind of France. Ragondin remembered the laments that had been Piaf's songs and *Orphée*, his favorite Cocteau movie. To quench his sorrow he drank beer and ate *croque Monsieurs,* fried ham-and-cheese sandwiches, by the handful.

Mme Leblanc leaned close to him on the drive back to Rebours, the gearshift grazing her thigh. Ragondin, for the first time in his life, was far more terrified than he was excited. His employer's wife was a strong woman and, like her husband, intimidating, so when she put her hand on his thigh, he left it there.

Suzanne Leblanc chuckled, displaying small, ferocious teeth, and declared, "My husband has balls the size of potatoes." And then, her eyes radiating an intensity that commanded assent, she asked, "Would you like to sleep with me?"

Jean Leblanc had once compared their conjugal bed to a worn-out anvil, and even though Ragondin had manifested since puberty an infinite capacity for depravity, on that day, staring straight ahead, he told her that he would rather keep his job.

Shards of blond hair curled professionally above furious blue eyes. "Salaud," she hissed and released his leg.

The next morning, Jean Leblanc waited until Ragondin had finished the half day he was contracted to work on Saturdays and then fired him, promising him a sojourn in the hospital if he ever spoke to his wife again.

Ragondin sat in one of the mill's two tattered armchairs with his feet on a low, oak coffee table in front of the fireplace. He waited for Vincent to change out of his work clothes and climb down from the loft. The bleached antlers of a dozen roebucks and the head of a

Russian boar with curved tusks as long as paring knives were hanging over the hearth. Spinning rods, a .22-caliber long rifle, varmint traps, and a brass horn rested pell-mell in the corners of the room. A quiet and constant sound of running water cradled the mill, a background melody intruded upon each spring by the sound of courting frogs and again in fall by the prattle of waterfowl. The smell of gun oil and burned wood dominated the room.

Ragondin listened for Vincent's uncle, knowing that Serge would inevitably question him about what he was doing, where he had been, and whom he was seeing. This was disconcerting to Ragondin, who had not poached the estate since cementing his friendship with Vincent. When he realized that the gamekeeper wasn't around, he settled deeper into his armchair and tried not to think about Suzanne Leblanc.

Vincent had shared with him the macabre history of the mill, dating from the turn of the century when it had been inhabited by a family from Bayonne, in the southwest of France. The miller, a big man who had lost his left leg to a Prussian cannon, had been an alcoholic whose family lived in nightly terror of his unpredictable behavior. As it turned out, their fears were well founded. One night, after drinking several bottles of absinthe, the miller retrieved his ax from the wood shed and killed his wife, four children, his dog, and a pig, for which he was eventually guillotined. Legend had it that on certain phases of the moon the spirit of the miller's wife slithered down the chimney wailing over the loss of her murdered children.

Ragondin's eyes wandered to the bookshelf above Serge's plank bed, which faced the river Avre. When Vincent first moved into the mill, his uncle had read out loud before going to sleep from the tales of Roland de Roncevaux, *Tristan and Isolde,* and the books of Alexandre Dumas, his voice carrying forcefully to the loft. From them Vincent learned about honor and chivalry and fell asleep to exquisite dreams about women who sipped dew and wore violets in their hair. Vincent had loaned Ragondin each one of the volumes at least twice, and they spent hours reliving the adventures of knights fighting the crusades, ladies in waiting, poachers, and their whores.

Vincent was upstairs on the mattress in his loft, pulling up his socks. The room, once busy with cogwheels and metal fittings, overlooked a hundred-year-old plane tree and beyond that a wheat field, in the middle of which two Italian poplars rose to the sky like the steeples of a church. A wooden ladder nailed to the floor provided access to his mattress, which lay below a dormer window carved into the roof. Before the dawn of each day, Vincent shared his dreams with the stars and observed the moon amble across the firmament.

From his loft Vincent inquired as to Ragondin's health and well-being. The two hadn't seen each other since the last dance, and Ragondin replied that he had shod eleven horses, pounded out a wrought-iron fence fifteen meters long, and been fired. Then he recounted his adventure with Mme Leblanc and the description of her husband's oversized testicles. Vincent commiserated with Ragondin on his loss of income, the rapacious behavior of middle-aged Alsatian women, and the particulars that conceivably could have applied to Mme Leblanc's desirability as a young girl.

Ragondin complained that on top of all that he had been busy dealing with the antics of his aunt, Tantine Artaban. It seemed that on Friday, about the same time Mme Leblanc was issuing her Teutonic demands, Tantine, unnerved by the neighbor's children who had been spying on her through her bedroom window, received the mailman at the door of her apartment by picking up the hem of her dress, raising it to her face, and pushing the material in her mouth. Because the mail carrier laughed when he presented her with her social security check, Tantine bit his thumb down to the bone.

Vincent shuddered remembering Ragondin's aunt, her narrow face and loose lips, the beige-colored eyes that floated vaguely inside deep, purple-stained sockets, and the mole under her nose, the size of a navy bean. Vincent looked down from the loft, his teeth white against skin the color of tobacco from a summer of outdoor labor, and rolled his eyes. He climbed down the ladder wearing a brown, long-sleeved shirt and gray boarding school slacks that ended at his ankles. The light inside the mill was soft against the earth colors of the brick chimney, Vincent's clothes, and the dark furniture. The friends shook hands.

They put on their jackets and caps and left for the village of Merlecourt, talking as they rode their bicycles, weaving back and forth on the dirt road, switching positions, pedaling with hands on and off the handlebars. The road, bordered by beech trees that connected the mill to the castle two kilometers away, meandered through fields and woods and across streams and over wooden bridges that, a decade earlier, had rattled under the shod hooves of gaited horses.

It was the middle of October and when Vincent shivered it took him a moment to recognize an inkling of fall in the air. Out of the corner of his eye he caught sight of a hare with black-rimmed ears as it stole from the shadows of a thicket into the field to feed on the woodbine next to the brambles. He pointed at it and his friend raised his arms pretending to take aim. A pang of hunger rumbled though Ragondin's stomach and he imagined skinning the hare and encouraging his Aunt Tantine to brown the dense red meat in butter and lay it to simmer on a bed of marble-sized onions in a cast-iron *cocotte*. He envisioned sucking the marrow out of the young hare's bones until they were white and brittle and perfectly hollow.

The low sunlight mirrored itself in a layer of cinnamon-colored clouds and fell back into the valley, casting an orange glow over the stubble. Earlier that summer they had drifted live grasshoppers down the river, allowing the current to swing the insects through the deep holes where the brown trout lay waiting. They had caught big fish in the quiet before dark and although neither talked much, the silences were never uncomfortable.

Vincent and Ragondin continued along the dirt road that skirted the castle's moat, pedaling in and out of immense shadows cast by hundred-year-old chestnut trees. The last of the sun's rays glanced off the castle's slate roof and crickets sang. Vincent pointed to the light already on in Robert de Costebelle's library.

The castle had been built in 1624 by a wealthy nobleman belonging to the court of Louis XIII for his Austrian wife, an opinionated woman who, unbeknownst to her husband, detested rural life and had vowed never to set foot on the premises. Her wish was granted when acute peritonitis cut short her marital obligations.

The castle changed hands twice before Robert de Costebelle's grandfather purchased the estate in 1847 for his mistress, a courtesan, whom he eventually married and later dispatched for reasons of infidelity by adding a measured dose of arsenic to her midmorning cordial.

The property bordered the state forest of Crothais and lay like a narrow hand next to a steep hill in an otherwise shallow chalk valley ten kilometers north of the town of Dreux. The village of Rebours buttressed the southern border of the estate while the village of Merlecourt, the castle's namesake, guarded the north. The Costebelles, the largest landowners of the department, owned eight hundred hectares of farmland, two hundred more of woods and pastures, and a fifteen-hectare park complete with a water garden and stables adjacent to the castle. A flint-stone wall, three meters high and one kilometer long, shielded the castle dwellers from the villagers' scrutiny. To the envy of every farmer in the valley, the rivers Eure and Avre braced the heart of the estate, protecting and nourishing it with fingers of running water.

At the end of a long meadow a poplar stand shadowed the road, its leaves turning in the breeze. The raft of clouds in the west filled with purple light. Behind the poplar trees the stables, protected by a coat of green ivy, stood empty. Visible in the last moments of daylight, the paint on the stall doors was dull from neglect and the damp, languid Normandy weather.

Vincent ruefully recalled the years when the pastures were filled with expecting mares and nuzzling foals, and how the saddle horses would push their heads out of the stables stalls and whinny for attention. So many times, he had saddled Nicole's pony while the thick inquisitive lips of the horses probed for lumps of sugar in the palm of his hand. He remembered watching with envy as she rode out over the pasture, her back straight, her auburn-colored hair dancing on her shoulders.

"Nicole's coming home," Vincent said.

Ragondin glanced over at his friend unsure if this was good news or trouble in the making. The relationship between the count's children and Vincent had always seemed tenuous to him.

Vincent had been raking leaves in the courtyard earlier that day while fantasizing about the dance when Count Robert's black Citroën 19 CV stopped under the eave of the abandoned stables. The count walked to Vincent gripping his silver-crowned malacca cane and after they shook hands he inquired about the worms. Vincent picked up a can filled with moss and presented the nightcrawlers he planned to use as bait on the trotline he would set in the river that night, after the dance. Count Robert had demanded eel for supper the next day.

Robert de Costebelle said with a touch of longing: "I'm told that eels migrate back to the Sargasso Sea to spawn and then die." He brushed the index finger of his right hand across his short gray, military mustache and suggested that Vincent use one of Serge's bottles of Côte du Rhone to marinate the eel meat. Vincent studied the old man's features, which were chiseled and shadowed like those of a statue. His thin lips and sharp bird nose, his small blue eyes that darted back and forth, quick as a badger. The count lit an L&M cigarette and told Vincent to add a handful of chopped carrots, shallots, half a cup of vinegar, fresh thyme, and parsley to the marinade.

The famous dish known as *matelote d'anguilles* was one of the count's favorites. Vincent had learned to prepare the dark wine stew during his years working in the castle kitchen and knew the recipe also called for a bay leaf, peppercorns, and a pinch of sugar, but saw no reason to mention it.

Then, taking him by surprise, Count Robert announced, "Nicole will be flying home on a new Boeing 707 jet plane."

Vincent grabbed the count's hand and shook it until the old man pulled away and said, "It's all right, it's all right." Vincent thought of the count's daughter as the sister of his childhood, a little girl with dark red hair and thin lips, whom he loved and who before leaving Merlecourt had kissed his cheek good-bye.

Nicole and Roland had been gone for five years, nearly a quarter of Vincent's life and during that time, except for the count and his butler, François, the castle had stood empty. Vincent had learned to live with the absence of his playmates, but as lonely as he had been for them his deepest regret had been for his employer, a proud old man who hadn't even allowed himself the company of a dog.

Vincent turned in the saddle of his bicycle and said: "I worry that Nicole will remember me only as the bastard son of her mother's maid." Distress strained his voice.

"Stop it," Ragondin said, ashamed for his friend. "She will remember you exactly as you remember her."

The unease of Nicole's return and the exertion of pedaling had brightened Vincent's face. He slid a hand between the buttons on his shirt and closed his eyes. "I would give a month's pay for a girl's hand on my chest," he said.

On a warm summer night that August he had, for the first time, touched the clay-colored breasts of a Moroccan girl during a ride at the town fair in Dreux. It had been a brief and memorable moment. When he called on her the following week a scowling brother dressed in a white djellaba met him on the doorstep of her parent's modest apartment and told him not to come back, that his sister had returned to Agadir. Now, longing filled his nights with erotic dreams and he would often wake up hungry for the coarse pleasures of his fantasies.

When darkness invaded the underbrush and slipped into the field, Vincent let go of the handlebars and took his feet off the pedals of his bicycle, locked his knees and stretched. His shoes were unevenly worn, as were all his shoes ever since the day Roland had accidentally dropped a carving knife on his right foot a decade earlier. The knife had sliced Vincent's middle toe off at the joint, leaving him to play goalie instead of striker on his school's soccer team. Neither he nor Roland ever forgot the action of the severed toe as it writhed under its own power on the kitchen floor. Roland had stepped on it and burst into laughter, remarking with his customary charm how the bloody digit behaved like a maggot. The extremity was displayed in a test tube filled with formaldehyde in the young Viscount's laboratory until his death.

The branches of the oak trees that canopied the main alley leading to the village filtered out any suggestion of light. Ragondin felt the wings of an owl brush against his face. The night bird screeched. They hurried on, hurtling through the tall iron gates, leaning into a tight right turn at the bakery and coasting downhill past the church and small houses roofed in flat red tiles that shaped the village of Merlecourt.

A dozen boys and girls stood in a loose group smoking, talking, and drinking beer in front of the bistro. The boys were for the most part thin and acned and bore the stains of nicotine on their fingers. The girls had painted many layers of makeup on unpolished white faces that lacked the serene texture of Vincent's Moroccan girl. The group acknowledged the arrival of Vincent and Ragondin with feigned indifference, a shuffling of the feet, free hands deep inside empty pockets.

"Go get us some of that château wine your uncle swills, castle boy," sniggered Claude, the son of one of Count Robert's gardeners.

"Talk to my ass, cretin, my head is busy," said Vincent walking past him and a heavyset girl whose arm was around Claude's waist.

Ragondin made a comment about cider and genes, but no one replied. An ironworker grows strong hands and thick arms, and although Ragondin was a small man and a bluffer at heart he possessed the means to back up his mouth and everyone knew it.

Claude was not the only villager who resented Vincent's access to the castle's amenities. Others were jealous of the fact that Count Robert had sent him to an expensive boarding school in Rouen and that he had passed both his baccalaureates in four years. The mind-set of a typical Norman is not one of tolerance, but of envy and mistrust. An overabundance of rain and a lack of sun had over the centuries generated skeptical dispositions. Some, particularly the older women in the village, regarded Vincent as strange because he had one green eye and one blue eye, considered by them to be a sign of evil. What upset the matrons of the valley was that Vincent's nonpareil eyes, like cabochon stones, gleamed under the lights of the dance hall and captured their daughters' imaginations.

Further evidence of his odd character was deduced from his penchant for night swims in the river Eure and his habit of conversing with birds, a claim advanced by the village priest who had observed Vincent lying on the ground in a pasture one summer evening surrounded by partridge. While some villagers were convinced that such peculiar behavior had to mean something, no one among them could say specifically what, which in rural France is reason enough for suspecting the worst. The truth was that Vincent had fallen asleep and was unaware that the covey had chosen him as a landmark.

But the real and largely acknowledged reason the villagers mistrusted Vincent Lebuison had nothing to do with the quality of his education, his eyes, or his peculiar connection with nature. What the residents of the valley could not tolerate was the fact that he was a German bastard, an illegitimate offspring and a constant reminder of a war that would require more years to recover from than they had to live.

It was said that soon after the Liberation, a woman reported to the militia that Marie Lebuison, Vincent's mother, had been seen with a certain major from Dusseldorf in compromising situations in the forest, on the estate, even in the castle. She steadfastly denied the accusations and refused to confess the name of Vincent's father.

She had promised her son that she would tell him the truth on his twenty-first birthday. But through no fault of her own it was a promise she could not keep. Marie Lebuison was killed in a car accident soon after Vincent turned fourteen. It was rumored that she and her companion were drunk the night they raced the train from Paris across the railroad tracks and lost.

The precipitous rhythm of a polka carried through the dance hall walls, adding a new dimension to the everyday conversation. The anticipation of the stag hunting season, with all its excitement and fanfare only two weeks away, along with the presence of young girls and fast music, excited the men, who drank deeply and argued more loudly than usual.

Vincent and Ragondin walked to the bar and stood in front of an array of bottles encased in mirrored shelves. Ragondin ordered his usual cognac and soda while Vincent asked Arnaud the bartender, a big man with olive-colored skin, for a bottle of Kronenbourg beer. Against a background of gray smoke, the whir of foosball and the clash of ivory billiards competed with the sounds of the band in the next room.

Ragondin's work clothes were sweat stained and dirty. "You stink like a badger," said Vincent. "So what?"

Ragondin replied. "How do you think you'd smell if you had been beating iron all morning?" He raised his head and ran his hand over his mustache, "I suppose I should use my severance pay to buy the clothes that will get me laid," he said, pleased at the thought.

"No doubt, my friend." Vincent patted him on the back and grinned.

Ragondin ordered another brandy. "Cognac makes me dream," he said feeling the comforting warmth of the liquor descending.

"About what?"

"Drinking and women," Ragondin responded. "The more I drink, the better I like the girls I dream about." He raised his glass and toasted the few women he had slept with and the many he had not.

"Count Robert told me this afternoon that I am officially enrolled in forestry school this fall," Vincent said. "He expects me to teach him about his trees when I come home at Christmas. 'The death of a tree is like the death of a man,' he told me. 'We anguish over it and then forget it.'"

Vincent smiled at his assignment. "Can you imagine that," he said to Ragondin, "Me teaching Robert de Costebelle about trees? He knows more about them than Serge, who knows more about trees than all the foresters in the region."

Vincent looked at his reflection in the mirror behind the bottles and wondered if Nicole would find him changed. He guessed that her real motives for coming home were all related to the count's failing health. During the past year he had on two occasions fallen into diabetic comas, surfacing each time weaker and less focused.

Ragondin started to roll a cigarette but the effects of the cognacs had gathered him into a different world. He put the yellow corn paper full of tobacco on the bar top, rested his forehead on his wrists, and told Vincent about his newest acquisition. The nudist magazines that he had been buying from the Arabs in Dreux came mostly out of Africa and of late, Vincent had been complaining about a lack of anatomical definition. Ragondin assured him that this latest issue, from Sweden, offered startling clarity. Vincent smiled, but the pleasure he might have otherwise derived from the cavorting of nymphets on the pages of a magazine had been overshadowed by the imminent return of the young mistress of the castle.

Ragondin looked up at the ceiling and started to say something about childhood infatuations, but forgot his train of thought, engrossed as he was with the immediate task of staying on his stool. Vincent stood and headed for the dance hall. Halfway there he stopped and cocked his head, inviting Ragondin to follow.

A depot during the week, the dance hall was a deep rectangular room next to the bar, decorated for the night with streamers of colored mealy paper, stained lamp bulbs, and round tables with red-and-white checked linens. Half a dozen waitresses wearing low-cut black dresses and white aprons waited on the tables with drink trays from the bar.

Farmers and local merchants danced to the music of a band that included an acoustic bass, a drummer, and two accordionists who referred to each other as "my brother-in-law," to acknowledge that each had slept with the other's wife. The girls wore short dresses and the pretty ones danced close to the floor fans, encouraging their skirts to fill with wind so as to show off their strong peasant legs. The married women wore conservative white lace blouses and danced formally with their husbands, who acted stiff and uncomfortable inside their tight-fitting Sunday suits. Sitting in rows of folding chairs, the village matriarchs surrounded the dancers, gossiping among themselves in hushed, secretive voices, their shadowed eyes registering the behavior of their neighbors from under traditional black bonnets.

Vincent and Ragondin leaned back against the partition and ordered beers from Lisette Moulin, Vincent's cousin, a pimply girl of seventeen with a craving for soft cheeses and older men. She complained of having been fondled and nodded at a group of tough young men, huddled in a corner. One of them noticed and waved his cigarette.

Lisette mentioned that she and her friends were going to the ruins later that night and invited Vincent along. He shrugged, knowing the girls would pretend to get lost in the underground tunnels that fanned out from what was left of a monastery once inhabited by Templar priests. Later, they would beg the boys to lead them to safety, affecting hysteria and promising favors. Once safely outside the dark passageway, the girls would renege and run away. Lisette was the exception. She loved to pay.

"Serge told me the deer were in rut," she said, "and since you know how to make those bizarre grunting sounds, you should join us."

Shaking his head Vincent said, "When a stag bells he wants one of two things: to fight you or fuck you." She made a face at the boys in the corner.

The band played "La Vie en Rose" in deference to the passing of Edith Piaf.

Germaine, the village plumber's daughter, whose small, freckled breasts Vincent and Ragondin had spied through her bedroom window during a village raid the summer before, smiled from across the room. Four boys surrounded her, including her brother, so when Vincent walked over, Ragondin went back to the front room and sat at the end of the bar, reluctant to confront the brother. Germaine's retarded cousin, Pauline, had taken a liking to Ragondin during the fireworks of the Fourteenth of July, and while she stared through opaque eyes at the festival of colors on the lawn behind the bistro he had removed her underwear. She had screamed, and Germaine's brother had punched Ragondin in the back of the head.

The competition for Germaine's favor in the dance hall turned out to be more trouble than it was worth and a few minutes later Vincent joined Ragondin at the bar, complaining that the girl had turned her back on him the moment he'd greeted her. He accepted a beer from Arnaud and Ragondin noted that Vincent's determination, like his, was waning.

The band played a tango and Adorée Painvin, Serge's girlfriend, stepped up on the foot rail and kissed them both on the cheek. She smelled of warm dough. Ragondin breathed deeply when she elbowed her way between them.

"You look so serious," she said to Vincent settling down and drinking most of his beer. "What are you thinking about?" She smoothed her thick, brown hair with a slow movement of her hand. Her red dress was rumpled from dancing.

"The river," Vincent replied.

Adorée put her hand on his. "You hide from the world in the river," she said. "It is the blanket you live under with the fish because you don't trust people. Serge does the same thing, only in the forest. You hide under the water, he hides behind trees. Each is the bed you choose to sleep in." Vincent pushed her hand away.

Ragondin rested his chin on Adorée's shoulder and asked where he hid. He asked because he loved listening to her speak, especially to him. She turned on her stool, smiled wickedly and said, "In a trough."

Adorée was a thirty-nine-year-old divorcée and the owner of the best bakery in Dreux. Her skin had the texture of milk and her eyes were brown and gentle as a newborn calf's. With full, velvety lips and generous breasts, she inspired every erotic dream in the valley.

Vincent's uncle and Adorée had been seeing each other for two years. And even though she also slept with Dr. Jobard, the count's physician, the arrangement was one that neither the gamekeeper nor the doctor ever questioned. In fact, the ménage fit Serge's notion that women were no better than men and men no better than monkeys. Dr. Jobard didn't care if Adorée had twenty lovers. He simply made sure that everyone in the region, other than his wife, knew she was his mistress.

A bead of sweat rolled down the side of Adorée's neck and caught on her collarbone before disappearing inside her dress. She followed its path with a finger and caught Vincent's glance.

"You need a girlfriend," she said, putting her hand on his leg and squeezing. Vincent looked at Ragondin in the reflection in the zinc and blushed. All he wanted at that moment was to be back in the mill with his dog, Jules. Ragondin, on the other hand, despaired for Adorée to touch him. But, she wrapped an arm over Vincent's shoulder and teased him further by asking if he wanted her to go into the dance hall and find him a girl. "When they hear it's the dark shy one everyone is always talking about, the fearless Lebuison who swims naked in the river at night, there will be a stampede and the dance will be over."

Serge, who had never been able to keep a secret, had told Adorée about Vincent's swims, just as he told Vincent that Adorée whinnied like a mare when they made love.

Ragondin asked her to find him a girl but she told him to find his own tart, and when Vincent said that he was going fishing for eels she replied that it was unnatural for a man to be without a woman, especially at his age. "That explains why you run around naked, showing yourself off," she said. It wasn't in Adorée's nature to harass, so when Vincent turned to her, his face red, she quickly raised herself off the stool and kissed him. "I'm just being motherly," she said. "Forgive me."

She touched his cheek with the palm of her hand and said, "What is it like, looking at the world from inside a river? You must see some odd things." She finished his beer.

"Last month I swam up on old man Cravic while he was diddling his niece on a bale of hay behind his barn," said Vincent. "His wife was in the kitchen thirty meters away."

"Cravic must be seventy years old!" Adorée exclaimed. Vincent grinned.

She stared at the crowd, the drinking, the arguing, and the laughing all blending into one raucous sound. She turned back to Vincent and asked about Serge.

"He's on patrol."

"Tell him I asked."

She kissed them both good night. "Christ," she said walking away. "The Cravic girl is only fifteen."

Vincent and Ragondin pedaled back to the mill on a path that paralleled the river. The fresh air sobered them.

Vincent felt his shirt fill with wind, tug at his belt, and billow at his back. A brocade of branches fell from the weeping willows and scattered on the river's surface where the water was deep and the eels were hunting. The sky lightened over a nearby valley and they counted out loud to fifteen before the peal of thunder reached them. Across the river, on Étienne Verdier's farmland, they heard the drone of machinery. Tractor lights cut across a distant field. The rains weren't due for two days but Verdier knew better. He would work until the weather came or the ground was turned.

Ragondin waved at the crossroads to the mill and continued on to Dreux while Vincent headed home. When he reached the river he stretched out the trotline on the grass next to the water and with the help of his flashlight he threaded the worms onto the hooks. The moon directed a beam of ivory-colored light across the river. A hen mallard, downstream from the eddy, cackled when the weighted end of the rope broke water. The duck's warning was acknowledged and repeated by others up and down the stream. But Vincent's intrusion into their world was brief. By the time the church bell rang twelve he was back at the mill and in bed asleep, dreaming of Nicole.

Chapter 2

Vincent pulled the trotline out of the river soon after dawn on Sunday morning. A breath of fog obscured the water. The weight of the line and the odd slanting cut it made across the surface suggested a successful set. Moments later, two brown bodies three feet long and as thick as a man's wrist shadowed the grass on the bank beside him. The eels had struggled in the night and twisted the dropper lines and leaders into tight balls of wire and rope. When he removed the hooks from their mouths they writhed and constricted their discontent in his hands. On the last hook a large perch spun out of the river, stiff and golden under an early sun.

He dropped his catch in a pail and returned to the mill where he set it next to the back door. The eels that lay coiled on top of each other stared at him through small black eyes. He pulled them out one at a time and threaded a braided rope through their gills, then hung them from the lowest branch of the fir tree that grew next to the kitchen. To neutralize the taste of the mud they lived in, he poured white vinegar through a funnel down their throats, and watched as they fought the rope.

Vincent covered the pail containing the perch with a wet kitchen towel and climbed up the wooden ladder that led to his loft. Tired from a week's work he fell on his mattress and went back to sleep. This time he dreamed of Roland, with whom he had shared all the adventures of his childhood.

His dream led him to a summer morning when he was twelve years old, shortly after the count and countess had taken Nicole to visit family in Vendée. When the count's sedan was safely beyond the main gates, Roland dragged Vincent to the garage where he soldered fifty meters of heavy-duty electrical wire to two square metal plates the size of copy books. After the welding was completed he cut the wire in half, inserted both ends into a plug, and waited for noon. Then, while Chef Gaston, François, and the rest of the help were in the kitchen eating lunch, he dropped the metal-plate terminals into the moat from a window in the count's library, and inserted the plug into a 220-volt socket.

The water boiled. Perch and pike, tench and baitfish rose from the mire at the bottom of the moat to the surface, upending scores of white bellies to the sun. The eels churned in the mud, clouding the water and sending streams of bubbles to the surface. Bigger fish and those on the edges of the electrical field darted in and out of the waterweeds, surfing on their sides with their gills and mouths stretched open before plunging back out of sight. Sooner or later every fish between the terminals quivered into view. The moat was iridescent. Roland was pleased.

They electrocuted as many fish as possible from the window and then attached a terminal at each end of a fourteen-foot wooden boat, taking turns rowing and netting, dumping their catch on the bank. Moving from one section of the moat to another, from one room of the castle to the next, from socket to socket, laughing constantly, fearless on the surface of the electrically charged water.

When they reached the pantry, the fuse blew and flames curled the paint on the cupboard where the countess kept her best Sèvres ware. They put the fire out with the help of everyone in the kitchen, and the next morning the fish were sold in Dreux, the proceeds of which, along with five strokes of the count's cane, went to repairing the damages.

Vincent woke from his dream to the sound of chimes beckoning the parish of Merlecourt to Sunday Mass. Standing on his mattress he opened the dormer window and pushed his head outside. A cloud cover stretched over the forest, and a late morning breeze drifted up the river dispersing the insect hatches and whorling the shallow water next to the bank. The eels were hanging plumb to the ground; the gravy-colored skin around their mouths had turned white, bleached from the vinegar.

Étienne Verdier, whose tractor Vincent and Ragondin had heard working the fields on their way back from the dance, drove his truck into the yard and stopped under the plane tree. He spotted Vincent in the window, waved, and asked if he had seen his sons.

"They are probably in church by now," Vincent teased.

"That'll be the day I win the trifecta," Étienne replied banging the truck door with an open hand.

Verdier, a big-boned man with a carapace of black hair and a weathered face, was a widower with two grown sons, Louis and Titi. His boys shared a wing of the family's farmhouse with a Polish woman by the name of Salomé Venard, a forty-seven-year-old streetwalker from la rue St. Denis in Paris. Étienne's wife, consumed with cancer, had begged the boys to move her out. But Louis and Titi, indifferent to her pleas, paraded Salomé through the farm, even into their mother's bedroom when Étienne was out working. It was common knowledge that Mme Verdier had died staring into the pockmarked face of her sons' whore.

Louis, the eldest, also known as Gros-Louis, was thirty years old and built like a Charolais bull with a head the size of a soccer ball. When drunk, he baited men into fighting him and, on occasion, would get so excited at the notion of inflicting pain he would wet his pants, a singularity no one mentioned in his presence.

Titi, two years older than Vincent, was as thin as the knife blades he had carried since the age of seven. At eleven he'd been suspended from school for carving his initials into the heel of a classmate's foot, and five years later was sentenced to three months in a correctional institute for amputating the teats off one of the mayor's cows.

Aside from their predisposition for violence, Titi and Gros-Louis shared three physical traits: thin black hair, eyebrows the size and shape of mussels, and small corn-colored teeth.

Verdier had plowed half the night and looked exhausted. He grumbled that one of his boys was overdue to replace him and said that he would be working across the river in case Vincent saw either one of them. He wearily turned the palms of his hands up in a gesture of disgust. "But, hey, I won't be holding my ass shut waiting." Then he asked Vincent when it was going to rain.

Vincent Lebuison was known in the valley for forecasting the weather and when he looked at the sky and predicted rainfall before dark Étienne believed him. His ability to make accurate prognostications dovetailed with his most coveted talent, that of diviner. To a farmer, the custodianship of land is far more important than patriotism, and Vincent's aptitude for tapping into underground springs of clean water was the leading reason why he had not been as persecuted as he might otherwise have been for being part German. Since the age of ten he had advised Étienne and others in the valley as to the location of their wells, and even if they didn't admit it they all suspected that his gift for finding water on the driest hill was magical.

Vincent performed his wizardry by holding a freshly cut willow fork and walking the terrain until, attracted by the magnetism of water, the willow branch bowed to the ground where the digging would begin. Étienne nodded, waved, and drove without hurry down the dirt road. To a peasant, a diviner is divine.

Vincent got dressed and watched a funnel of crows take shape behind Étienne's harrow. He imagined the funereal-looking birds as musical notes, rising and falling, arguing and fussing over the slugs and worms upended from under the earth. He felt sorry for Étienne, who with no one to keep him company tended to his tractor as he would a mistress. A cold-hearted mistress that despite allowing him the linear pleasures of harrowed fields, constrained his back, and occasionally the mechanics of her own engine, to laborious perversities. Étienne Verdier was a tired and disillusioned man with little to look forward to. His only passion other than playing the French horn was running stags behind a pack of hounds in the forest of Crothais as a member of the local hunt club. Occasionally, when the moon was full, Étienne played his instrument, of which he was a master, and when the wind blew from the west Vincent could trace the plaintive sounds of the old man's solitude back to his farm.

Vincent fired the gas stove in the kitchen, a small room with a round table in the center and four wooden pegs sunk into the walls for hanging the empty chairs. A window looked out onto the plane tree. He set a kettle of water on the flames to boil and walked to the outhouse at the edge of the woods. Serge had not been home since the previous afternoon and Vincent hoped he would take his time, maybe even go to the bistro and not return until after lunch. As much as he enjoyed his uncle's company, Serge was strung tighter than a leg trap, and there were times the mill was too small to accommodate his energy.

The count's first driven shoot of the season was only a week away, and Serge had been patrolling the estate every night. The young, gray partridge were once again vulnerable to those poachers who hid small spaniels in their game pouches during the day and at night allowed them to cast over the land, interpreting the wind until the mere notion of a roosting covey drifted across their course. Then, with dogs on point and the partridge under an age-old spell, the men, holding either end of a net, would shroud the unsuspecting birds and wring their necks.

On his way back from the outhouse Vincent removed the perch from the pail. Inside, he flattened it on the cutting board next to the stove and lifted the filets. A sparkle of scales washed down the white porcelain sink. When the water in the kettle had come to a boil, he made chicory coffee and drank it with milk and sugar out of a heavy-bottomed pickling jar.

A little later, Vincent took off his clothes and went outside. To the east the wall of clouds that had stalled over the forest was falling into the valley. The breeze had died and waves of gnats swarmed in and out of the ivy. He held a rubber hose above his head and turned on the faucet. The water ran hot and then river cold.

Secretly pleased with the way his body had developed over the summer, Vincent turned the water off and went to the plane tree where he loosened a sliver of beige-colored bark and crumpled it to the ground. It was a tremendous tree with heavy, sprawling boughs and wide leaves that shaded the lawn. He had climbed it a hundred times and fallen asleep on its bottom limbs. A kingfisher flashed blue against the green backdrop of a willow tree and disappeared around a bend in the river. Vincent stretched his arms and legs until his skin burned, flaunting his body because it excited him. The fragments of light that fell through the leaves cast gray outlines on the grass. He relieved himself, drawing patterns around the designs, remembering when he was young how his mother would hold him between her thumb and forefinger and aim at things, like he was doing now. "Pow!" she would exclaim. "We got it!" He would look at her proudly, and she would shake the last drop off for a job well done.

Inside the mill Vincent dressed and then sharpened a short-bladed paring knife. He walked out to where the eels were hanging and ran his thumb down the body of the closest one until he found the small, unprotected depression in its rib cage. He pushed inward, hard, and burst the eel's heart. Careful not to cut too deeply into the meat, he made a circular incision below its neck and rolled the skin down its body. When a measure of hide was peeled, Vincent wrapped a sheet of newspaper around it for purchase and, with both hands holding the newspaper, sat down all at once. The entire skin came off in one piece, inside out, white and dull, like a lemon rind.

He skinned the second eel and carried the pinkish-gray meat into the kitchen where he stripped the guts and cut the flesh into steaks. After assembling the marinade and mixing it with the meat, he pan-fried the perch filets in butter and washed them down with a glass of hard cider. The perch tasted clean and sweet from having lived in the quickest part of the river. He made a plan to visit his fishing hole later that afternoon.

Once a week since June, Vincent had added pieces of meat to a metal can that hung from a limb reaching directly over the deepest pool in the water garden. Flies laid their eggs on the carrion, which then hatched into maggots that fell onto the surface of the water through holes he had drilled in the bottom of the can. Circadian showers of maggots teased the fingerlings into a state of constant expectancy. Vincent fished the water garden with a cane pole and small gold hooks. Serge loved the tiny silver fish and ate them by the handful like French fries.

Vincent stood up when he heard his uncle's car crossing the bridge next to the sluice gates. The vehicle sounded like it was going fast, which meant Serge was in a foul mood. He turned on the gas stove and refilled the water kettle to make more coffee.

The car stopped under the plane tree and Maurice Corneille, a federal gamekeeper with a thick mustache that crowded his face, and his assistant, a little man with no hair on his head, climbed out of a Citroën 2 CV truck, the same as Serge's but in better repair. Corneille waved at Vincent standing in the doorway. "Get over here," he said, "your uncle is hurt."

As Corneille's assistant lowered the tailgate of the truck, Vincent ran over to them, feeling the same apprehension he had experienced the morning he found out his mother had died.

Serge was stretched out on a tarp with his head resting in the shadows on a pillow of hay. A section of shredded sock, stiff and dry with black blood, stuck out of a jagged hole in the right sole of his boot. The two men carefully pulled Serge out of the truck. Grass stains covered his clothes and a line of red spittle ran out of his mouth and grooved his chin.

When Serge's body had cleared the tailgate, Vincent took over for Corneille's assistant, feeling as though someone had blindsided him on the soccer field. Serge's left hand, swollen and bloody, was a shade of blue that

Vincent had never seen before. It didn't look much like a hand, and Vincent felt his stomach heave.

While they carried Serge into the mill Corneille ordered his assistant to the castle. "Tell Count Robert what happened, and call Dr. Jobard. Hurry."

They laid Serge on his plank bed and he groaned. Vincent pulled off his uncle's shoes and unbuckled his belt because he had read somewhere that it was the right thing to do.

"Merde!" said Corneille, looking down at the bed. The sheet under Serge was turning pink. Vincent stepped back and stared at the spreading stain that was working its way slowly down the side of the bed. Serge was pissing blood. He remembered seeing staghounds piss blood after being kicked by horses. Most died.

"What happened?" Vincent didn't recognize the horror in his voice.

"I spotted his empty car on the south side of the Roberta Woods. We went looking and found him in the ditch between the road and the wheat field. I'm not sure, but I think that whoever did this to your uncle somehow closed a window on his hand and dragged him until something came loose." Corneille asked for hot water.

Vincent brought back the kettle he had readied for coffee and looked down at his uncle's body covered with bruises and protuberances that appeared on the verge of breaking through the skin. They removed the bottom sheet and cleaned him as best they could. Corneille didn't think the hand was broken but the large, purple bruise below the rib cage upset him.

"I'm sure he wasn't run over," he said. "It was probably a glancing blow. The swelling though, that's not a good thing."

Corneille rested his hand on Serge's stomach, which caused the injured man's eyes to fly open. "Stop!" Vincent yelled as he stepped between them. Corneille put his big, hard hands on Vincent's shoulders and held him until he stopped shaking. Then Corneille turned toward the fireplace and sat down.

Vincent covered Serge with a blanket and looked down at his small, pinched face. His uncle's curly black hair was matted to his forehead and beads of sweat had formed on the snuff stains under his nose. Vincent leaned closer and whispered his name. Serge's closed eyes fluttered but he didn't answer.

"He can't hear you," said Corneille quietly. "Wait for Dr. Jobard."

Vincent turned back to the gamekeeper and asked him if he had any clues. "Tire tracks," was all Corneille said. "And when my assistant gets back we'll take prints.

Now listen to me. Serge is as tough as they come. He's going to pull through."

Vincent tilted his head and looked at Corneille through his green eye, his bad eye, the one he referred to as his German eye. With a tremor in his voice he said, "I would hate to be the one who did this to my uncle."

Chapter 3

The uncertainty of Serge's breathing brought back memories of the shallow breath of a roebuck Vincent and his uncle had once come upon, shot in the stomach by a poacher and left on the ground to die. The deer's black eyes had been concealed behind a cloudy veil, and underneath the tawny hide, beleaguered muscles jumped and twitched out of control. Serge cursed the hunter's carelessness. When he leaned over and stroked the roebuck's neck there was compassion in his voice. "Forgive me," he said. And then he drew his knife across the little deer's throat.

Vincent couldn't look at the worry etched on Corneille's face so he closed his eyes and recited the Lord's Prayer under his breath as he had been taught to by his mother. The picture of Serge's body being jerked off the ground and striking the car fender, like a string puppet, played over and over again in his mind. So he prayed faster and faster, hoping the accumulation of pleas would hearten God's compassion.

Finally, longing to be alone, he went outside to the back of the mill where the smell of impending rain filled the air. He watched as dark squall clouds rolled down from the forest into the valley in stubborn unison. Vincent breathed deeply to rid his lungs of the stench of urine and pain that had overtaken the mill.

Great storms, encouraged by the evaporation of two river systems, were common in Merlecourt. Vincent remembered, as a child living in the castle, watching in wonder with his face pressed against the windowpane of his bedroom as gusts of wind drove the tall Lombardy poplars into each other creating gingerbread patterns on the lawn. He had witnessed, more than once, moments of pure revelation when night burned white inside the clouds as lighting unveiled the secrets of its shadows.

The leading edge of the front followed the count's car into the courtyard and within moments a flood of rain erased the entire landscape behind him. Vincent ran to the Citroën sedan, holding an umbrella and Count Robert, looking gaunt in his gray jacket and cravat, ducked under it.

Once inside the mill, the count crossed the room and touched Serge's forehead with the tips of his fingers. He looked to Corneille for answers. The federal gamekeeper was not sure how Serge had managed to get his hand trapped inside the door, but he did know that a car had dragged him across the wheat field in front of the

Roberta Woods. He mentioned finding tire tracks in the stubble, drew a figure eight in the air, and said that whoever was driving had left Serge for dead. Count Robert looked down at his gamekeeper's broken body and cursed. Corneille glanced at Vincent; Robert de Costebelle never swore.

The count clutched the pommel of his cane. "Who would do such a thing?" he demanded of them.

Corneille shrugged and put his hands in the pockets of his corduroy pants. "My guess is that it was poachers, or maybe a carload of drunks joyriding after the dance."

Count Robert looked around the room, his eyes absorbing every familiar detail. He knew that professionals didn't drag a man behind a car for pleasure. "Poachers are much too conscious of time to do such a thing," he said, his eyes narrowing.

Corneille looked out the window. "This rain isn't going to help," he said. "The tire tracks in the stubble are going to be impossible to read."

Dr. Jobard, a short, bald man in his mid-fifties with small hands and a pronounced stomach, hurried in out of the weather carrying a black bag and dropped an open umbrella on the floor, oblivious to superstition. He shook everyone's hand with solemnity before going to Serge's bed without saying a word.

The storm relocated on the far side of the valley and a wedge of blue sky pried open the clouds. Then, the rain stopped all at once and steam rose from the ground, cooling the earth in a slow but resolute surrender to fall.

Corneille turned to Vincent. "There's more," he said. "Jules is dead. I'm sorry."

Vincent felt the count's hand on his arm and tried swallowing the lump that rose in his throat. He went to the window and watched the courtyard fill with light.

Corneille shook his head and said that Jules had been run over, probably trying to protect Serge, and that even with a broken back the dog had managed to drag its hindquarters the length of the field during the night to be next to his master.

"I had to shoot him," the gamekeeper said with discomfort. "I'm sorry, but there wasn't any hope . . . just pain."

Vincent turned from the distressed looking faces and ran outside and stood under the plane tree. The sun had fully emerged and was flooding the courtyard with light. He remembered that when he first moved to the mill, Serge had allowed Jules, who at the time was just a puppy, to sleep with him. Vincent hugged the big tree, pressing his cheek against its trunk, and watched the clouds above him sail over the valley, taking with them the radiance that had been Jules's life.

Corneille's assistant and François, Count Robert's butler, arrived in separate cars. François, whose nose jumped out of his face like a bulrush, walked to Vincent and handed him the keys to the Citroën that Serge had been driving. Corneille came out of the mill shaking his head. "Serge is awake and pissed off," he said. Corneille looked at the estate car and admonished François for having moved it. He told him he would have to show the police exactly where he had found it. Thin and gray and momentarily confused, François looked back and forth from Corneille to Vincent, blinking and swallowing, and then he stuttered an apology for having interfered with the investigation.

Corneille reassured the old servant. "Don't worry, François," he said, putting a hand on the butler's shoulder. "Serge is in there cursing a blue streak." Then he turned and motioned Vincent to his vehicle. "I'm going to bury Jules in the dog cemetery," he said.

Vincent looked away from the car that had brought his uncle back to the mill. Somewhere in the back under the tarp was Jules, his closest friend. He asked Corneille if Serge had said anything about the attack, but Corneille shook his head and slipped behind the wheel. He told Vincent that Serge had said to come back the next day and Corneille did not insist, knowing he would be wasting his time.

Inside the mill the room had the metallic smell of alcohol and blood. Count Robert and Dr. Jobard stood at the end of the bed. "Save your breath for farting, Jobard! I'm not going to the hospital," Serge exclaimed as Vincent walked in. Indignant, the doctor paced and told the gamekeeper that he didn't have a choice, that he was an imbecile, and that he could die without proper care. Count Robert raised his hand and said that he wanted to be left alone with his gamekeeper. Dr. Jobard and Vincent went to the kitchen and sat across from each other at the table in silence. Relieved that his uncle was acting normal, Vincent burst out laughing at the farting comment.

The doctor wasn't amused and told Vincent to grow up. But Vincent couldn't help himself. It was like one of those nightmarish times at the castle when he and Roland had started laughing and couldn't stop and eventually were asked to leave the room. Vincent excused himself and went outside.

The rain had washed the trees of summer pollen and the sky was now a shade of blue Vincent had not seen since spring. François, the only employee on the estate who didn't hunt or own a gun, leaned against Serge's car and bowed his head. "A bad thing happened here last night," he said. "It reminds me of the war." François hated violence, having witnessed too much of it. He had been deported in 1941 to Czechoslovakia where he worked in a steel factory fabricating armor plating for German tanks. There he had been persecuted, not so much by the German soldiers, who were common men following orders, but by the Nazi youth, monster children with guns who regularly committed acts of atrocity. Once he witnessed five of them—the oldest was sixteen—arrest a Jewish woman and her baby boy, shave the woman's head, and strangle the child with its mother's braids.

Dr. Jobard emerged from the mill and went to his car, muttering that he'd be back before dark to take Serge to the hospital. Count Robert followed and told Vincent that his uncle didn't want to see anyone, but that he was going to call Adorée anyway. He wanted Vincent to wait until she arrived, and then to meet him at the castle. He nodded in the direction of Jobard. "The doctor is right, Vincent. Talk to Serge and make him understand the gravity of the situation." François opened the door and the count folded his long, elderly body into the car and rolled up the window, his profile a caricature of authority.

Serge lay between the sheets with his eyes closed. He had pushed the blanket off the foot of the bed and folded his arms over his chest. He hummed. There was no melody, just confused sounds, like those Vincent used to hear late at night when as a senior in boarding school he patrolled the lower formers' dormitories. His uncle's humming was entirely out of character and it upset Vincent, until he realized that Dr. Jobard must have given him morphine for the pain.

Serge opened his eyes and looked vaguely around the room. His pupils were dilated and he talked slowly, as if a weight rested on his tongue. He said that he was having a dream, and each time he closed his eyes the dream resumed exactly where he had left off. Serge looked into his nephew's face with a confused smile.

Vincent did not like seeing his uncle withered and helpless between the sheets of his narrow bed. For the first time since he had moved to the mill years before he felt uncomfortable in his uncle's presence. Serge sensed Vincent's discomfort and placed his hand on his nephew's. He said that he would be all right soon and not to worry. Vincent cast his mind back to another time when things had not turned out all right, the night his mother died.

The room had been gray from a dawn light seeping through the folds in the curtains that morning. Vincent woke to the countess leaning over his bed. She was wearing a beige-colored robe and her thin blond hair was pulled back so tightly it altered the shape of her face. At first he did not recognize her.

She told him in French that his mother had been in an accident the night before and that she was so sorry. The countess sat on the edge of the bed and stroked his hair. It had been a car accident she said. His mother didn't suffer. The pale face above Vincent bore the veneer of a pearl; a morning breeze parted the curtains and her words broke his heart. The countess's eyes were so sad that he turned away and hid his face in the pillow, numb with fear. She stroked the back of his neck and whispered how sorry she was and how she had loved her Marie. Bursting with grief Vincent sat up and wrapped his arms around her. He sobbed against her shoulder and when she leaned back he lay on top of her, held her down and frantically pushed his hips into hers.

Vincent blushed at the memory, drawing a picture in his mind of the Countess de Costebelle, the most beautiful woman anyone in the village had ever seen, with her head buried in his pillow. She had kept her arms around him and never said a word. When he quieted she covered him with a blanket, kissed his forehead, and tiptoed out of the room.

Shortly after the funeral Vincent's belongings were moved down a flight of stairs to a room on the third floor of the castle that overlooked an alley of linden trees. Roland gave him his best knife and Nicole her undivided attention. A week after the funeral, François told him that he had overheard Count Robert talking to Serge about a possible adoption and Vincent lay awake every night fantasizing about becoming a member of the de Costebelle family.

Vincent heard the estate tractor and went to the door to greet Jacques and Hubert, the count's gardeners, stubborn men who kept to themselves and complained openly about their jobs behind their employer's back. The gardeners usually avoided Serge, who didn't allow anyone to criticize Robert de Costebelle. In this instance, the men must have known that the gamekeeper was in no condition to object. They went to his side and stared down at the broken body under the sheet without saying a word.

Jacques Labûche was a small man who looked and smelled as if he had slept in a pile of manure. His brown eyes blinked in a face filled with welts and scarlet furrows fertilized by Pernod. Proud of the fact that he had not gone to bed sober in twenty years, Jacques liked to brag that he could scythe a hayfield as level as a billiard table in one-third the time it took anyone else in the valley.

Hubert Muserole was twice as big as his partner but forever deferred to the smaller man. He had red-rimmed blue eyes, a long nose that ended in a small knuckle of cartilage, and a thick lower lip, which he licked like a sow. He lived in the guardian's house inside the main entrance gates with his wife and his thirty-three-year-old son. Hubert's daily diet included half a kilo of lard, a loaf and a half of farm bread, and two liters of Algerian red wine. He walked as deliberately as time permitted, and if he wasn't in Jacques's immediate footsteps he could be found in the background, shitting down the side of a log.

The gardeners joined Vincent in the kitchen. Jacques pointed at the Calvados bottle and Vincent filled two small water glasses while he told them what he knew. "He's been fucking every married woman from here to Calais," Jacques declared. "I'm surprised this didn't happen sooner." The gardeners left the moment their glasses were empty, driving off as they had come, with

Jacques at the wheel and Hubert on the jump seat behind him.

Serge called his nephew in a low voice and waited while he fetched a chair from the kitchen. Vincent sat at the head of the bed, his face close to his uncle's. "I pretended to be asleep when they were here," Serge said. "I feel like hell, so it was easy. Every part of my body, including my dick, feels like it's been soaked in gasoline."

Vincent asked him for the name of his assailant, to no avail. Serge admitted to foul play and that there had been two men in the car. But he also said that if he volunteered their names Vincent would have to lie to the police and he didn't want them meddling in his affairs. Serge's eyes looked beyond Vincent, into a space of their own. "But," he said, "I promise you that we will make them wish they were dead long before they are."

The gamekeeper settled back into his pillow and, after telling his nephew to be quiet, closed his eyes. Vincent took a deep breath, knowing from experience that there would not be another word said about the incident until his uncle was ready.

"Imagine a March morning soon after the fog lifts off the feeder creeks," Serge said in a low melodic voice.

"A morning when the first crocuses of the year struggle out of the ground and unfold golden under a young white sun. Imagine kingfishers darting downriver and the river leaving its bed and stretching across the blue-green grass of spring." He stopped for a moment to make sure Vincent was following. Then he closed his eyes and continued.

"I lie awake in a cave in which rows of stalagmites spring like narwhal tusks out of a carpet of moss. Standing over me is a beautiful woman wearing a light blue cape that falls from the top of her head to the toes of her feet. She comes to me and tells me her name is Lanner. She has high cheekbones and a narrow nose, and her skin is so thin I can see the blood coursing through the veins of her hands.

"She waves to me and I follow her down a corridor to a room where twenty other women sit under an immense crystal carving of a bird with topaz-colored eyes. A girl hands me a gourd full of wine while another covers my shoulders with a feathered blanket. There is nothing to say, so I sit and watch these women with odd-looking bird faces watch me. I drink from the gourd and almost immediately fall asleep. When I wake up I am naked under the feathered blanket, in a circular room that smells of forest mushrooms. There are animal skins on the floor. A door opens in the wall and Lanner comes to me holding a pewter bowl.

"'Goat's milk,' she says. 'Drink it. It will give you strength.' She walks to the end of the blanket. 'You may get up,' she says. 'We have examined you. I am familiar with your body.'

"I stand and she hands me the bowl. The milk is rank. Lanner turns to the door and claps her hands and the rest of the women enter and stand facing me. The bird women look into my eyes and slowly, in unison, allow their robes to fall off their shoulders. Naked, these women stand splendid and unashamed, their long legs white as frost and their breasts polished eggshells. Lanner says, 'We want you to be our mate.'"

Serge opened an eye, grinned at his nephew and closed it. He said he was going back to his dream, that his mission was to fuck each and every bird woman there and that he would let him know how it went. His voice began to lose intensity and Vincent leaned closer. "My boy," Serge murmured, "they have long raven-colored feathers on their heads and black down between their legs; best of all, they preen each other from morning to night. You'd love them."

The morphine had freed a corner of Serge's soul and inspired a vision of its own. Vincent rubbed his head and tried to imagine what their feathers would feel like. His uncle sighed as he slipped deeper into sleep. Vincent returned the chair to the kitchen and heard Adorée's Fiat brake to a stop. "Oh, Serge!" she said, running to his bed. "You look awful."

Chapter 4

Vincent stopped the Citroën next to the bronze statue of a life-size wild boar that was mounted on a granite pedestal. It overlooked the water garden, a puzzle of small islands, backwaters, and creeks that in summer filled with white-flowering lily pads. He ran his hand over the verdigris *solitaire* and looked for Jules's grave, finding the small rectangle of fresh earth under a weeping willow next to still water. A great blue heron rose out of a tangle of cattails and climbed into the sky.

By design a place of beauty and reflection, the water garden had also been the setting for Vincent's only fight with Roland. They'd wrestled next to the statue of the boar in the summer that Nicole's King Charles spaniel drowned in the moat. A week after it was buried, Roland had insisted, much to his sister's dismay, that the dog be exhumed and autopsied. When Vincent rose to her defense the ensuing commotion was brief. Roland was older and heavier, but he was also fat and slow. A truce was called on top of the grave of Blanche, a beloved griffon that had belonged to the count's father, and Roland opted to dissect a frog instead.

With the exception of that one fracas, Roland had been Vincent's best and only friend since the day they'd first met on the bridge that spanned the castle moat. Always the leader, Roland led the son of his mother's maid down a long and colorful road filled with plots and pranks and conspiracies that more often than not ended with a meeting of the count's cane. Vincent would remember his brief relationship with the young master of the castle with all the exaggerations that time imparts on the memories of a child.

Like the weather disturbances so familiar to Normandy, however, one catastrophe was followed by another. Twenty-seven days after the accident that claimed Vincent's mother, Roland de Costebelle slipped in a fountain next to the castle, knocked himself unconscious, and drowned in fifteen centimeters of water. He was sixteen years old, reading Frank Slaughter books, and spending his free time in a walk-in closet on the third floor of the castle that he had converted into a laboratory. There, with the help of zoology books, scalpels, and bottled ether, he operated on the rabbits and snakes that Serge had taught Vincent to trap.

A few days before the accident Roland had anesthetized a cock pheasant and, except for its tail feathers, plucked it bare. The bird regained consciousness naked and crazed, a prisoner in a glass jar. Vincent had begged Roland to kill it but his pleas were ignored in the name of science. The pheasant lived for two days. On the third morning Vincent wrung the bird's neck and carried it to the kitchen where the chef braised it for what became the viscount's last supper.

On that fateful morning, Vincent came upon the countess kneeling next to a fountain outside the south wing of the castle, with Roland's head cradled in her slender hands. When he tried to touch his friend a scream, as terrifying as the keening of a strangled rabbit, escaped from the countess's throat. The memory of that sound and the picture of Roland's face, inert and blue in her lap, invaded Vincent's dreams with dreaded regularity for the rest of his life.

He had responded to the countess's pain with tears of his own, but for weeks after Roland's death whenever Vincent tried to console her she refused to see him. Finally, one evening before the sun had set, he gathered his courage and stepped into her room. Wrapped in a shawl, she was sitting at the window overlooking the fountain in which her son had drowned, staring at a place above the trees that she had chosen as her own. When she didn't answer him he fell to his knees and awkwardly made his way across the carpet until he reached her. Overcome with sorrow, he rested his head in her lap.

"Madame la Comtesse, please forgive me. I should have been with him," he begged.

Vincent felt her legs harden under his face. A sob escaped from inside her, a long and terrible moan. She turned away and when the sound of her loss became insufferable, he stood and left the room, closing the door on the stranger he loved and that he would never see again.

Soon after Roland's death Vincent was moved from the castle back to the family farm for reasons that he never fully understood. It was François who took him aside and said that his presence upset the countess in a manner he couldn't explain, and that Count Robert had decided that Vincent should go live with his uncle and aunt for a while. Mortified, the young man's eyes filled with tears. He wondered out loud what he had done to offend anyone.

"Nothing, Vincent. You did nothing at all," replied François.

Monique Moulin, who advocated prayer and arduous labor, put her nephew to work cleaning the yard, the cattle barn, the chicken coops, and anything else that caught her fancy. After each evening meal he was expected to read aloud from the Book of Lamentations. His aunt's favorite topics of conversation were the scriptures, the sins of her peers and, more to the point, Vincent's lineage, the disgrace of which she never let him forget.

Roland's accident intensified the anguish he felt over his mother's death and, with no one to turn to, his fears encroached on his appetite and eventually on his health. The countess's rejection, the shame of being a German, and the guilt he felt for not having been at Roland's side the morning of the accident made him so ill that he was bedridden for weeks. Alone in a windowless room adjoining the pigsty, his condition was exacerbated by his aunt's dim world of condemnation, the stench of manure, and the absence of the slightest thread of compassion.

Merlecourt had defined the boundaries of his youthful world for ten years. Unaware that his life there had been contingent on the fancy of others, his heart broke when fate returned him to his own.

Unbeknownst to Vincent, Count Robert was kept apprised of his well-being by Serge and François, and when he heard how Vincent was being treated the count arranged for him to be sent to boarding school in Rouen. To further protect Vincent from his aunt, Serge insisted that his nephew be moved to the mill during his vacations.

The countess remained in her room for three months after Roland's death. In October she took

Nicole to London, and a few months later she convinced her husband to move to New York, where she had decided they would start a new life. He joined her there in the spring, and for a year the castle stood empty.

Count Robert's correspondence with friends in Europe expressed his dislike of New York and his opinion that the women there talked like girls, the girls like women, and the men about their money. He refused to qualify what he ate in America as food, and although, for his daughter's sake, he tried to conform to the mores of his new home, there was nothing that Nicole or the countess could say or do to make him appreciate the particulars of that city. The more he expressed a longing to return to Normandy, the more adamant the countess became in her desire to remain. Consequently, the divorce came as no surprise to anyone. Count Robert went back to France and his daughter remained in America with her mother. Nicole had visited her father briefly three times since his return to Merlecourt, but each time Vincent was away at school.

Vincent left the dog cemetery and drove to the castle where François was waiting for him in the front hall, the smell of red wine strong on his breath. Vincent handed the butler the eels in their marinade, pointing at the purple stain on the front of his cream-colored jacket. François pushed the vexing finger out of the way and asked about Serge.

"He's dreaming of women who look like birds," Vincent said, proud of his uncle's apparitions.

François led him through the living room to the library, where the count and his guests had once walked on Aubusson carpets under the glitter of crystal chandeliers. All that remained was the seventeenth-century oak wainscoting. Everything else had been sold at auction and replaced with replicas and furniture from the region. The sofas and Louis XV chairs, the bronze andirons, the fine serpentine tables and commodes, the gilt-framed Courbet, the Millet, and the two Degas pen-and-ink studies now belonged to a Chicago businessman.

In the divorce settlement Count Robert had willingly given half his fortune to the countess and returned to Merlecourt from America a poorer man. He closed down two-thirds of the castle, sold the horses, reduced the estate staff from twelve to five, syndicated the partridge shooting, and retired to his library. Close friends still came and went, but the fine luncheons, the parties, and the general ambience of revelry that had dominated Vincent's childhood were relegated to history.

Vincent stood in the doorway to the library holding his cap in both hands waiting for François to announce him. Count Robert was working at his desk on what everyone presumed to be his memoirs. Hundreds of books, protected by woven mesh brass panels, were encased in the walls. The smell of leather and parchment was an integral part of the room. It reminded Vincent of his childhood.

The count waved him to a couch in front of his desk and, turning to François, asked for a whiskey and soda for himself and cider for Vincent. "François and I are very upset," he said when the butler was gone. "The difference is he's drunker than a duck and I'm not."

The library, a powerful, mystical place that one entered by invitation only, was Vincent's favorite room in the castle. He looked at the false panel in the bookcase, which, when opened by pulling on two counterfeit medical volumes, led to a secret underground tunnel.

Every once in a while, when they were young, the count would open the panel and allow Roland, Nicole, and Vincent to enter the dark passageway. The count's father had, for safety reasons, condemned the tunnel before it reached the moat, but that didn't matter to the children. They could wander far enough inside the cool, damp opening in the earth to encourage dreams. Too proud to admit that they were terrified by the stories they'd heard of robed priests and black knights, Vincent, Roland, and Nicole would hold on to each other, clutching candles that invariably blew out. Vincent imagined himself as the Count of Monte Cristo, urging Nicole and the countess under the moat before turning back to avenge the murders of Count Robert and his son.

Robert de Costebelle caught the young man's glance. "No one has been down there since Roland's accident," he said, taking a deep breath. Vincent sat on the sofa without the need to say anything. The count stood and handed him a long rectangular box, wrapped in brown paper.

"It hasn't been used in a long time, but I had it cleaned and it works," the count said, sitting back down.

Vincent held the box across his lap while he fished a knife out of his pocket. The brown paper hid a leather gun case, inside of which lay the stock and barrels of a box lock, sixteen-gauge side-by-side Robust. The sweet smell of gun oil that stained the felt lining rose to greet him. The wood was scratched and the barrels had lost most of their bluing, but when he put the gun together and closed the breach, the sound filled him with delight. He stood and mounted the stock to his shoulder until the count was satisfied that it fit.

"Hold your hand farther out on the fore end. You want to be stretched in a straight line from your eye to the end of the barrel," the count instructed, walking around Vincent, pushing and poking his arms and chest.

Count Robert handed him half a dozen boxes of number-seven waxed cardboard shells. "Shoot some crows," he said. "They're easy to hit and hard to kill."

Vincent thanked him again, cased the gun, and stood awkwardly in the middle of the room looking out the window. The swallows that had been hawking mosquitoes above the moat earlier had been replaced by bats attracted to moths drawn to the library lights. He caught a glimpse of a small flying body and remembered how Roland would cast spinning lures at bats on summer nights and how the tiny flyers, taking the moonlit sparkle of metal for an insect, would hurl themselves at the lure. He recalled their pathetic, high-pitched screams as the treble hooks dragged them to the ground.

Overwhelmed by memories, Vincent was startled by the anger that strained the count's voice. "There hasn't been anything to compare with what happened to Serge since the war," Count Robert said. He walked back and forth across the room. "Fights, yes, but nothing this malicious." He stopped and shook a finger in Vincent's face. "I will not allow anyone in my employ to keep secrets from me," he said and added that he would personally drive Serge to the hospital in the morning if he was not up and about.

François knocked and then walked in with the drinks. He stared at the gun case with the disgust he relegated to all weapons. The cider, pressed the year before from the estate's apples, was dark and milky. Vincent took a swallow and asked the count if Serge had said anything about the attack. "Your uncle is taking the blame for what happened. He said he'd been negligent, and that he would handle it when he felt better." François shook his head and left the room.

"Serge heard laughter coming from the car while he was being dragged," the count added, "but when I offered to help he told me he had family for that. That means you, son."

The uneven sound of a single-engine plane flying low over the forest caught the count's attention. He stood and looked through the window at the stars. "I always wonder about the pilots of night planes . . . who they are, where they're going, and why they are flying under the cover of darkness," he said. Vincent followed his gaze until he picked out the white taillight of the aircraft. He was aware that the count's attraction to airplanes was not based on idle curiosity but on his experience as a pilot in the First World War.

The count sat back down at his desk. "Some men become pilots because they love birds," he said. "I became a pilot first and then learned to love birds."

In 1915, when Robert de Costebelle was eighteen years old, he was sent into combat, after a mere four hours of piloting instruction. On that first outing he engaged in a dogfight he would have lost except that his adversary's plane ran out of gas, a common occurrence in the First World War. The viscount scored eleven wins after that, but a year later, on July 14, Bastille Day—a holiday he did not condone—his luck ran out high above the flatlands of Picardy. He never saw the German Fokker, but suddenly he felt his Spad buckle and a thin line of holes sprang through the fuselage toward him. It wasn't until he force landed his crippled plane in a hay field that he felt the blood in his boot. A twelve-year-old boy by the name of Étienne Verdier jumped off his plow horse and pulled the pilot out of the cockpit moments before the Spad caught on fire. He wrapped Robert de Costebelle's shattered leg in a potato sack and helped him to his house. The knee turned septic and the young viscount fought osteomyelitis for eight months in a military hospital outside of Paris. After the war, Count Henri de Costebelle found the young man who had saved his son's life and granted his family an indefinite lease to Merlecourt's farmland. Étienne Verdier had cultivated the property ever since and Count Robert had spent the rest of his life anchored to a cane.

The count drank from his glass and lit a cigarette. His immediate concern was Serge's well-being, but he couldn't overlook the partridge shoot that was to take place in a week. In the likely event that Serge was still bedridden, he asked Vincent to take the gamekeeper's place. The young man had been a beater on and off for a decade, and had loaded the count's shotguns on numerous occasions. He knew what to expect from both sides of the line. When Vincent looked doubtful the count raised his hand and said that Serge would brief him on the details.

"This will be your first important job for me," he said. "I expect you to do well."

Vincent was proud that Robert de Costebelle had chosen him but worried that in eight days he would have to transport, feed, and count on thirty men, men he had known all his life, to follow his orders. Leading a driven shoot was a thankless job, particularly after the midday meal when beer and cider filled the beater's bellies and dampened their fortitude. Vincent knew that even after he influenced his men into moving birds, the success of the shoot would still be at the mercy of a roving fox, a change in the weather, and, most of all, luck.

"I suggest you run the shoot from the left wing," said the count. "And that you find someone reliable to work the other end. You'll want to choose this man carefully. Driven shoots, like infantry maneuvers, begin and end on the flanks." The count took a thoughtful drag on his cigarette and exhaled. "What about the Verdier boy, Titi, the younger one?"

Vincent nodded but knew better than to accept; he was sure that once in the field Titi would team up with his brother Louis and take over the shoot. He asked Count Robert for a day to reflect on his choice, and the meeting was over.

Vincent left the library with the gun case under his arm and made his way through the darkened living room, eager to show his present to Serge. François stood at the door leading to the front hall. He paused for a moment and then walked quickly through the living room. Vincent put his hand out to talk to him but the butler shook his head and walked past him into the library without knocking. Surprised, Vincent followed him to the doorway, reacting to the butler's failure to properly announce himself. The count turned in his chair and stubbed out his cigarette in the ashtray.

François rubbed his hands together. He bowed his head and spoke quickly, as if he were throwing away something dirty. "Monsieur le Comte," he said. "I just received a call from Dr. Jobard. Serge is dead."

Chapter 5

Ever since the death of her brother, Ragondin's father, Tantine Artaban's behavior had been unpredictable. Most of the time she was childish and agreeable to her nephew's wishes, but there were moments when she acted as if haunted by demons. Ragondin didn't know if her rages were triggered by past slights and jealousies, or if the hysteria she welcomed was merely passing entertainment to a demented mind; either way, many of her actions troubled his sense of reality. Over the years he had learned to anticipate situations that would set her off, and ignoring her promises to behave, always drove her to church on small departmental back roads to allow the fewest opportunities possible for her to stick her head out the car window and insult the passersby.

That Sunday, Ragondin's aunt, wearing a black dress and a gray scarf over her thin, unruly hair, received Communion while her nephew waited at the bistro for Mass to be over. The reassurances she sought relating to her ultimate salvation were rendered by the village priest, Father Ménardeau, in exchange for the donation of weekly tithes and her unwavering devotion to the church's deity.

After Mass she cooked Ragondin a shoulder of lamb stuffed with spinach for lunch. Over salad and cheese she admonished him for poaching and reminded him that a similar inclination had ultimately killed his father. Then, girlish in her manner, she held his hand and told him that she loved him and, unaware that her brother had already plundered her stash, planned to leave him the coins she had sown inside her mattress. Later she read him poems by Musset, whom Ragondin loved. Finally, when the afternoon drew to evening, she drank a bottle of mulled wine and fell asleep in her chair.

Ragondin went back to the bistro in Merlecourt, where the men were discussing the upcoming stag hunting season and the condition of the young hounds of the year. Arnaud was polishing glasses. He looked worried. "There's been an accident at the mill," he said when Ragondin walked in. "I have no details except to say that Dr. Jobard has been summoned." Ragondin ran out of the bar, jumped back on his bicycle and pedaled hard toward his friend's house.

A low sun cast a glow on the square grave-like bales of hay in the pastures next to the river. The shadows of the plane tree stretched over the thatch roof, canvassing the mill. He knocked on the door, mustered his courage and entered, calling out Vincent's name without conviction. Serge's bed had been stripped and a bitter odor rose from the mattress. Ragondin climbed the ladder that led to the loft, backed down when he couldn't find Vincent, and then went out to the larder. He thought about drinking from a bottle of opened white wine cooling next to a block of ice but didn't dare. He went back into the mill and decided to wait until Vincent, or Serge, returned. After stoking the chimney he sat in front of the fireplace under the steady gaze of the Russian boar. A dozen different possibilities crossed his mind.

Minutes later, Vincent burst into the mill and ran through the room, pausing at his uncle's bed, calling Adorée's name. Fear had pulled the skin on his face tight against his cheekbones. When he ran out the back door, Ragondin followed. Vincent tripped over a garden hose that lay stretched out on the ground next to the larder. He traced it to the metal washtub, and warily dragged the nozzle out of the water. Serge's sheets rose to the surface, folding and unfolding before slowly ghosting away in a medium of excrement and blood.

The headlights of the Citroën carved a path of light down the dirt road leading to the blacktop that would take them to Dreux. The car smelled of snuff and of

Jules, of grease, and of a finality that Vincent felt in the pit of his stomach. He steered the car hard into the corners. A man walking his dog jumped out of the way and raised his fist. Vincent rubbed his right arm in an effort to remove the fluids from the washtub that were now drying and pulling on the hair on his forearms. He recited Hail Marys under his breath over and over as fast as he could until he felt Ragondin's hand on his shoulder. In a halting voice, he recounted what had happened. "I won't believe he's dead until I see him with my own eyes," he said, looking at his friend for reassurance. Ragondin moved his hand back to his lap and stared through the windshield. There was nothing to say.

Yellow streetlights stained the deserted facades of the town's nineteenth-century buildings. The flicker of black-and-white televisions filtered out from behind the slats of closed shutters and cast an eerie light on the potted geraniums that embellished the window sills. The bourgeois of the city sat in respectable comfort with their backs to Vincent's suffering and their eyes on the news. In the commercial district middle-aged men shuffled silently in and out of the train station bars, pausing to joke with whores in doorways. The smell of lamb fat, perfume, and cigarette smoke drifted through the car's windows, evoking the salacious pleasures of night.

Vincent stopped in front of the well-lit hospital on the hill overlooking the town of Dreux.

They ran through the swinging doors and elbowed their way through the crowd in the emergency room until Vincent stood with his hands on the admissions desk. A middle-aged nun wearing a black habit was filling out forms while fending off a mother cradling a young girl. Vincent leaned over the desk and spoke in a measured voice. "Where can I find Serge Lebuison?" he asked. The nun, without looking up, told him to wait his turn. Vincent repeated his request; this time raising his voice. The woman made a hissing noise and, lifting a pair of small, black eyes to his, told him to sit down or get out.

Vincent screamed at her: "Tell me. What have you done with Serge Lebuison?" The nun stood up, her round face pinched and mean. The crowd protested, pushed from behind, muttered threats. A heavyset farmer told Vincent to shut up or he would kick his ass. From deeper in the crowd someone else suggested calling the police. The farmer took a step forward but Ragondin turned and raised his fists in the man's face.

The nun called for help. People yelled for Vincent and Ragondin to leave. A black orderly and a short blond nurse ran into the room. The orderly, a thin man with prominent cheekbones, took Vincent by the arm and, in an accented voice that rolled out of his chest from Central Africa, told Vincent to follow him outside. Vincent ripped his arm free and stood ready to fight. A hand lightly touched his and he looked down at the young nurse. She had a pretty face and the lids of her blue eyes opened and closed like those of a porcelain doll's. "I'll take you to your uncle," she said. Her voice was calm and composed.

Vincent motioned for Ragondin to wait and then he followed the nurse down a brightly lit corridor. He kept his eyes on her, mesmerized by the curls of straw-colored hair poking out from under her starched white bonnet. Vincent inquired about his uncle as they walked beneath a twin row of fluorescent lights.

"They brought him down a short while ago, Monsieur," she said. He stared at her. No one had ever called him Monsieur before. Turning to face him the nurse then quietly said that she was sorry, that this was the morgue. She opened the door.

Sitting behind a desk eating a sandwich and drinking from a liter bottle of beer was an emaciated man with a prominent Adam's apple that bobbed up and down as he swallowed. In the background a ceiling light reflected off a chrome operating table with a metal drain that disappeared into the floor. Next to the table was a roll-away desk on top of which scalpels, forceps, metal bowls, and an electric saw awaited. Except for a few strands of hair caught in the saw's blade, the room was immaculate. A strong smell of chemicals made Vincent sneeze.

The mortician looked up, visibly annoyed. The nurse introduced Vincent as M. Lebuison's nephew and the man ran a finger down a list of names on a sheet of paper on his desk. He said that he hadn't started working on Serge Lebuison yet and, wiping his mouth with the back of his hand, stood and shuffled over to a second door behind the operating table. He was taller than Vincent and wore black, knee-high rubber boots with his pant legs stuffed down inside them.

They followed the man through the door. Vincent felt like he was walking in slow motion. Green sheets covered corpses on two metal tables. The man scratched his head, seeming to have forgotten where he had put the body. He pulled one of the sheets back and exposed a woman's head. Her face was bloated and purple. Her tongue, fat and black, filled her entire mouth. He turned to Vincent with an amused expression. "Strangled on a chicken bone," he said matter-of-factly. Then he reached over and pulled the sheet all the way off the second corpse.

Vincent looked down at his uncle's battered body and was embarrassed. He moved to cover Serge back up and then paused when he realized, with relief, that the nurse had left. Serge, who looked cold and helpless beneath the harsh white light, had an erection. Speechless, Vincent wished he hadn't come.

"Had a big dick," said the man. "Often the case with little men." A bitter taste rose in Vincent's mouth. He looked into the man's eyes and called him a son of a bitch. The mortician made a rude gesture and left the room.

Vincent stared at the man whose house he had shared for five years and felt ill. He drew the sheet back over his uncle and turned to leave, but then remembered something from his youth, a gesture of peace, a concession to the dead. He picked up the sheet and gently rubbed his thumb between his uncle's cold eyes. When Vincent lived at the castle the count had sometimes made a furtive sign of the cross on Vincent's forehead before sending him up to bed, a mark intended to ward off any evil that might befall him during the night.

Vincent walked back alone down the long corridor leading to the admitting room. The young nurse with the blond curls stood next to the black orderly behind the desk. She told Vincent how sorry she was and the man looked away, as if grief were contagious. Ragondin joined Vincent and without saying anything put his hand on his friend's shoulder. The nurse followed them to the door and explained that Dr. Jobard and Mme Painvin had brought Serge to the hospital and that Adorée had left in tears.

Vincent touched her arm. "You know Adorée?" he asked. Her skin had the texture of cream.

She looked up at him with bright round eyes. "I buy my bread from her bakery," she answered. The girl's bonnet barely reached his chin.

Her arm felt warm in his hand when he asked her name.

"Mélanie," she answered, and looked away. He let her go.

Vincent thanked her for helping him; he knew that the police would have come if she hadn't intervened. He introduced himself and Ragondin to the girl.

She let out a small giggle and touched the sleeve of his shirt. "I know who you are," she said. "Mme Painvin has told me about you."

They said good-bye.

"Call me sometime," Mélanie whispered, standing in a wedge of fluorescent light.

Vincent drove down the hill into town and, after dropping Ragondin off at his aunt's flat, parked in front of Adorée's bakery. She owned an apartment above her shop; he didn't know which one. Vincent called out her name several times, but there was no answer. Angry, he walked over to the metal roll-down door of the bakery and banged on it with his fists. He called her again. Lights went on up and down the street and a man's voice yelled out into the night. Vincent didn't care whom he woke. He cursed God loudly until he heard the sound of feet running down the stairs. Adorée came out in her bathrobe and pulled him by the shirt into the building.

They climbed the staircase to the second floor and when they reached the landing the light automatically blinked off. Adorée guided Vincent into the parlor, where they stood for a moment, awkwardly holding onto each other. Then she took him by the hand and walked him into her bedroom.

He sat on the edge of the bed while Adorée went back and locked the front door. Serge had described her bedroom: a long, carpeted room with high ceilings and burgundy-colored curtains, pen-and-ink drawings of young girls in diaphanous dresses on the walls, and a single high-backed armchair facing the side of the bed she slept on. The very bed that Serge and the doctor had been sharing for years. An ebony prie-dieu inlaid with a carving of the Virgin Mary stood in a corner of the room. The clothes she wore at the time of Serge's death lay neatly folded on the elbow rest, with her panties on top of the pile, directly below the benevolent gaze of the Blessed Virgin.

Adorée sat down and rested her head on Vincent's shoulder. He asked her what had happened; he had only been gone an hour. She moved into the armchair and explained that after he left Serge had talked for a while, then rested until Jobard returned. The doctor had wanted him to go to the hospital and there was a scene. Then a strange look had crossed Serge's face. "Something just busted loose in here," he'd said and touched his midsection. A moment later he vomited blood. Jobard tried to bring him back but he was gone.

Tears filled Adorée's eyes and she looked away. Vincent got down on the floor and laid his head on her lap. She was warm and soft, like his mother, and a few minutes later he felt the tension in her quiet. Her tears came slowly at first and then poured out in uncontrollable heaves. He wrapped his arms around her knees. Toward the end, and perhaps because he held her as the countess had once held him, comforting Adorée gave him strength. When her sobs subsided she made Vincent lie down on the bed and covered him with a blanket. She turned off the lights and went to the bathroom. He heard the toilet flush, and the sound of her muffled sobs.

That night Vincent dreamed he was back in boarding school, in the dormitory he had shared with eleven other students. It was a hideous dream that he had struggled through for many years. In it he was ill and restricted to his bed because the school's rules forbade the use of the bathroom after the lights were out. In the night, his cramps were so painful that he got up and stumbled down the row of metal beds, past the dorm master's room, and into the communal bathroom. He didn't make it to the toilet. Just inside the door he fell to his knees and was sick, as sick as he had ever been in his life. He curled up on the bathroom floor with his face on the tile and prayed to God for mercy, promising him his life if he were not caught.

The dread of being discovered prompted him to use his hands and clothes to clean up the mess. Too scared to turn on the lights, he worked in the dark. When he finished he balled up his pajamas, hid them in his locker, and crawled back to bed. He was so weak that he didn't hear the bell the next morning and woke up surrounded by jeering roommates, holding their noses and giving him the Nazi salute.

Then, Vincent was standing in assembly in front of the entire student body. There, humiliated as never before, he listened to the Jesuit headmaster deliver a sermon on cleanliness and godliness. It was a long sermon, one that encompassed all the particulars of what boys do to themselves and to each other—particulars that, according to the priest, would see them all in hell. Vincent had stood with his chin on his chest, certain it would never end. When it did, the student body whistled and hooted and chanted: "Lebuison caca, Lebuison caca."

Vincent woke in a sweat and sat bolt upright in a bed that wasn't his. He tried to focus on the noise that was coming up from the street below. Adorée, already dressed, handed him a cup of coffee. He could see that she had spent a long time in front of the mirror and he was about to tell her how nice she looked when a loud crashing sound came up from the street. It was Monday, market day. They listened as insults rose up and inundated the apartment. Adorée opened the curtains and allowed a gray morning light to enter the room. Vincent got out of bed with his clothes still on and followed the light to the window.

Farmers were in town to buy, sell, and barter their wares. Fishmongers who had left the English Channel during the night were unloading trucks crowded with iced-down fish and seaweed-packed crustaceans in wicker baskets. Local vegetable and fruit growers had begun to fill the marketplace; the hollow resonance of hooves on stone pavement mingled with the sounds of rickety carts. Small groups of Arki Arabs, back from fighting for France in the Algerian War, hurried along with copper trinkets carried in cardboard suitcases and colorful carpets draped over narrow shoulders. Vincent could see the wealthy buyers, the hotel owners, and the restaurateurs drinking coffee in the bistro overlooking the market, ready to deal the moment the stands were open for business. Housewives would arrive at nine when the square was filled with flowers and cheeses, vegetables and meats, farm girls and fowl. The needy would begin shopping at noon, when the trucks were being reloaded and bargains were there for the asking.

Vincent looked at the egg-shaped depression in the sheets where Adorée had curled up next to him. He had never slept in a bed with a woman before other than his mother. They talked over a second cup of coffee and Adorée's smile was gentle and understanding. He told her about returning to the empty mill and his trip to the hospital with Ragondin, about the pretty blonde nurse who had helped him.

Adorée stood up from the dining room table. They could hear activity in the bakery below. Vincent followed her downstairs and accepted a chocolate-filled croissant from a tray fresh out of the oven. She raised her face for a kiss and promised to see him at the church services.

He walked to the door, stopped, and asked her if Serge had told her anything before he died.

She paused without looking at him and slowly shook her head. "No," she said. "He didn't tell me a thing."

Chapter 6

Bernard Auverpois, a French national born and raised in Algeria was a fourth-generation *pied-noir.* A lieutenant with the police force in Dreux, Auverpois was waiting at the mill with Maurice Corneille when Vincent returned from town. The lieutenant, staring myopically through thick metal-rimmed glasses, shook the young man's hand with more vigor than necessary. He had lost what little humor he was born with as gradually as he had lost eyesight and as permanently as he had lost his homeland. As a retired rugby player for the French national team, Auverpois loathed wearing glasses as much as he despised Charles de Gaulle for granting Algeria its independence.

Vincent told the lieutenant what he knew: that other than the usual fines for fishing out of season, and the eviction of a family of overeager English tourists who had demanded a tour of the estate, Serge had not mentioned anyone or anything out of the ordinary. Auverpois seemed surprised. He impatiently told Vincent to think before he spoke, but Vincent had nothing to add. The policeman mumbled an obscenity and commenced to methodically search through Serge's belongings. When he found half a dozen wire nooses and three pouches—the kind rabbits rush into—he became accusatory. "I bet you and your uncle eat deer and hare, even pike and trout, all year, don't you?" As he spoke an old scrum scar on his forehead turned scarlet. Hunching his shoulders he turned to Corneille and said, "I have never met a privately employed gamekeeper who didn't poach for profit." He poked Vincent in the chest with a short, stiff finger.

"I believe that Lebuison and his killers were partners," the lieutenant said in a thick North African accent. "He was killed over the divide."

The poaching accusation took Vincent by surprise. Of course they ate game year-round. It was customary for every keeper in the region to bring home animals that had been wounded or confiscated for being taken illegally. But the implication that Serge had poached for profit was insulting. The protection and proliferation of game on Robert de Costebelle's estate had been the focal point of his uncle's entire career.

"Gamekeepers are like gypsies," Auverpois insisted, squinting his eyes. "They would steal their sister's children if they were worth something."

Vincent wished Serge had been in the room to defend himself. His uncle would have hit Auverpois. Or if he had been in another mood he would have mimicked the policeman's manner of speech, as he sometime did over drinks when he would describe a woman's ass and it sounded like the village butcher peddling a rump roast.

"Policemen," Serge liked to exclaim, "have the morality of politicians and the imagination of compost."

Vincent refused to acknowledge Auverpois's accusations. He stared at the red-faced policeman, who was listening to Corneille express emphatically that he had known Serge for years and that, irrespective of his faults, he did not poach or deal with poachers, other than to apprehend them.

The intervention didn't satisfy Auverpois, who moved to the front of the room, with purpose, as if walking on to a playing field. He had a murder to investigate and no clues, not even a set of decent car tracks. On top of that he had to deal with an impertinent kid who thought he was someone he wasn't. Halfway out the door Auverpois turned and ordered Vincent to be at the police station at two o'clock the following afternoon to fill out a deposition.

Ragondin passed Corneille and the lieutenant as they drove away from the mill. Once inside Ragondin described to Vincent the summer night he witnessed the policeman batter two Algerian boys with a spring-loaded blackjack outside a dance hall in Dreux. The boys had invited a couple of local girls to dance. When the girls refused, two workers from the Renault factory got into a fistfight with the Arabs. Auverpois arrived on the scene and beat the Algerian boys unconscious. They were taken to the hospital in an ambulance.

Outside in the larder Vincent found the makings for lunch: an earthenware platter of St. Daniel ham, a round of ripe Muenster cheese that promised an olfactory adventure, sweet butter, and a jar of *cornichons*. Under the Douglas fir where Vincent had hung the eels a ladder of flies clung to the abandoned ropes. He waved his arms to disperse them. Beyond the swarming flies the midday sun cast brilliant rays on the stand of birch trees that buttressed the mill.

Ragondin placed a loaf of bread and a bottle of cider on the table. He mentioned that when he had gone to school in the village his classmates had called the big purple flies *mouches à caca*—shit flies. In early December, when the insects surfaced on every windowpane of every house, the boys used to catch them by the dozens. Weekly contests involving *mouches à caca* culminated in a winner-take-all Christmas tournament. The rules were simple. On an agreed count each contestant popped a fly into his mouth. The object was to keep it alive longer than anyone else. If it flew out or died, the contestant lost. If a competitor swallowed his *mouche* the rules provided for a replacement. "I made it to the finals one year," Ragondin said. "But I sneezed and my *mouche à caca* blew out my nose and flew away."

Ragondin buttered his bread and heaped ham on his sandwich, squeezing the two halves of bread until yellow butter oozed out of each end. Vincent cut the Muenster and made a face. The cheese exuded a wonderful and indecent smell.

A loud knock at the door interrupted coffee. A moment later, Monique Moulin, Vincent's aunt, flung the door open and marched into the room with her friend, the widow Béton, following humbly behind. The women were dressed in full mourning attire, their starched, black dresses rustling loudly with each step. Mme Béton clutched her rosary and a bar of black chocolate, which she handed to Vincent. She smiled and greeted Ragondin. Monique Moulin didn't acknowledge either, but instead, with an ill-tempered expression etched on her face, snorted her disapproval. "Why didn't you call me?" she chastised Vincent. "I am your only family, your aunt, your blood. I had to hear about my brother's death from my friend here, instead of from my kin." She nodded at Mme Béton.

Ragondin busied himself with cleaning the kitchen table and took his time moving the food back into the larder. Monique's uneducated peasant voice rose into a shrill as she recounted the things she had done for her nephew—taking him in after his mother died, caring for him when he was sick, allowing him to live in this hovel against her better judgment.

"What do I get for my kindness?" she screamed. "Nothing! Not even a phone call!" Vincent was certain that if Mme Béton had not been in the room his aunt would have hit him.

He looked at her and closed his good eye, his blue eye, just as he had done every time the Jesuits priests had accused him of being German. Composing herself with a shudder, Monique Moulin turned away and proceeded to rummage through her brother's belongings. Without saying a word, she opened drawers, ran her hands under Serge's clothes, turned over pictures, leafed through the pages of his books. Mme Béton, embarrassed, hugged her rosary against her chest. Vincent hated his aunt for violating Serge's privacy, but he didn't protest, knowing from experience that the quickest way to get rid of her was to ignore her. When she finished her inspection she sat on Serge's bed, stroked the pillow, and sighed out loud, as if on cue.

Mme Béton, a retired schoolteacher who had recently become Father Ménardeau's housekeeper, had a dry, wrinkled face across which her mouth stretched like a thin horizon. It made her seem bitter and intransigent but in reality she was a gentle, kind-hearted woman. She had taught geography when Ragondin and Vincent were young, and stood up for them at different times in their lives—Ragondin for being the son of a poacher, Vincent for being the son of the enemy.

Monique, on the other hand, was considerably younger, with a smooth, round face, turned-up nose, plump cheeks, and a heart-shaped mouth that was either admonishing sinners or preaching the word of God. She was, as Serge liked to call her, "a sanctimonious whore." Vincent's uncle had also offered up the idea that Monique was diddling the priest, an accusation they both found hilarious.

When Monique realized that Vincent was not going to console her, she jumped up from her brother's bed and called him a bastard, spitting the words into his face. Vincent said nothing and she went back to her rummaging. Stopping in front of a small tarnished bowl in which Serge had stored his change, she declared that it belonged to Mémé, Vincent's grandmother.

Mme Béton sat down next to Vincent and implored him to disregard his aunt explaining that she was upset, that she loved her brother and didn't mean what she was saying. The old woman hesitated and then in a low voice urged Vincent to pray for his uncle, to pray for God's love and forgiveness as they had prayed together in school when Vincent was young. "In the days ahead, Vincent," she continued, "when you are saddest, do not hesitate to call on Father Ménardeau. He cares, and he will listen to you."

Monique looked at the kitchen floor and muttered, "Pigs." Vincent wondered how her husband kept from slitting her throat. Impatient to be on her way, to revel in the condolences of the villagers and display her grief in public, Monique Moulin announced that she had talked to Father Ménardeau and arranged for the funeral service to be held at eleven o'clock, two days hence. She wanted Vincent there early, dressed in a suit and tie. After church there would be a lunch at the farm for family and friends. Glancing over at Ragondin she declared that he could come, but then added that Adorée Painvin was not invited. "She's a harlot!" said Vincent's aunt. "My dead brother's harlot!" Monique wiped away an imaginary tear and begged God to forgive her brother's sins, of which Adorée was but one of many.

Mme Béton stood and placed her hand on Vincent's shoulder. She reminded him that his uncle was in good hands. Vincent kissed her cheek. On her way out Monique stopped in front of the sterling silver change bowl, turned it upside down and stuffed it into her purse. "I'm returning this to the farm, where it rightfully belongs," she said, opening the door and leaving without waiting for a reply. A copper coin rolled across the desk and fell onto the floor.

Chapter 7

After his visitors left, Vincent joined Ragondin in the kitchen. He split half a baguette down the middle, buttered one side, pulled the dough out of the other, and placed Mme Béton's chocolate bar in the hollow. "My aunt has an infinite capacity for self-pity," he said. He cut the demi-baguette in two, handed Ragondin his half, and added, "She is also a cunt."

"Five hundred years ago she would have been screaming insults at Joan of Arc."

"Screw her," Vincent said. "I have something more important to discuss. I want you to be my wing man this Sunday. What do you say?"

For the son of a poacher this was a great honor, and Ragondin confirmed his gratitude by shaking Vincent's hand and then embracing him. His newfound status would inspire both resentment and envy in those villagers more qualified for the job, and this delighted him.

When the afternoon sun was low and the shadows dark and specific, Vincent walked his friend to the door. He said they would go to the Roberta Woods the next morning. And then, his eyes bright with anger, said, "I'm going to kill the men who murdered Serge."

Ragondin shrugged. "I doubt you could kill anyone, Vincent. People like you don't kill unless threatened and backed into a corner." He didn't say this to question his friend's courage or wound his pride; he said it because he believed it to be true.

Vincent sat in an armchair in front of the fireplace after Ragondin left and fought the sleep that rushed at him. His mind, on the edge of consciousness, drifted back to a spring afternoon when he was twelve years old. That day, out of curiosity and because he was sure he would pass unnoticed, Vincent had, from a distance, stalked his uncle while he made his rounds of the estate. For reasons he couldn't remember, Vincent decided to circle ahead of Serge and wait for him in the water garden. He ran through the understory next to a maze of ponds and rivulets and, guessing his uncle's path, climbed a willow tree overlooking a tributary of the river Avre. Minutes later Serge stopped in front of the same tree. After leaning his shotgun on its trunk, he lay down on the bank and stared into the water. Overjoyed that he had gone unnoticed, Vincent quietly made himself small in the elbow of the limb he was sitting on and watched.

Serge rolled up his right sleeve and slowly lowered his arm into the water. From his vantage point Vincent could see all the way down to Serge's hand, which had slipped below a large brown trout suspended in the current, fanning its tail. He watched his uncle's fingers gently touch the trout's fins, tickle the fish's belly, and slowly move up its sides. It seemed forever before Serge's fingers found the gills, but when they did, they closed like a talon. In one sweeping motion the fish came flying out of the water and onto the bank. Vincent held his breath.

Serge stood up, rolled down his sleeve, and brushed the grass off his shirt. He pushed a pinch of snuff into each nostril and looked over the water garden. Then, without hurry, he walked away, leaving the big trout flopping in the grass directly below his nephew's gaze. When Serge had disappeared, Vincent climbed down the weeping willow, picked up the fish, and carried it to Chef Gaston.

"Merci, young Lebuison," the chef said. "Madame la Comtesse asked for trout earlier this morning. Your uncle told me you'd be over."

The round tin of tobacco that never left Serge's shirt pocket had slipped between the cushion of the armchair Vincent was sitting in. When he opened the metal box the release of familiar smells brought on the tears that had been welling up ever since François had announced the tragedy. Vincent sat with his face in his hands, his shoulders shaking. Much later, when no more tears would come, he leaned back and rested his head on the back of the chair, allowing the silence of the mill to accept his grief.

Before going to bed that night, Vincent walked to the bank of the river Eure and tested the water with his hand. A thin layer of fog stretched across the surface. Without giving it much thought he took off his clothes and waded in, his feet sinking through the mud to the gravel floor below. He shivered. The water temperature had followed the change of seasons.

For years Vincent had gone swimming naked in the river almost every summer night. And, perhaps because he was a diviner and a predictor of rain, he had overcome his fear of dark water and become part of the river, as if he belonged to the family of fishes. There were many nights, when the moon was full and the owls hunted low over the fields, that he didn't get out of the water until dawn. Now, even the mud, which at first had felt queer, even repugnant, excited him. One Saturday after a dance in the village he'd stripped off his clothes, paddled through the current into an eddy and, with his chest resting on the warm grass of the bank, made love to the mud. The next morning he woke up mortified, convinced his member would rot off.

The river swirled around his body and took him to a hundred familiar places. He passed through cold and warm pockets of water, feeling the fresh evening air clean against his face. Drifting with the current he watched the fog rupture and mend itself with his passing. He wondered if Nicole would swim with him as she had when they were children. High above his head, stars speckled the sky.

When he neared the trunk of a willow tree that had toppled into the river during a summer storm, he pulled himself out of the water and climbed onto the bank. The sound of a dog barking in Rebours reminded him of Jules. Finally the cold night air sent him running back to his clothes and home to the mill.

Vincent put a match to the kindling in the fireplace and warmed his hands in front of the tall, young flames until his chill disappeared. He longed for the sound of his uncle's voice, the comforting suddenness of a sneeze, a cough, a curse—anything to ease the loneliness the swim had been unable to dispel. To fill the emptiness of Serge's bed, he climbed in between the fresh sheets and thought about the bird women in his uncle's dream, the count's shoot, and Nicole's return. When his mind became a continuum of future plans and patchy memories he fell asleep, his head accepting his uncle's pillow as his own.

The next morning Ragondin and Vincent met early. After a cup of coffee they ran from the mill to the Roberta Woods, as the crow flies. They ran for ten minutes through pastures and woodlots, climbing fences and jumping creeks. Even though Vincent's gait was hampered by his severed toe he was light on his feet, Ragondin had to push himself to keep up. When they reached the woods they sat on the ground and leaned back against the stump of an oak tree that overlooked the scene of Serge's murder.

The narrow stubble field where Vincent's uncle had been left for dead was bordered by woods on the one side, a dirt road on the other, and, closest to them, an ankle-high alfalfa field. When the sun was firmly planted in the sky and the stubble had turned white, Vincent shook his head and told his friend that he simply could not imagine his uncle ever walking into a situation that would kill him. He repeated what Serge had told Count Robert about the sound of laughter rising above the noise of the engine of the car that was dragging him to his death. Vincent wondered out loud who could be so perverse?

"Probably someone we know," Ragondin said matter-of-factly. He stood up and stretched.

They walked through the green alfalfa field to the road and followed the shallow ditch where Serge had been found. Vincent stared at the washed-out tire tracks in the stubble, and guessed at the imperceptible depressions of his uncle's body. He stopped next to the dense, green foliage at the edge of the woods and shivered, imagining his uncle lying on the ground watching Jules dragging his hindquarters toward him.

They came away from the wheat field convinced that Serge had been waiting in hiding. Most likely for poachers who had inadvertently left hints of their whereabouts. It was difficult for either Vincent or Ragondin to imagine the gamekeeper being outsmarted by anyone.

They pushed through the brambles and walked into the underbrush. The upper leaves on the hardwoods had turned colors, but the lower halves of the trees were still green and rich with falling sap. They found the terrier's droppings a few meters away, next to the walnut tree that Vincent's uncle had leaned against. Serge had peeled off a square of bark, and scattered the shavings between his feet, a habit Vincent imitated. Ragondin stood on the trampled ground and pointed at the trees that drew away and framed a view of the road and the scene of the murder.

They walked slowly to the roundabout in the center of the Roberta Woods where the estate's pheasants were kept in large aviaries fashioned from chicken wire and netting. The structure was evidence of a once-robust breeding program, but over the years the number of birds had dwindled from five hundred to a brace of cocks and a dozen hens intended for the kitchen. The pheasants greeted Vincent by running back and forth inside the aviary. He shoveled corn out of a drum, freshened their water, and buried the carcass of a dead hen whose tail end had been violated and then devoured by her peers.

There were deer tracks under an oak tree next to where Vincent buried the bird. Ragondin counted seven does and recognized the imprint of a large stag. They checked and re-checked the hoof prints until there was no doubt in either mind. Three years earlier, at the end of a long chase, the same stag had jumped a barbed-wire fence, tearing a triangle of horn and meat off its rear hoof. The wound had healed leaving a permanent scar. The stag's spoor was easy to identify.

Ragondin felt his heart beat a little faster. The markings belonged to Monsieur, a red stag that at last count carried a rack of sixteen tines, making him the largest and one of the most sought-after royal stags in France. Ragondin knew that it had been his father's most cherished ambition to poach Monsieur, but he didn't mention this to Vincent. The stag's coat was graying, but his hindquarters were still as powerful as a stallion's, and when the weather changed and the season turned to hunting his story was told and retold on the streets of the towns and villages, beside the hearth of each farmhouse, and inside every bar in the region.

The Haute-Normandie Hunt Club had been running hounds at Monsieur for ten years, ever since he was a spike, to no avail. Season after season, the stag had eluded the pack with an ease that both baffled and challenged the best hunters in the province. Monsieur had legendary stamina and was an accomplished artist at backtracking. On occasion he was known to stretch out flat on the ground with his antlers on his back and his nose under the leaves to keep his scent from rising into the path of the oncoming dogs. At other times he simply vanished.

Over the years, strong, determined men and the best deerhounds from every hunt club in France had been invited to help bring Monsieur to bay, all with the same inevitable results. When the gray winter afternoons succumbed to shadows and the hunt horns fell silent, the venerable stag had invariably transformed a fine day of hunting into a memorable one, his methods of evasion worthy of a magician.

Vincent told his friend of a night earlier that summer when his uncle had been approached by a poacher who wanted to ingratiate himself with Serge. The man had reported that a group of wealthy sportsmen in Paris had formed a syndicate with a large cash pool to be awarded to anyone in France who delivered to them the head of a stag with a rack of fourteen points or more. The prize was worth two million francs, more than enough money for one man to kill another.

Ragondin had also heard the rumors of a ransom on Monsieur's head, but there was so much hearsay floating around the valley, especially regarding the business of poaching, that he hadn't paid much attention.

Serge had corroborated the man's story. Fat, rich bourgeois from Paris wanted to hang the heads of royal stags on their walls. Vincent was equally sure that evidence of Monsieur less than a hundred meters from where his uncle had been murdered was no accident. Serge had taught him that coincidences were only relevant in the Bible.

Ragondin studied the droppings near the tracks under the oak tree and estimated they were four days old. Since it was the beginning of the rut, he felt Monsieur had led his does down from the forest into the Roberta Woods, a safe distance from the rivalry of younger bucks. If Vincent was right, poachers had been watching the herd's movements, seen these same spoors, and waited at the edge of the woods for Monsieur. When Serge had questioned their motives they murdered him.

The friends agreed that as soon as the shoot on Sunday was over they would concentrate all their efforts on finding Monsieur—and the men intent on killing him. The breeding season would be in full swing, and the stag wouldn't be quite as wary. Vincent had every intention of being present when the poachers made their next move.

Chapter 8

Sunlight filtered through the canopy of the hardwood trees to the ground where the red stag had herded his does. Vincent and Ragondin walked through the light that was falling in bold streaks and moved out from under the woods toward the village by way of the river.

Partially hidden behind a tangle of nettles a young doe was drinking, with her front legs spread wide on the bank. They stopped and watched until the little deer had taken from the river what she needed. The pastoral scene reminded Vincent of the day Serge slit the throat of the roebuck that had been gut shot.

"I am going to see Father Ménardeau," he told Ragondin. "I want to understand why God took my mother and Roland, and now Serge from me."

Ragondin didn't see the point. He thought the priest was a charlatan and insisted that it was Ménardeau's smooth complexion and sad brown eyes, not his piety, that had been prompting women to confessional ever since Father Bonnechair had retired with the gout.

"That penguin has been poking the wives of all the farmers in the valley. He knows a lot about blow jobs but doesn't know holy from shit." Ragondin looked at Vincent and realized he wasn't listening.

Vincent was walking quickly, his uneven gait even more pronounced at this pace, a frown on his face.

When they reached the church they saw the tall figure of Father Ménardeau climb out of his car and walk into the rectory. Vincent felt remorse for having cursed God out loud on the street in front of Adorée's apartment. He would seek pardon for his blasphemy, talk to the Father about the deaths in his life, and beg forgiveness for his sins. He would seek absolution through confession and be purified by eating the body of Christ the next day at Communion. He felt a weight lift off his shoulders.

Ragondin reminded Vincent that Father Ménardeau's weekly sermon invariably focused on his favorite topic: the role of the Church in a totalitarian society. And that Ménardeau had been in favor of changing the delivery of the liturgy from Latin to French, a movement newly blessed by the clergy but rejected by many parishioners, including Robert de Costebelle.

"He meddles in politics and swells the heads of the working class," the count would say. "Now he wants to rob the wonder from the Church and flaunt the frailties of its beliefs by stripping Mass of its garments. He's a damn Communist!"

Ragondin left Vincent to his quest for arcane answers and went to the bistro. He did not see Catholicism as a forum for understanding life's indignities, but rather as a slow surrender to a malevolent authority, with hell as its grisly alternative. The allegiance to nature that they had both embraced, and often discussed while fishing, made sense to Ragondin, who was more intrigued by the transparency of a flower blossom than the agony of a man-god nailed to a tree.

When Vincent knocked at the rectory door Mme Béton greeted him with the news that the Father was absent. She played with a dust rag and wouldn't look him in the eye, visibly unsettled at having been asked to lie. Vincent kissed her wrinkled face and told her not to be concerned, that he'd come back another day.

He walked toward the heavy, hand-carved oak doors that led into the seven-hundred-year-old Norman church struggling to understand God's deplorable choice of emissaries and capricious attitude toward death. Out of habit, he knelt down onto the cold stone floor, crossed himself, and recited the Lord's Prayer. Vincent thought about all the pleas that had been forwarded to heaven over the centuries from this very spot, and wondered how many had been answered. He stared at the colored light falling through the stained-glass windows, hoping for a sign from above. While he waited a blue jay, chased by a thrush, entered the church through the open doors in the vestibule. The birds flew through the rafters and brushed against the statues of saints. Vincent watched, knowing the thrush had no real designs on the larger bird. It was only a show, an accepted ritual, comparable to the performance enacted under this same roof every Sunday. After a while the birds found the sunlight and flew out the way they had come, taking with them a measure of his faith.

Vincent went to the village bakery to buy chocolate éclairs for Mémé, his grandmother. Inside, the room was warm and filled with the odors and memories of his boyhood. M. Dupont, the baker, was old and stooped. Flour obscured his disheveled eyebrows. He expressed his condolences and refused to take Vincent's money, solemnly adding an extra pastry to the bag.

Vincent walked to the bistro and nodded to the women on the street who crossed themselves as he passed. He asked Ragondin to tell the beaters chosen by Serge for the count's shoot to meet him there at noon the day after the funeral. Men in the bar offered him drinks that he turned down, and their best wishes, which he accepted.

Outside the village, flocks of wood pigeons rose out of the harvested fields under a cloudless October sky, settling back moments later in an expansive sweep of steel-colored wings. As he walked into the farmyard Vincent noted with relief that his aunt's car was gone.

The wall that fortified the Lebuison farm was held together with lime. Built in 1785 from stone and straw, it measured three meters high and one meter deep. The original purpose of the fortification was to protect the farmer's family and livestock from packs of roving wolves and bandits. Now it served to shield the inhabitants from the inquisitive eyes of curiosity seekers.

The main house was a long, narrow, two-story stone building with a tile roof, three chimneys, and flower boxes on the windowsills. Vincent went inside and walked under the hand-hewn oak beams to the center of the room, where he placed the éclairs on the dining room table. He went to his grandmother, who was quietly rocking in her chair in front of the fireplace, and kissed her twice on each cheek, as was the family custom. Mémé was eighty-six years old, frail, and twisted with arthritis.

Her voice trembling with sorrow, she acknowledged Vincent's presence. "My boy has gone to heaven," she said.

Vincent stroked her hand and told her about the birds he had seen in the church, painting a pretty picture. Then he went to the kitchen and found a plate for the éclairs, which he placed on his grandmother's lap. He sat on the floor in front of her rocking chair. Her legs, tightly bound in brown-colored stockings, were so thin her shoes appeared improbably large.

He looked at her and remembered that once she had been recognized as the fastest chicken-plucker in the valley. As a boy he had watched her hang fowl, four at a time, by their feet from a rafter in the stable and, one by one, cut out their tongues with a pair of scissors, bleeding them into a trough, the blood to be mixed later with gruel for the pigs. With fingers flying as fast as knitting needles, Mémé had started at the legs and worked downward, turning the room into a whirlwind of feathers.

She used the same method to bleed and pluck ducks and geese. But rabbits were handled differently. Before skinning them she bled them by carving one eye from its socket with a sharpened spoon, saving the blood to thicken her soups and sauces.

Mémé picked up an éclair off the plate, her fingers almost as wide as the pastry, and pushed it, end first, into her mouth. The expression of pleasure on her face momentarily softened the lines of pain etched there by time, the loss of a daughter, and now the loss of her only son. She looked at Vincent and smiled, her mouth a toothless hole. As she sat staring absentmindedly out the window she asked Vincent to help her dress Serge for church. She wanted her boy to look his best. The tears that fell from her eyes ran down a dozen wrinkled paths to the corners of her mouth and slipped over her chin.

Back at the bar Vincent drank a beer and listened to the commiserations of Arnaud. The rest of the men in the room averted their eyes and drank in silence, undoubtedly wishing Vincent would go away and leave them to their pleasures. Fluorescent light flared over the shiny dome of Arnaud's head when he leaned from the waist to return a glass to its rack. The bartender's face was troubled as he searched for the right words. Haltingly, and with as much sincerity as he could muster, he told Vincent that the terrible accident involving Serge would one day be just another memory, one in a long list of sad events in an even longer life.

"It wasn't an accident, Arnaud," Vincent said closing his good eye. "Serge was tortured and then killed." Arnaud nodded his head, looking even more troubled. Sensing hesitation in the bartender, Vincent added, "What've you heard about the murder?"

"I haven't heard a thing, but I know poachers." Arnaud glanced over at Ragondin before continuing. "Their hearts and minds are not complicated. They believe that the land and the animals that reside on it belong to everyone; they take game to feed themselves and their families, and they hate the authority of those who would deny them." Arnaud paused a moment and added, "They poach to test their manhood, as well as to level the injustice of social laws. Such men can be dangerous when cornered. Isn't that so Ragondin?"

Before his friend could answer Vincent shouted, "I'm going after the men who murdered my uncle!" His voice rang out. "I will torture them as they tortured Serge and then I will kill them!" The words came out of his mouth of their own volition. All the men at the bar turned and stared at him. Realizing that he intended to commit murder they averted their gaze and went back to their drinks.

Arnaud later told Ragondin that at that moment he recognized the change in Vincent's eyes as a coming of age, a transformation usually misunderstood for its banality and for the violence with which it is sometimes manifested.

The bartender reminded Vincent that Merlecourt was a small village, that it was only a matter of time before rumors surfaced and names were mentioned. He looked around to make sure no one was listening before he offered his help, and asked Vincent not to let anyone know. "My wife would cut off my balls," he said sheepishly, "if she thought I was helping you." Vincent knew that Arnaud's wife would not allow her husband to help a German.

The friends walked out of the village under a warm autumn sun. A magpie rose off a roadkill in the main alley leading to the castle. François met them at the door. He told Vincent that his visit would have to be brief. Count Robert was in bed with hypoglycemia and needed rest. Everyone at Merlecourt believed that the count, out of loneliness, was gradually letting himself die, a concern to which the count took umbrage.

While Ragondin remained in the pantry, Vincent went upstairs to the master bedroom and knocked. When he was summoned, he opened the door. The old man's face was slack and without color.

Count Robert waved Vincent toward him. "I have been dreaming, but I can't remember about what," he said. "For years now, when I dream I see myself as a thirty-year-old man instead of what I have become. I also see my friends as young men and women. Even when I dream about the present, my characters have young faces."

Not sure how to respond, and intent on stating what he had come to say, Vincent blurted out in a rush of emotions his theory on the death of his uncle. Count Robert, interrupted in his thoughts, looked puzzled.

"You're looking for noon at two o'clock," the count said after a minute. He shook his head. "Let the police do their work." And, before Vincent could tell him that he had asked Ragondin to help him run the shoot, the count raised a hand and closed his eyes, ending the meeting.

They drank hard cider with François in the pantry. Vincent retrieved his shotgun and put it together. François eyed him and warned him not to put any bullets in the gun until he was outside. Vincent broke the action and pretended to load the chambers before dropping the shells in his pocket and closing the breach. François was not amused.

"I was going to give you some news, but now you can go look for it up my ass," the butler said. He stared at Vincent until he apologized.

"All right, then," François said, placated. "Mademoiselle Nicole called. She's driving out in the morning."

Vincent asked him how she sounded. He tried to contain his excitement. François sat on the pantry table and lit a cigarette, taking his time. He told Vincent that at first he hadn't known whom he was talking to, that Nicole's voice had changed. She had an accent, he said, but not like Madame la Comtesse. More like a child using grownup words.

Vincent wanted to know if she had asked about him.

"Why would she do that?" François said, punishing him for pretending to load the shotgun.

"Come on, François. Stop being an old dick."

"You're not endearing yourself to me by being rude," the butler said.

Vincent gave him the finger and waved at Ragondin to follow him out. He would see Nicole the next day. On the way to the mill he shot at a jackdaw swirling low in the fading light, and missed.

Later that night a coastal wind rustled the tree tops and rattled the windows. From his bed Vincent watched the clouds chase each other across the sky. He slept, and then woke to the sound of a high-pitched moan just before dawn. It sounded like the countess grieving on the lawn next to the fountain where Roland had drowned, but he knew better. It was either the miller's wife wailing for her children or the solicitations of a vixen in heat.

Chapter 9

The next morning the mood of the town people in Dreux mirrored the weather, which was overcast and threatening. Vincent bought supplies for the mill from merchants complaining about the upcoming winter, stopped at Adorée's bakery for a brioche, and went to give Lieutenant Auverpois his deposition. At the police station the officer on duty, a man with parchment-colored skin, took Vincent's statement. Auverpois was out of the office on assignment. The civil servant's eyes were gaunt and lifeless from pushing papers all his life. He ushered Vincent into a small room that smelled of corn-paper cigarettes and black ink, scowled at the stack of reports on his desk, and explained that since they hadn't found Serge's shotgun, Auverpois assumed the killers had stolen it. Then he glared at Vincent and reprimanded him for not showing up the day before, when the lieutenant had been expecting him.

"Auverpois can go screw himself," Vincent said, angry at himself for forgetting about Serge's shotgun, a twelve-gauge Darne that would fetch a good price. The functionary glanced at the door as if expecting to see the lieutenant, and then burst out laughing. "I wish that on him every single day, and twice on payday!"

Although some people in the village had been envious of Serge Lebuison for his position at Merlecourt and others had disliked him because of the harsh manner with which he dealt with poachers, the gamekeeper's social standing was considerable. For that reason, with the exception of Count Robert, the entire village attended his funeral.

Ragondin stood behind the last pew, near the door, with a view overlooking the landscape of heads facing the altar. Vincent, wearing his only suit, a dark-blue tattered holdover from boarding school, was seated in the front row along with Monique Moulin; her husband, Sebastien; their daughter, Lisette; and Mathieu, Monique's pink-faced sixteen-year-old son. The farm boy, ill at ease anywhere but on a tractor, fingered an angry boil on his neck. Lisette smiled at Vincent and then buried her nose in the Bible. He wondered if she had gone to the forest the night of the dance and if so, with whom. When he leaned over and asked her she nodded, and with an impish grin, whispered the names of two married men.

Sebastien Moulin, a big man with a round, weathered face and graying, yellow hair, sat slumped over in the pew. His shirt collar dug into his neck like a wet belt, and the moment his wife wasn't looking he loosened it, popping the top button off in the process. Monique Moulin remained kneeling on the stone floor for the duration of the service and despite the effort she put into praying, drying her eyes, and crossing herself, she found time to steal sideways glances at the congregation.

Father Ménardeau stood tall and handsome behind the pulpit. He looked down benevolently at the upturned faces of his flock, crossed his hands on his chest and greeted them. Speaking in mellifluous tones he reassured his congregation that they were the loyal ones, the mourners, the friends of the dearly departed who had cast aside personal obligations to pray, as one, for Serge's salvation, and his acceptance into the kingdom of heaven. The priest reminded his parishioners to render homage to God and to forgive those who were not in attendance. The words rolled out of his mouth like wet marbles.

Focusing on the stained-glass windows above the heads of the parishioners, Father Ménardeau went on to applaud Serge for having lived under nature's mantle. A moment later he frowned in the direction of Adorée, and condemned the gamekeeper's sinful indulgences.

Vincent turned around in his pew and was greeted with a checkerboard of veils, black dresses, and unfocused eyes. Everyone had set his or her face in a mask that fit the occasion. Ragondin caught his glance and grinned.

On the way to the altar for Holy Communion, Vincent sensed the focus of the entire congregation on his back—a broad back belonging to the nephew of the murdered man, but also the vulnerable backside of a bastard. Vincent received the Sacrament on his knees. Father Ménardeau safely delivered the body of Christ into Vincent's mouth without looking him in the eye.

Back in his pew, Vincent saw Nicole, partially concealed behind a black tulle veil, waiting her turn in the aisle. Because of the count's disdain for Ménardeau, he had not expected her to attend the services and had assumed she would meet the mourners at the cemetery with her father. The profile behind the veil didn't belong to the girl he had said good-bye to five years earlier. That girl had possessed a narrow face and big teeth. What he saw as she faced him on her way back to her seat was a young woman with soft lips, dark auburn hair, and eyes that rested like burnt almonds on her cheekbones. He craned his neck to follow her until his aunt pinched his leg. My God, he thought, she's beautiful.

Vincent, Sebastien, and the gardeners, Jacques and Hubert, carried the simple pine casket down the center aisle, through the oak doors, down the stone steps, and into a waiting hearse. Vincent glanced up to see gray clouds progressing over the black slate roof of the church's steeple. The undertaker stood between the pallbearers and the hearse, buffing raindrops that were beading up on the black hood of the car with a chamois cloth. Vincent knew Serge would have much preferred to be buried upright under a tree in the forest.

Father Ménardeau, partially obscured behind a cloud of incense, followed the coffin as far as the church doors, where he exchanged the brass censer for an umbrella. Serge's family stood in a cascade down the stairs and shook hands with the congregation. Vincent took his position at the end of the line. Ragondin, who had slipped out early, was situated with his back against the stone wall overlooking the church. He watched the women nod their way solemnly down the steps and into the courtyard. The men, relieved that the ceremony was over, shook Vincent's hand or slapped him on the back. Rain fell intermittently.

Father Ménardeau paid particular attention to Nicole when she passed through the oak doors and stood before him. He held her hand in both of his and rewarded her with his most charming smile. He said how pleased he was that she was home and how much the village had missed her and that he was sorry that

Monsieur le Comte could not attend the services, and was he not well? The priest leaned closer, his smooth face capturing the gravity of the occasion. Nicole replied without emotion that her father was fine, removed her hand from his, and moved down the line.

In contrast, she was courteous to Monique Moulin and took time to say a kind word to each member of Serge's family. When she reached Vincent she lifted her veil, removed her hat and, beaming like a child, raised her arms and wrapped them around his neck. They hugged while the village looked on and smiled. Nicole leaned away and her auburn hair fell in folds down her back. Vincent looked into her eyes and saw the little girl whose hand he used to hold. He kissed her on both cheeks, and their years together came rushing back. She pulled his ear and told him how happy she was to see him.

Nicole stood next to Vincent while the last mourners offered him their sympathies and welcomed her back. The men, holding their hats at their sides, shook her hand and nodded their heads. The old women who had worked at the castle curtsied. Aware of her social standing she walked next to Vincent directly behind Father Ménardeau in the procession to the cemetery. If Monique Moulin was offended at being upstaged she chose not show it.

"You're beautiful, you know," Vincent said as they walked through the main street leading to the cemetery. Nicole's head was level with his eyebrows. She blushed and put her hand in his.

"You and I have taken this walk before," she said speaking to him in both French and English, mixing the languages together as she had done all her life. "First for your mother, and then for Roland." She paused and squeezed his hand. "I'm so sorry, Vincent."

Vincent didn't know how to respond. He only knew that he was grateful she was next to him, and realized he should have waited to talk to her instead of trying to find answers from Father Ménardeau. The events of the last days welled up in his chest and he stared straight ahead.

Nicole squeezed his hand again. "I'm here, Vincent," she said. "I'm home. It will be just as before."

Count Robert was waiting in his black Citroën sedan outside the cemetery. When the hearse drew near, François opened the door and Nicole went to her father. She offered him her arm and they walked to the graveside, past the villagers, who bowed their heads in deference to his loss. Count Robert looked exhausted. His lips trembled as Serge was lowered into the ground. In the distance the church bell rang the hour, highlighting the passing of time. Father Ménardeau paid his respects to the count, who nodded but looked away, unobtrusively straightening the index and small finger of his left hand, a gesture believed to ward off evil.

When the pine box disappeared into the ground the villagers collectively crossed themselves. Monique and Lisette each dropped flowers on the casket and Vincent added a small leather pouch containing a corkscrew and three wire nooses. Serge had always said that if a man had the wherewithal to snare a rabbit and open a bottle, he would rest in peace. Count Robert accepted the villagers' condolences and placed his hand on François's shoulder as they walked slowly back to the car. He barely nodded at Father Ménardeau, who was visibly offended.

Nicole politely refused Sebastien Moulin's invitation to lunch and lingered with Vincent at the gravesite after everyone had left. The intense moment of joy they experienced at first seeing each other had passed, leaving Vincent feeling awkward and uncertain about what to say next. They stood in silence side by side.

Ragondin's presence interrupted their thoughts. When Vincent introduced him Nicole registered surprise, recognizing his last name from years of overhearing her father and Serge condemn the Artaban family of poachers. In contrast, her smile was radiant and she said that it made her happy to know that Vincent had a best friend. Taking both their hands she invited them to walk with her, commenting that cemeteries were condominiums for the dead.

"America certainly didn't wash the cynic out of you," Vincent said. He turned to Ragondin and explained that when Nicole was nervous or upset she would talk fast and say just about anything.

"Did you see Monique?" Nicole continued with a mischievous smile. "She couldn't hide the fact that she was weak with glee at all the attention she was receiving. My bet is that she'll be slipping off her chair by lunch."

Nicole announced that she was going to spend the semester studying at the Beaux-Arts in Paris and that she would be driving out to the estate on weekends. When they came to the portal guarding the estate, she turned and asked Vincent to come and see her the next day. He agreed, raised her hand in his, and kissed her fingers. When Nicole told him that he had never done that before, he kissed the corner of her mouth.

Her eyes brightened and looked into his. "Let's meet tomorrow after lunch," she said. "At the island?"

Chapter 10

The splendors of a lifestyle that had once belonged to Vincent came flooding back during the short walk from the village to the farm. For a decade he had lived in opulent elegance and slept under the roof of the most powerful family in the valley. Until Roland's tragic death, the Costebelles had loved him and nurtured him and over time had educated him to appreciate beauty and grace. His reunion with Nicole reminded him of the enchanted life he led before her departure for America.

Sebastien Moulin greeted Vincent and Ragondin at the door to the farm. Like all the Moulins, Sebastien was heavyset and of fair complexion, dedicated to hard labor and stubborn as a wrench. An even-tempered man who walked with a limp from having forgotten his right leg under the wheels of a plow as a teenager, Sebastien was responsible for the day-to-day running of the farm. When it came to business decisions and financial concerns, however, it was common knowledge that Monique wore the family pants. "My wife would shave an egg to save a franc," her husband would brag.

The Moulins cultivated alfalfa and corn on the high ground and ran Norman cattle on the fertile pastures next to the river. Surrounding the main house and farm buildings was an orchard that produced four thousand liters of hard cider every fall, two-thirds of which were distilled into apple brandy. The Moulins' Calvados was recognized as the best in the valley.

Ragondin followed his host to a table filled with glasses, ice, and Pernod while Vincent went to his grandmother and kissed her, smelling the years and anguish on her thinning hair. Too frail to leave the house, she had waited in her rocking chair next to the fireplace for the family to bury her son. Vincent knelt at her side and told her how much he had wanted her to be at the services. "People from all over the region were there," he said. "The church was filled with flowers. Mme Béton played Bach on the organ, and the altar boys chanted the kyrie like a covey of angels. You would have been so proud," he added.

He brushed his grandmother's short white hair with his fingers and kissed her forehead. When he told her she looked beautiful, Mémé smiled, and her ageless eyes filled with tears. He put his hands on hers. The joints of her fingers were shiny knots of arthritic pain, which she rubbed unconsciously from morning until night. Vincent looked into her eyes, watching his grandmother's mind drift in and out of reality until she leaned toward him in a moment of lucidity. Her lips trembled when she told her favorite grandson that any night now Monique would be wheeling her out onto the balcony.

It was still a custom among peasants in the region to abandon the elderly outside on a balcony, or in front of an open window on any given night, to encourage the onset of pneumonia, God's recipe for a relatively peaceful death. Vincent told her that he would never allow such a thing to happen, but in truth he knew he couldn't prevent it. Mémé opened her mouth and gummed her knuckles.

Ragondin stood with Adorée listening to Vincent's two middle-aged cousins from Rouen, civil servants in separate branches of the post office, argue over wages. The room slowly filled with the acrid smell of gray tobacco. Étienne Verdier, sullen and quiet, joined them and the conversation inevitably turned to the opening of the stag hunting season, less than two weeks away. As usual, Verdier came to life the moment the topic of venery was broached. He loved comparing the relative stamina of French and English dogs and delighted to argue with those who found the sport cruel. On hunting days he reverted to silence, allowing his horn to express the depth of his passion.

Father Ménardeau kept a hand on Mathieu Moulin's shoulder while talking to him earnestly about shameful, personal pleasures, pointing every so often at the festering boil on the boy's neck as a manifestation of the evils of puberty. The younger children had been fed first and were outside doing their best to avoid the adults. The women, with the exception of Adorée, busied themselves in the kitchen. The table was set for twelve.

Monique did not hide her agitation at her husband for inviting Adorée to lunch. Serge's mistress not only offended her sense of righteousness, but Adorée was the thirteenth guest at her table, a number that upset Monique's superstitious peasant blood. Although she didn't dare vent her anger out loud for fear Father Ménardeau might reprimand her beliefs, she instructed Lisette to eat in the kitchen, and vowed to make her husband pay for his indiscretion.

Sebastien Moulin walked Vincent to a corner of the room and announced in a low voice that though he understood that this was neither the time nor the place for such a conversation, he wanted Vincent to know that he was prepared to buy the farm after Mémé passed away. Vincent didn't understand what he meant.

"In theory the farm still belongs to Mémé," Sebastien said, "but after she dies it will belong to her descendants. Your mother left you her share, as did Serge.

Your aunt and I own one-third." When Sebastien was finished explaining the intricacies of the inheritance, his big pink face beamed at the thought of owning the entire farm. Turning to his guests, he clapped his hands and announced that lunch was served.

Plates of pâté, smoked ham, and veal *rillettes* were displayed on the dining room table. Radishes, sliced tomatoes, cucumbers, and olives colored half-a-dozen earthenware bowls. The men seated themselves and rolled up their sleeves while the women carried in bottles of wine and cider. Loaves of crusty farm bread lay like railroad ties across the plastic tablecloth. Father Ménardeau, impatient to say grace, sat at the head of the table with Monique on his right and the wife of the eldest cousin on his left. Adorée sat next to Vincent and Ragondin, at the far end of the table. The moment "Amen" was uttered a dozen working hands reached for the food; not another word was spoken until the plates were full. The men used their pocket-knives and, except for Father Ménardeau and Vincent, held their forks in their fists while they ate. Sebastien hugged a loaf of bread against his chest and cut two thick slices before passing it on. Vincent did the same for himself and Adorée. When she commented on Nicole's looks, Vincent blushed.

"She grew up straight and is more attractive than her mother. More French." Adorée pinched the skin on the top of his hand. "Watch yourself, Vincent."

After the crudités came deep oval platters of chicken poached in cream, and tureens brimming with French fries. Adorée leaned over to Vincent and said under her breath, "The bitch is too cheap to serve red meat!" Vincent stood up and carried a plate of food and a glass of wine that he cut with water to Mémé in front of the fireplace. She tilted the plate and spooned the cream into her mouth.

The conversation at the table centered on the weather, the harvest, and the price of grain. Father Ménardeau credited God for the earth's bounties and man's greed for its shortcomings. His tongue made wide circles inside his mouth. A green salad, Camembert, Brie, Gruyère and a ripe Pont-l'Évêque followed the chicken course. Mémé fell asleep with her hands in her plate. Étienne, who had been drinking steadily in silence, spoke of missing Serge. Adorée pressed her leg against Vincent's. She had been waiting for someone to bring up her lover's name. Suddenly, sensing an opportunity to showcase her grief, Monique Moulin let out a wail. "Will someone tell me who killed my brother!" She buried her face in her apron and sobbed, hunched over her plate. So studied was her portrayal as the bereaved sister that Ragondin tried to suppress a laugh and choked, remembering what Nicole had said.

"Courage," said Father Ménardeau putting his hand on Monique's. He glared at Ragondin.

Everyone had an opinion about why or how Serge had been killed. The second cousin was in favor of the "drunks after the dance" theory; his wife looked at Adorée and declared that a jealous husband had killed him. "Poachers murdered Serge," Étienne said firmly, crossing his arms in front of his chest. But he spoke quietly and no one paid him any attention. One of the cousins volunteered that gypsies had ambushed Serge. It was customary in the region to blame everything from stolen chickens to missing children on the persecuted people with brown skin who journeyed from one country to the other in horse-pulled wagons. This instigated a heated discussion.

Father Ménardeau raised his hands to quiet the table. When he had everyone's attention, he restated the first half of his sermon: "Serge was a man who lived in harmony with God's creatures. He was in His eye." Ménardeau paused and the women took it as a sign to begin clearing the table. But he tapped his fork on a plate so they stopped and turned toward him in unison.

"However," he continued, closing his eyes, "there was also violence in Lebuison, and God summoned him accordingly." He opened his eyes and slowly looked from one face to the other. "Now Serge is gone. And the count is ill. His son has been dead five years and his daughter is living in America. The future of the estate looks bleak." The priest's voice was deliberate and hushed with concern.

Ragondin shook his head and muttered an obscenity in his wine glass. Adorée looked at him and, for the first time that day, smiled. Father Ménardeau shook his head in pity.

"It would seem to me," he said in a reflective voice, "that when Count Robert passes on, Mademoiselle Nicole will sell." Étienne Verdier looked up in alarm, but the priest raised a hand to reassure him.

"Fear not, Étienne, our social laws support the working class. You will keep your farm. But what will become of the village? Do we not depend on the castle for work and the consumption of goods? Look at what happened when Count Robert went to America for a year. The village withered. We lost a grocery store, a plumber, and a farrier."

"Then why, Father," Ragondin inquired, encouraged by Adorée's approval, "don't you tell your boss to leave

Count Robert the hell alone? Hasn't he done enough harm by taking Serge?"

"Don't be rude, Ragondin," said Monique Moulin, her ill-tempered face reddening.

Vincent raised his hand and all eyes turned to him. "Count Robert is fine. I see him every day. He is sad, as I am sad, because he loved Serge." Vincent paused and looked at the guests seated at the table. "Everyone here knows that the count's foremost concern is for the people in the valley. He proved that during the war." Vincent's heart rose to his throat. Adorée's knee nudged him on.

"Believe me, Count Robert will never let the village down." He stopped speaking and then added forcefully, "He is a Seigneur."

Father Ménardeau opened his mouth and said, "Sadly, though, Robert de Costebelle has not been to confession or taken Communion in . . ." But Vincent stopped him.

"My uncle is dead," he said, gaining confidence, "and this lunch is in his honor. Why not remember him, and celebrate his life instead of questioning the motives of a good man?"

Ragondin banged his fork on his plate in approval. The noise was deafening. Vincent hid his shaking hands under the table.

"My son," replied Father Ménardeau, "of course you are right. We are here to mourn your uncle and I can assure you that he is in the Almighty's good hands. Come to me for guidance. These are demanding times, and the future appears uncertain. I feel it my duty to mention the possibilities."

"I came to you yesterday, Father, but you chose not to see me."

Father Ménardeau interlaced his fingers and, with his chin on his chest, replied: "Mme Béton told me that you had stopped by. Unfortunately I was away at the time."

"That's not true," Vincent replied, looking the priest straight in the eye. "I saw you entering the rectory before I knocked on the door. I won't be back."

Monique scowled at her nephew. Father Ménardeau kept his dark eyes fastened on Vincent's, waiting for the younger man to turn away. But just as Vincent had held Lieutenant Auverpois's stare, he now held the priest's. Ménardeau glanced down at the table and then back up at Vincent, who had not taken his eyes off the clergyman's face. "You are mistaken, my son. I was not there. I hope you will reconsider."

Agitated by the priest's arrogance and the tension of the moment, Ragondin said in a stage whisper that he hated a liar. The faces around the table lit up with astonishment.

No one had ever called the village priest a liar before. The men stared at their plates and the women looked alarmed, as if Ragondin's words would see them all in hell. Father Ménardeau's expression never changed.

Monique stood up and marched into the kitchen. The other women took away the cheese and brought back clean plates and freshly baked fruit pies. Lisette Moulin served coffee and Sebastien's Calvados. When Father Ménardeau smiled thinly at Vincent, he realized then that the priest's powers were greater than the truth.

The torpor of digestion slowly settled over the table. Anxious to return to their fields, Étienne and Sebastien fidgeted in their chairs. Mathieu left the table on the pretense of going to the bathroom and didn't return. Adorée, a little tipsy, leaned against Vincent's shoulder. Ragondin was drunk. Finally, Sebastien stood and raised his glass, a toast to his departed brother-in-law. Everyone followed suit except for Adorée, who sobbed quietly in her hands. They drank.

The instant their glasses were back on the table, Sebastien concluded in a loud voice: "My tractor awaits me."

Father Ménardeau left quickly without shaking hands with either Vincent or Ragondin, concentrating instead on wiping a food stain off his black *soutane*.

When everyone else had left, Sebastien and Monique walked with them outside. The clouds had moved out of the valley and patches of blue sky brightened the courtyard. Sebastien put a hand on his nephew's shoulder and inquired about his future. There was friendly concern on his face, but not on Monique's.

Vincent explained that the count had asked him to act as the estate gamekeeper through the upcoming shoot. Then he would go to forestry school.

Sebastien looked over the orchard and told Vincent that he would need his services, that the old well was almost dry. He hoped that Vincent could locate water, and not too deep. After all, digging was expensive.

"Don't worry, Uncle Sebastien," Vincent said looking over the land. "There is plenty of water here."

Monique's face darkened when her husband told Vincent that he should consider the farm his home. "I told him," Sebastien said turning to his wife. "It's only fair he should know. When the time comes, we will make him an offer."

"Over my dead body," Monique replied returning to the house, unaware of the grin on her nephew's face.

Chapter 11

Vincent and Ragondin walked back to the church, where Vincent had parked the car, and drove to the mill on the narrow roads and trails that webbed the estate. They stopped the Citroën often to walk the fields they would be leading the beaters across on the day of the shoot. The decadent fragrances of fall rose out of the earth to greet them. The rains of June had been replaced in July by the infinite azure of thirty cloudless days when the unmerciful sun had dried up the irrigation ditches and bred rocks in the fields. In August, evening thunderstorms had saturated the earth again and the ground filled with dandelions and stinging nettles. Vincent had spent long hours on the tractor, pulling the mower in ever-diminishing circles, stopping once or twice an hour to shake off the insects that billowed out of the grass, flew into his shirt, and marched through his hair. He hated the tractor, which he said softened him, jarred his kidneys, and knotted his neck from looking back at what he had mowed. Vincent liked pitching hay, cutting firewood, and hammering nails.

The two friends walked close together through the pastures and talked about the mechanics of the shoot. Serge, Vincent explained, had always emphasized the need to control the terrain first, and then exploit the wind by choosing the correct order of the drives. Before a shoot he always offered a toast and then a prayer to St. Hubert, patron saint of hunters. He appealed for good weather, hard-flying birds, and sober guests.

During their survey of the hunting fields of Merlecourt they came upon the carcass of a hare that had been bled by a marten, a pigeon with its breast picked clean by a bustard, a white-headed crow dead on the side of the road, and nine coveys of partridge. The doves and quail of the valley had already flown south, a sign of early winter.

Ragondin could tell that, for the first time, Vincent was looking at Merlecourt with objective eyes, seeing more of the estate's shortcomings than ever before. The meadows and woodlots, the rivers and streams no longer defined his childhood playgrounds. There were fallen trees in need of cutting, splitting, and stacking; fences to repair; ditches to drag; roads to be graded; alleys to be cleared of debris. On and on the list grew until Vincent was overwhelmed. He and Ragondin found the gardeners emptying the tractor-trailer at the estate dump. Jacques laughed when Vincent outlined the work to be addressed. He elbowed Hubert, and mocked that it had taken Vincent years to finally notice the disrepair the estate had fallen into since Count Robert's return from America.

"We've been using the same equipment since you were born, Vincent. To do the job correctly we would need ten million francs worth of modern machinery and the help of two more men."

"But the place is a mess!" Vincent said, throwing his hands in the air.

Jacques leaned against the tractor, pulled a pack of cigarettes from his pocket, took one out and offered one to Hubert. He lit them both by cupping a match inside the palm of his hand.

"We do what we can with what we have," he said to Vincent, blowing smoke in his face. "Understand? So don't take yourself so seriously." Hubert nodded and dug into a fresh load of trash.

"I'll talk to Count Robert. I know he'll agree with me," said Vincent, his face reddening at the gardener's insolence.

"Don't be an asshole," Jacques replied. "The count knows better than you the condition of the estate. Why upset him?"

Vincent drove back to the mill angry with Jacques and Hubert for their lack of concern, and embarrassed because up until then he had looked at Merlecourt through the eyes of a child. He had taken for granted that the estate would somehow take care of itself and live up to his ideals, just as he assumed after the death of his mother that he would become a part of the Costebelle family.

Vincent and Ragondin walked to the weir and stood watching waves of rolling water flow from one river into the next. Ragondin closed the gates noting that the oak planks that stretched across the sluice were water-logged. Rivulets of water sprang out of the fissures in the wood in graceful silver arcs. Vincent had always thought of this water-fountain effect as a magnet for the sun.

He stared at his reflection in the water and his eyes were hard, like those of Maurice Corneille. He knew that Jacques was right: how could he blame Merlecourt for its frailties?

The bistro was crowded with men who had taken time off from work to meet with Merlecourt's new game-keeper. The bitter odor of beer and sweat and tobacco packed the room. Old-timers drank wine at the bar and told stories of drives on the estate in the twenties when the count's father, using black powder, a loader, and a matched set of Damascus-barreled shotguns, thought nothing of shooting thirty brace of partridge a day. The young men talked about the fall harvest, politics, and women.

Vincent left Ragondin at the bar and walked over to the table of a farmer who was explaining to his twelve-year-old grandson what would be expected of him on the day of the shoot. A good beater, the farmer was saying, is a man who listens to orders and then carries them out on strong legs. His job is to do whatever it takes to move the birds to the guns. The old man told his grandson to listen to Monsieur Vincent and not to play around; a shoot was serious business and a mishap could get someone shot.

Vincent shook the hard, bony hand of the peasant who for three-quarters of a century had grown, harvested, and lost crops with forgotten regularity. Vincent told the wide-eyed boy that his grandfather had encouraged more partridge over expensive guns than anyone else in the room. The farmer acknowledged the compliment with a nod of the head and wondered if Monsieur Vincent wanted to tell young Henri about driving birds.

Vincent nodded remembering the first time Serge had explained to him the procedures of the shoots. It seemed to him that the conversation had taken place a lifetime ago. His mother had still been alive.

"After we gather early next Sunday," he said looking the boy in the eyes, "we are going to fan out and solicit those coveys of birds living on the perimeter of the estate to reestablish quarters in the center of the property."

Ragondin laughed at his friend's choice of words but he was proud of Vincent, who spoke with the eloquence of someone who had graduated from a tough Jesuit boarding school with both baccalaureates to his credit. Some of the men closest to Vincent had stopped talking and were now listening.

"Later, after the guests have eaten," Vincent continued, "and Count Robert has placed them behind the shooting stands, we are going to stretch out, a kilometer away, in a line about two hundred meters wide. You know what a net looks like, Henri?"

"Oui, Monsieur," the boy replied in a low, almost frightened voice.

"Well, that's what we will be, a human net moving toward the shooters, with ends that will fold in and out like wings, herding the partridge into and up over the guns."

Vincent accepted a beer from Arnaud and, after raising his glass in the direction of the men at the bar, drank half of it.

"Each guest,"Vincent said to Henri, "will shoot at the covey coming toward him with his number one gun, turn around, receive a fresh gun from his loader, and shoot again at those birds that make it through the line." He looked down into the face of the boy, who glanced at his grandfather for support. "The best of them will shoot two partridge in front and another brace of birds departing."

Vincent laughed and placed a hand on the boy's shoulder. "But only a handful of shooters in all of France can do this with consistency. Even fewer with grace."

The men in the bistro laughed and their high spirits filled Vincent with confidence. He stood for a moment next to the farmer and his grandson who would one day inherit the family farm, the work that goes with it, and a life devoted to the land.

"I watched Monsieur le Comte shoot eighteen birds in a row one day," said another elderly beater. "He handled the gun like a violin." The heads in the bistro nodded up and down in agreement.

"Finally," Vincent said, turning back to young Henri, "when we beaters reach the guests, the dogs are sent out to retrieve the game and a new drive begins."

One of the men listening to Vincent nodded in approval and mentioned Serge. The room fell silent. The same man recalled the days when Count Robert and Serge, who acted as his loader and chauffeur, were gone five days a week for months on end, traveling through France shooting birds.

"Serge claimed that during those years he ate the finest food money could buy, and he slept with the best-looking maids in all of Gaul." The men raised their glasses and toasted his memory.

Vincent knew then that the beaters were going to support him, if only in deference to his uncle. He went over the order of the beats, the procedures for starting and stopping the drives, and fixed the time of the Sunday meeting at the Verdier farm. The men came up to him one by one and wished him good luck. After he shook the last hand he left for the island where he would later meet Nicole, taking with him two hard-boiled eggs for lunch.

Vincent walked the path between the woods and the river, across from the pasture where Étienne had been working the night of the murder. The warm October sun had revived the grasshoppers of summer. Moorhens flushed from inside the river banks and ran across the water in a dazzling display of webbed feet. Wide patches of scythed water reeds floated downriver toward him.

The island, densely wooded with pine trees and mixed hardwoods, was a hundred meters long by fifty meters across at its widest point. Downstream it tapered into a thin tail of land that overlooked a gravel bar. Vincent sat on the bridge that linked the island to the mainland and looked for fish in the pool under his feet. Twenty meters upstream was a wooden barrel that Serge had partially sunk in the river next to the bank to trap water rats. The drum was half full of water and there were apples floating inside as bait. The rats would detect the sweet, enticing smell of rotting fruit, climb up to the lip of the barrel and jump in, eventually drowning and sinking to the bottom.

A light breeze blew up the valley, carrying the fragrance of warm hay and the songs of birds preparing for winter. As a child, the island had been Vincent's favorite place to play on the estate; a place for roughhousing, sandwiches, bottles of Orangina, and long swims across the reflections of sunlit trees. In the fall, when he and Roland weren't fishing or shooting ducks, Vincent would help Nicole gather colored leaves, which she pressed between the pages of her poetry books.

Vincent lay down on the bridge and watched the clouds slip through the branches above his head and dozed off. He woke once, turned over and stared down at the almost imperceptible flow of water between the wooden slats. He heard Serge's voice say to him: "Rivers are fountains of sap bred in the ventricles of clouds. Their purpose is to drag all of man's follies to the bottom of the sea." Vincent went back to sleep and dreamed that he was buried alive with his dead uncle inches from his face.

The church bell in Merlecourt rang the half-hour and woke him. He stood up with the dream still in his head. It would be at least thirty minutes before Nicole arrived, so he removed his clothes, stretched his arms high above his head, and slowly let himself fall off the bridge into the river. The water wrapped itself around him like a blanket of ice. He pushed off the bottom and broke through the surface gasping, beating the water with his fists.

"Some things never change," Nicole said from the bridge above him, smiling and waving a paper bag. "I thought I'd have lunch here and wait for you, but you beat me to it." She wore a blue summer dress that reached just below her knees. When she crossed the bridge and sat in the grass on the far bank, he caught a glimpse of white underwear.

Vincent forgot about the icy water and allowed the current to carry him to an overhanging limb well below where she was sitting. He held on to the branch with one hand and covered himself with the other.

"Too late for modesty," she said. "I watched you undress." She looked at the river and added, "We used to swim here all the time, remember?"

"As if it were yesterday."

Kicking off her shoes, Nicole stood and turned around. "I'm coming in," she said, pulling off her dress.

She stood tall and lean, her tanned skin the color of ginger and except for a pair of small, white cotton panties, she was naked. He could tell, by the way she shook her hair, that she wanted him to admire the changes that had transformed her from a knock-kneed teenager into a desirable young woman. She hesitated for a moment, then, careful of the nettles, tiptoed to the bridge, where she stood facing him with her arms crossed over her chest. Nicole's body was smooth and gilded by sunlight. Vincent closed his green eye and stared through his good eye, his blue eye, at the slight aperture between her thighs, a sight for future reverie.

"How cold is it?" she asked.

"Just right," he said clearing his throat.

"I bet," she hooted, and let her hands drop to her sides as she looked into the water.

Nicole stood naked in front of him, a radiance of dewy gold, with only a pool of deep, green water between them. Her hair fell forward hiding her face. She smoothed the fabric of her underwear with her hand, and he imagined her hand to be his.

Her breasts reminded him of small melons from Cavaillon, young and supple, growing at a slight angle from each other. She glanced at him and blushed. Crossing her arms and taking a deep breath, she closed her eyes and jumped into the water feet first. Vincent had never seen a vision so perfect, even on the pages of his best nudie magazine, and when she was inside the river he slapped the water with his hand and let out a shout of delight.

Nicole surfaced and splashed over to him, shrieking, "Oh my! Oh, Jesus, it's freezing!" She grabbed the branch above his head. Water ran down her face and into her mouth.

"What are you staring at?" she asked.

"You," he replied. "Have you no shame?"

She cupped her hand and sprayed him. "None!"

Nicole slipped under water, bobbed up, and leapt at his neck. She wrapped her arms around him and he felt her breasts on his chest. "God I've missed this place and you and everyone," she said. The current sent them spinning around each other while he held onto the branch and she his neck. Vincent felt the muscles in her legs and the softness of that part of her thighs he had been staring at. Her body entwined around his and the closeness overwhelmed him and he let go of the branch.

They swam back to the eddy and climbed out of the river and sat side by side in the mud. "Nothing has changed," she said playing in the shallow water between her legs.

"You have," he said pointing at her breasts, his eyes wide and staring. Nicole scooped up a handful of mud and he scrambled to his feet. She laughed and covered her face with her free hand.

"So have you!" she said grinning. He wasn't hard, but he felt heavy from the waist down, and he didn't dare look. She dove back into the cold water and swam upstream to the bridge.

They dressed, sat on the pine slats, and shared her sandwich and his hardboiled eggs. A water rat swam across the river.

"Papa asked me to invite you over for a drink before dinner."

"Okay," he said, watching the rat angle toward the barrel. "I'll come at seven."

"Good," she answered, and got up to leave, her dress clinging to her wet legs. She reached down and mussed his hair. "You can meet Eric. He's driving out from Paris." She walked across the bridge.

Vincent took his eyes off the river and looked at her.

"Who's Eric?"

"Eric Potter. I know him from America."

"You like him?"

"Yes," she said as she tossed her hair back. "He's going to work at the Morgan Guaranty Trust in Paris." She waved.

He watched her walk through the pasture, as light on her feet as her mother, and then sat back down on the bridge just as the rat climbed up on the bank, peered over the edge of the barrel, and jumped in.

Chapter 12

Robert de Costebelle sat in an armchair of the living room reading a copy of *Le Figaro*. François paused at the door before announcing Vincent. He had opened a bottle of pink Taittinger in honor of Nicole's return. The champagne chilled inside a crystal bucket on the table in front of the couch. Count Robert tossed the paper on the carpet and motioned Vincent to the couch. "I was just reading about Vietnam," he said. "You'd think the Americans would have learned from our mistakes at Dien Bien Phu. They are walking in our footsteps." He searched for his lighter in his jacket pocket and lit a cigarette. "To paraphrase Jean de la Bruyère: 'Men are animals, but generals are animals someone forgot to tie up.'" He looked at Vincent and added, "It is, as usual, a matter of ego: the killing kind."

Vincent sat on the edge of the couch, his knees level with his chest. He felt uncomfortable in his worn work shoes and frayed, gray herringbone jacket. His fingers, a cat's cradle of cuts and scars, embarrassed him. He hid them between his legs. When the sound of laughter and running feet carried through the ceiling down to where they sat, the count glanced up. Vincent followed his gaze, suddenly uneasy that he wouldn't measure up to Nicole's American friend.

"She brought with her a young man from New York," the count said indulgently. "She seems to like him."

"Do you, Monsieur?"

"He's clean cut, went to Yale University. Very American." Count Robert shrugged. "I really don't have an opinion, but I trust her judgment." He sat back in the armchair and looked at Vincent through a breath of smoke.

"Lieutenant Auverpois was here this morning," he continued. "He is of the opinion that drunks attacked Serge. I didn't tell him your theory." The count paused, rubbed his mustache and added, "I don't like him."

"He insinuated Serge was poaching," said Vincent.

"Corneille told me. He's also worried that under the right circumstances you might break the law to avenge your uncle." The count looked at Vincent. "Should I be concerned?"

"I would never do anything to displease you, Monsieur."

More laughter from above interrupted the conversation. Vincent coughed and changed the subject, mentioning his choice of Ragondin as his wing man on the upcoming shoot.

"You can't be thinking straight," Count Robert exclaimed. "The man's a poacher. His family has been stealing game from Merlecourt since before the First World War. Poaching is in their blood. The Artabans are thieves."

"I know that, Monsieur," said Vincent. "But Ragondin is indebted to me and he knows the property as well as I do. Maybe better. I don't question his loyalty."

Disturbed by Vincent's sense of allegiance, the count paused. Then he said, "If you insist, bring him by tomorrow. I want to talk to him," he paused. "Understand, though, if I hire him and something, anything, goes wrong, it is you I will come looking for."

"Oui, Monsieur."

The count acknowledged Vincent's reply with a frown and then chuckled at the gaiety that was filtering down from above. He stood and reached for the bottle. "I don't know what they are doing up there, but I'm thirsty." He opened the champagne and filled two flute glasses.

"Santé!" said Vincent standing. The wine was pink and cold and dry, and the bubbles were sharper than those in cider.

The count took a swallow and said that he needed a full-time gamekeeper. He would have to hire someone reliable and he was counting on Vincent to teach him all he could about the running of the property before enrolling in forestry school. Vincent stared into his glass and didn't answer. He wasn't Serge, but he knew he was qualified for the job. When he lifted his eyes Count Robert was looking at him with an amused expression on his face.

"Of course," he said, "I could probably arrange for you to start school this spring instead of in two weeks." He picked up the bottle and topped off their glasses. "That would give us sufficient time to find someone reliable, wouldn't it?"

"Yes, Monsieur le Comte," said Vincent standing taller.

"Good. It's settled then. You'll take over for Serge. Here is a list of your duties." Count Robert handed him a sheet of paper, which Vincent folded and put in his breast pocket. "If you have any questions come to me." The count stood in front of him and put a hand on his shoulder, just as he had when Vincent was a child.

"By the way," he added, "you are now on full salary. And when you find someone to help you, I'll pay him your old wage. Remember, work begins at dawn and ends when it is finished."

"Would Monsieur mind if I kept Ragondin?" Vincent asked quickly.

The count took his hand off Vincent's shoulder. "Good God, man," he said shaking his head. "You're inviting the fox into the chicken coop."

"He's my friend, Monsieur. He'll do what I say, and I trust him."

"Well, I can't say I commend you on your choice." Count Robert studied Vincent for a sign of indecision but the look in the young man's eyes reminded him of his uncle's determination. It was a look of infuriating stubbornness, one the count had lived with and secretly admired for decades.

"I reserve judgment until tomorrow," he said running his fingers through his short gray hair.

Vincent shook his hand until the count's expression changed to one of quiet seriousness. He tugged on the lapels of Vincent's jacket to get his attention.

"One other thing," he said. "I know you're thinking about Serge, and what he said regarding blood and family. I encourage you to pursue his killers. Revenge is the legacy of young men. But remember that you are not above the law, and that your first obligation is to me." He puller harder on Vincent's coat and took a deep breath.

"And, in the name of God, be careful. If you get too close to these men they'll kill you without hesitation. They've proven their worth."

Nicole walked into the room wearing a long, fawn-colored dress with a neck bordered by white lace embroidery that met between her breasts. The man following her looked older than Vincent had expected. Blond and handsome, he wore gray trousers, a fitted blue blazer, and a striped tie. He looked like all the do-good prefects Vincent had loathed at boarding school.

"Eric, this is Vincent Lebuison, my oldest friend." Nicole spoke in a little girl's voice and giggled when the two shook hands. "We were born on the same day! Look, Vincent, Eric gave me a present." She stretched her neck toward Count Robert and Vincent, and they admired in silence the flat band of gold that lay on her throat.

Vincent recalled the gift that Nicole had sent him during his first year at boarding school. It was a deer-skin pouch containing eleven agate marbles and a note wishing him Merry Christmas. Below her signature was a postscript that read: "I kept one to remember you by." The marbles were rare, or so the seller in Paris had told her. When Vincent held them to the light streams of colored crystal buried in the stone came alive. Each agate traded for twenty of the glass kind and forty of those made from clay. Vincent lost them all within three weeks, and he wistfully followed their destiny through that winter until the best shooter in school owned them all. A semester later only two remained in circulation; by then they were well used, chipped, and opaque.

Eric told him he was glad to make his acquaintance. He spoke French with a heavy American accent.

"And I am glad to meet you,"Vincent answered in halting English, which prompted them all to laugh louder than necessary. Eric stood next to Nicole, who smiled while the count filled their glasses. "I hear you spear fish with a fork tied to a broom handle," said the American.

"Only big fish. I miss the smaller ones," Vincent said, wondering if she had told Eric about their swim that afternoon. He thought about her standing lovely on the bridge, about how the sun had sparkled off her skin, and about how, when she slipped her dress back on and tossed her hair, that part of the river she had borrowed had rushed off of her—and he knew she hadn't said a thing.

"I have an announcement to make," said the count standing. "Vincent is Merlecourt's new gamekeeper."

Nicole clapped her hands and Eric congratulated Vincent, expressing envy that while he would be working in a small office in Paris Vincent would be running through the woods. Nicole's friend made a toast and

Vincent saw that the American was losing his hair. He's going to look like a fucking egg before he's thirty, he thought to himself, pleased with the image.

Vincent left after the Count set a time to see him the next morning. Nicole accompanied him to the front door and kissed him loudly on both cheeks. Then, in a voice from America that he didn't much like, she said, "Come by and see us tomorrow. We won't leave for Paris until after lunch." She didn't ask him what he thought of Eric, and he didn't volunteer his opinion.

Chapter 13

A cold, stubborn wind rumbled down from the North Atlantic that night, shaking the village of Rebours and upsetting the quiet of dawn. Ragondin listened to the rain from under the covers, imagined the cold, and dragged a pillow under the sheets for comfort. In the next room he heard his Aunt Tantine fighting wine-induced devils in her sleep. Suzette, his gray-and-tan ferret, wrapped her tail around his neck and settled on his chest. A throb of longing for something he couldn't immediately place brought back memories of his father and mother, and of the thatch-roofed house on the outskirts of the forest where he had grown up.

Ragondin yearned for those years when his father had taught him how to set traps, dig pits for wild boars, adjust nooses at the exact height off the ground to catch hares and pheasants, even roebucks. When his mother left them, his father moved them to town to his sister's apartment, where everything had begun to change for the worse. In Dreux, Jérôme began drinking in earnest and making mistakes he had never made before, thoughtless acts that eventually killed him. Ragondin wrapped his arms around Suzette, listened to her small chirrups of contentment, and fell asleep. At the sound of the first village rooster crowing, he woke.

To the north, the wind and rain that streamed across the dormer window reminded Vincent of the winter nights at boarding school when doors and windows blew open and no one in the dormitory had the courage to get out from under the covers to close them. The storm passed over the valley and was replaced by a chill that bled through the walls and settled on his bed. At seven o'clock he got up and stuck his head out the window to a gray sky and pastures lacquered in hoarfrost. A flock of rooks mewed and cawed above the river, somersaulting over the limbs of trees, adjusting the angle of their wings to the wind. It was too early in the year for such a storm.

By the time Ragondin bicycled to the mill Vincent had made coffee, built a fire, and started a cider stew in the Dutch oven. The two friends sat in the armchairs under the boar's head, drank chicory coffee from pickling jars, dunked buttered pieces of farm bread and lumps of sugar into the coffee, and talked. Ragondin mentioned again the bounty of two million francs on Monsieur's head. Vincent said that he didn't know anyone who would kill for money.

"If they thought they could get away with it, Jacques and Hubert would strangle their own mother for that kind of a reward," Ragondin said, rolling a quantity of gray tobacco into a finger of yellow paper.

On the way to the castle to meet Count Robert, Ragondin pointed out some of the hiding places his father had used when he poached Merlecourt. Jérôme Artaban's insatiable lust for the count's game drove him to take chances that had landed him three times into Serge's custody. Ragondin remembered well the hours in Tantine's apartment listening to his father vent his hatred toward the Costebelles and all the rich landowners of the region. His loathing was not steeped in logic but rather in the deep-rooted belief in the parity of mankind, and Jérôme's interpretation of justice had been narrowed down to the equal sharing of nature's bounty.

As they approached the castle Ragondin was nervous and blurted out, "I have to tell you that I don't like Count Robert. My father went to jail because of him."

"Your father went to jail because he was a poacher," Vincent replied sharply. "Besides, you hated your father."

"I did hate him. Now I miss him." Ragondin laughed when he saw apprehension on Vincent's face.

"Don't worry. I'll work for you because you cook a good rabbit."

Ragondin took Count Robert by surprise when he told him that a valuable edition of Baudelaire's *Les Fleurs du Mal* had disappeared from the count's library while he was living in New York. Ragondin said that he had seen it a year ago in someone else's house.

"And whose house would that be?" the count replied, more annoyed than interested.

"M. Dufossé, the funeral director in Dreux. He lives in a restored farmhouse in the forest overlooking Merlecourt with his wife and three children."

The count frowned. "I know where he lives," he said. "He dressed my son for burial." Ragondin lowered his head and ran his hands around the beak of his cap, wishing he had kept quiet.

"When did you get invited to his house?" the count demanded.

Without raising his head, Ragondin said that he hadn't been invited. Rather, he had gone in when the Dufossés were out.

"I don't like what I'm hearing, Vincent," the count exclaimed without taking his eyes off Ragondin. "Take him back to town."

Ragondin glanced quickly at Vincent and then begged the count not to think he was being insolent. He admitted that at one time or another he had broken into almost every house in the valley. He had eaten left-overs and drunk from open bottles of wine, but he swore he'd never stolen anything. The book he had seen on M. Dufossé's desk had the count's name in it.

"Have you ever been inside the castle before?" the count challenged.

"Only once, Monsieur, when you and Mme la Comtesse were in America." The count wanted proof, and Ragondin described the 7.65 mm automatic pistol Count Robert kept in the righthand bedside table, and the Fragonard nude in his bathroom.

"Well, at least he's had some education," said the count, looking at Vincent. He tapped his cane on the ground and turned back to Ragondin. "Tell me, when you saw my Baudelaire at M. Dufossé's that night, did you take the time to read any of the poems?"

"Non, Monsieur," Ragondin laughed relieved that the count was talking to him, "not that night. But I have read *Les Fleurs du Mal.* I like Rimbaud better, particularly *Une Saison en Enfer.*"

"Really? Well I'm not surprised you like that little wretch. Your morals are comparable."

The count recited from one of Rimbaud's prose poems: "'Do I know nature yet? Do I know myself?—No more words. I bury the dead in my belly . . .'" Then he looked at Ragondin to continue.

"'Shouts, drums, dance, dance, dance, dance!'" Ragondin said waving his cap above his head, grinning.

The count suppressed a smile and nodded his approval. "Your knowledge of poetry surprises me," he said.

The count turned to Vincent. "You may hire him, and I wish you the best of luck. But I would lock up everything of value." He looked back at Ragondin. "Be certain that I will be monitoring your every move."

"Oui, Monsieur," Ragondin said, backing out of the room.

Vincent and Ragondin drove to the Verdier farm. The ground was wet from the rain and the birds had spread out to feed in the stubble. They walked through the adjoining fields until they flushed a covey of partridge, first into the wind, then downwind, then over a wood-lot, and finally out of a cornfield. They watched closely as the partridge adapted their flight patterns to avoid obstacles such as trees, telephone poles, even roads.

Vincent knew that each species of bird had its own command of distance and that before every drive it was important to study their preferences in relation to the terrain. Barring the unforeseeable, he now felt confident that he could fashion his men into a seine, keep it intact for the duration of eight drives, and move scores of partridge over the guns on Sunday.

After lunch in Dreux with his aunt, Ragondin headed back to the mill. On his way he stopped his bicycle in Rebours to avoid a gathering of children skittering across the street on their way to the candy display in the grocery store.

Émile Dumont, the village butcher, was carrying half a veal carcass on his shoulder to the cold room down the block from his store. Ragondin stopped again and, joking, said that he would take the loin chops if the butcher didn't want them. Dumont replied that he would eat them himself if he could afford to. Without warning he turned serious and said that the rumors circulating in Dreux had it that a gang of poachers from out of town had killed Serge.

"We plan to find out," Ragondin said, and bicycled off.

Ragondin walked into the mill just as Vincent swung the Dutch oven away from the fire and lifted the lid. The aroma of cooked meat and vegetables reached him first.

Then he noticed the potatoes, the carrots, turnips, onions, and a healthy lamb shoulder all rise to the surface of the cast-iron pot, influenced by the circular motion of a long wooden spoon. Vincent grinned.

"I could eat lamb every day of my life," said Ragondin.

"You'll get tired of it soon enough," said Vincent, ladling food onto the plates. "We'll be eating out of this pot until the new vegetables reach the market in March."

"Someone told me you cooked for Charles de Gaulle," Ragondin said, folding a piece of bread he had soaked in sauce into his mouth. The stew clung to the end of his mustache.

"I made the salad dressing that day, that was about it."

"I remember the summer parties at the pool," Ragondin said. "The beautiful cars, the music, the dancing, elegant ladies. I'd sneak onto the estate and watch from inside the woods. Important people filling their faces with whiskey and wine and carrying on like we do in the village. Once, one of those aristocratic-looking women stumbled over to where I was hiding, pulled up her dress, and took a leak next to me. She wasn't wearing underwear!"

"Rimbaud would have liked that," Vincent laughed. "I can't believe they taught him at vocational school."

"They didn't. My aunt used to read verse when I was growing up. She could recite stanza after stanza of all of the great French and Russian poets. Now she reads the labels off her bottles of wine." Ragondin paused and then added with a smile, "My favorite Rimbaud poem goes like this: 'for girls the most enchanting lurk in a dark crack where tufted satin grows.' It's named: 'Our Assholes Are Different.'"

"You know you got the job because you recognized the Fragonard and knew that poem."

"No, I got the job because you begged for me." Ragondin finished the food on his plate. "How was it living in the castle?" he asked.

"Just what you'd imagine it to be."

"I can't. It would be like living in a museum. I bet you had to drop your pants, once in a while."

"I did not," Vincent said, his face reddening. "I was polite, that's all." He remembered the laughter when Roland and he spiked the punch during the countess's garden parties, that delicious sense of conspiracy and that laughter—sometimes insane and terror-driven, prompted by the threatening menace of the count's cane. But he also remembered the pony the countess had promised to give him for Christmas when he was eight years old and how he had gone to the paddock every day for weeks and brushed it until the colt's coat gleamed like an otter's. Then, three days before the holiday, she changed her mind and gave the horse to the daughter of her dressmaker in Paris. When Vincent cried and went to Nicole for comfort, she sided with her mother, saying it was a wish he should not have indulged in to begin with.

That night Vincent dreamed the same dream, over and over. Each time it started with the sound of a dog baying in the predawn darkness. Then he would see Jules sitting on the hood of a parked car, howling at the moon. Inside the car there were men laughing. Vincent, watching himself through the eyes of an onlooker, would open the car door and fire his gun. In the time it took the shot to travel through the barrels, the interior of the car lit up and Vincent recognized his victims. In each dream what differed were the faces of the men he shot. Sometimes it was Jacques and Hubert, other times it was Étienne and Sebastien, or the Verdier brothers. Once the light revealed Count Robert and Father Ménardeau sharing wine out of a chalice.

He woke at dawn and while he lay in bed watching the sun rise through the dormer window he worried that his appetite for revenge was driven by blood. Bad blood, German blood.

In the morning, while Ragondin made the rounds of the estate, Vincent went to Dreux and bought two pairs of calf-length canvas pants, three shirts, knee-high wool socks, leather walking shoes, and a dark brown corduroy jacket—the traditional uniform of a gamekeeper. Before meeting Ragondin at the bistro in Merlecourt he stopped at the butcher shop and bought pig's feet for lunch. Over beer, the two friends argued about how to cook them: stewed in white wine, or fried in bread crumbs.

Some of the men who were assigned as beaters gathered around Vincent and he bought them drinks. Titi Verdier stepped forward and said too loudly that he would have a good laugh when the partridge flew backward over the beaters' heads and the shoot was a failure. There was a general guffaw. Vincent stared at the young Verdier troubled by the outburst and offered him a drink. Titi shook his head, flailed his arms, and caricatured a beater fending off birds flying in the wrong direction.

"Thanks for the encouragement, Titi," said Vincent, maintaining a composure he didn't feel. Enduring ridicule from a man he had known all his life, particularly when wearing his new jacket and his gamekeeper's badge for the first time, made him feel like a fool.

"Who do you think you are, a gamekeeper?" asked the younger Verdier, planting himself in front of Vincent. "I'll tell you. You're an ass kisser. That's how you got the job." He made pucker sounds and waved his hands, taunting Vincent. Everyone in the bar had seen the Verdier brothers pick fights like this with other men, and each time things had gone from bad to worse. Both men liked to inflict pain and didn't mind getting hurt in the process. About the time Vincent realized his options were narrowing, Gros-Louis called from the other end of the bar, "Calm yourself, brother. Let it pass."

Ragondin chose that moment to step around Vincent. His head bobbed up and down with every word. "Fuck you, Verdier," he yelled in fury. "If the count hadn't talked to the judge, you'd still be in jail for cutting off cows teats."

"Listen to that, Louis. The hunchback of Rebours speaks," said Titi, shuffling back and forth, nodding and pretending to drool.

Just then a loud voice announced, "Leave them alone and get back to work." Étienne Verdier stood inside the door to the bar, his clenched fists hanging at his sides.

"Mind your own business, old man," said Titi glancing over and shrugging off the warning.

The men in the bar shifted in their seats and buried their faces in their drinks. With blood pounding behind his eyes, Vincent stepped up close enough to smell the garlic on Titi's breath. "You don't scare me, Verdier," he said staring into his eyes.

"Hey, brother, castle boy here is pretending he isn't scared," said Titi staring back at Vincent. "So why is he trembling?"

"Get out of here, both of you, or I'll have you arrested," said Étienne to his sons. There was dirt on Étienne's boots and rancor on his breath.

"Come on, Titi," said Gros-Louis, standing up to leave. "You made your point."

The beaters whispered to each other and Titi grinned at them, clicked his heels, and saluted Vincent. "*Deutschland über alles!*"

Vincent punched Titi in the middle of the face as hard as he had ever hit anyone in his life. Titi collapsed into a heap on the floor, bounced back on his feet, and reached for his knife. But before he found it Gros-Louis dropped a heavy arm over his shoulder and whispered in his ear. Titi wiped the blood off his nose, looked at Vincent with a smirk, and spat on his shoes. Gros-Louis pulled him out of the bar. A moment later Vincent heard them laughing.

"Sons of bitches," said Étienne.

On the way back to the mill Ragondin told Vincent, who was not as privy as his friend to the local gossip, the embellished details of a story that had mesmerized the villagers all summer. The trouble that had been brewing for several years between Étienne and his sons had come to a head after the sale of a spring steer. It seemed that Titi and Gros-Louis had disappeared for ten days after driving the animal to auction at Les Halles in Paris, leaving behind their woman, Salomé Venard, in their apartment. On the Tuesday following the sale, when Étienne discovered that the money had not been deposited in his farm bank account, he went to his sons' quarters, a wing of the farm he had not visited since the death of his wife.

He had not laid eyes on Salomé since then. However, the old man was firmly aware of the steady stream of men through the apartment, particularly on weekends, and was convinced the woman was whoring for his sons. Each time he questioned them, they insisted the visitors were simply friends.

When no one answered his knock, Étienne stepped inside and was greeted by a virulent stench of urine. He covered his face with his handkerchief and walked through the parlor into the kitchen, where he found

Salomé sitting on a wicker-bottom chair in the far corner of the room. A bare light bulb hanging from the ceiling revealed half a dozen cats lying on the stove, and that many more on the floor.

"Where are your sons? I'm hungry!" Salomé complained, looking at him through shiny, feverish eyes. "Feed me!" she demanded. The skirt of her thin, colorless dress had been gathered in a gray ball between her legs.

Étienne didn't answer and Salomé turned her attention to a sore on her thigh, picking at it with her fingernails. Red hair sprang out of her head like brambles, and her pale blue eyes darted from Étienne's face to his pants. She smiled through thin, bloodless lips.

"I'm hungry!" she said again, but he wasn't listening. The smell of rank butter and cat piss made him crazy. He took her by the elbow and dragged her out into the courtyard. "Move," he yelled, pushing her toward the road. She covered her head with her forearms. "Get off my farm. Leave my boys alone!"

Étienne went back inside, cursing. Piles of reeking garbage and empty bottles littered the floor; a mound of coffee grinds clogged the sink, and the stains on the bed sheets were unlike any he had ever seen. He took a broom and drove the cats outside, breaking half a dozen glasses and a pitcher of sour milk in the process. Then he opened the shutters and stood for a long time looking over the land he had spent a lifetime tending. A cold spring wind whistled past his ears, blew through the apartment and out the door. Étienne felt old.

When Gros-Louis and Titi returned a week later, they found Salomé Venard starving in the hay barn. The boys moved the whore and her cats back into their wing of the farm and for the first time openly defied their father's authority. When Étienne confronted them about the stolen money they bragged that they had spent the proceeds of the sale at the racetrack in Paris. They joked often about it at the bistro.

Vincent and Ragondin sat in the kitchen eating the pig's feet. Ragondin was mopping up the wine sauce with his bread. Vincent, who had left his appetite at the bistro, had given Ragondin all but a mouthful of his share. The quickness with which the argument escalated had paralyzed him, and now that it was over he was filled with remorse. "Of course you should have hit Titi. I should have kicked the shit out of him when you had him on the ground," Ragondin said.

"I don't know. We grew up together. I don't understand what I did to make him act that way."

"Listen, when Titi was a baby Gros-Louis used to pick him up by the feet and drop him on his head for the fun of it. His mother drove him to the hospital at least once every six months. The last time he was in there the doctors screwed a metal plate into his head. He's not only an asshole, he's abnormal."

After Ragondin left for Rebours Vincent walked to the Italian poplars in the wheat field and shot a rabbit. The sun was low in the valley and the temperature was falling. He raised his quarry to his face. Through the warmth of its coat he could smell the woods and leaves and the dirt that it had slept in. He turned the doe upside down, rubbed the softness of her underside to his face and then squeezed her warm, inflated belly inciting a stream of hot urine to the ground.

Vincent returned to the mill and gutted the rabbit next to the larder. The blood vessels that ran through its parchment-thin ears made him think of Lanner, the bird woman in Serge's dream. As he hung the rabbit by a rear leg on a hook in the larder, he heard a car cross the bridge. It was Adorée.

Agitated, she asked in a loud voice where he had been. Vincent didn't know what he had done to make her angry. "What's wrong?" he asked her.

"Don't act stupid and don't tell me you haven't been

to Dreux. I've seen you from my shop. What is the matter with you?" she said, twisting his ear. "Remember me? I'm the woman who took you into her bed and shared your grief. Why haven't you been in to see me?" Adorée was wearing a short black dress with a round, white collar. When she finished speaking her voice faltered.

Vincent put his arm around her shoulders. He had been so preoccupied about Serge and the shoot that he hadn't given thought to anyone or anything else.

Adorée let her head fall on his arm. He gave her a glass of wine, reflecting to himself that it had only been three days since they had sat together during lunch at the farm. She wanted to know about Nicole and he said she was fine and had a boyfriend and that he didn't want to discuss it further.

"She came into the store the other day and asked about you."

"What about?"

"Oh, everything. If you had a girlfriend, what you had been up to, if you had mentioned her to me. You know, girl talk. She stayed an hour and ate three brioches."

Adorée took a mirror from her purse, checked her lipstick, and talked to her reflection. "Just before she left we were laughing about something and she said, 'Isn't he pretty?' I assumed she was talking about you. She said that you had been swimming together. Is that true?"

"Yes."

She smiled at the mirror. "Did you behave yourself?"

"None of your business."

Adorée made a face, got up, and thanked him for the drink. Vincent promised he would drop by on Monday. At the car she turned and took him by the collar.

"Give me a kiss."

Not waiting for an answer, she wrinkled her nose and pulled his face down to hers. He had to lean way over but she knew where to stand and how to fit against him in an odd and comforting way. A faint smell of butter rose from her hair. After she kissed him gently on his lips, she smoothed her dress and got into the Fiat.

"That was nice, Vincent," she said, and left him standing in the shade of the plane tree.

Chapter 14

On the morning of the shoot Vincent watched from the kitchen as the sun burned off the fog that rose from the warmer waters of the river Eure. He shaved and drank coffee, pulled on a clean white shirt and a black tie in deference to his state of mourning, and dropped Serge's clasp knife into a pocket of his corduroy jacket for luck. At eight o'clock he met the beaters and Ragondin in the courtyard of the Verdier farm. The men, who had arrived early, stood in small groups, talking and smoking, waiting for direction. Vincent shook hands all around and discussed the order of the drives. He assigned Hubert and Gros-Louis to the tractor-trailers that would transport the men from one beat to the other, and asked everyone to keep in line and listen for the horn. Before starting the flanking maneuvers, Vincent took Gros-Louis aside. "Is he going to follow my orders?" he asked, gesturing in the direction of Titi, who was acting sullen.

"I'll handle him," Gros-Louis assured Vincent.

The beaters climbed into the trailer and sat close to each other, commenting on the cold and exchanging jokes, the condensation from their breaths mingling with the smoke from their cigarettes. At different times, on different edges of the property they jumped to the ground, spread single file into the field, and began moving partridge into position for the morning drives. The sun melted the frost and the men took off one layer of clothing after the other until they were in shirt sleeves. An hour later they had pushed eleven coveys to the middle of the estate.

They returned to the farm and Vincent commented to Étienne on the large number of birds, a pleasant surprise after the early summer drought. The beaters exchanged good-natured comments on various subjects, everything from the flavor of partridge braised over cabbage to the attributes of some of the local women.

"Plump little things," said one of the younger men referring to the birds. "They remind me of Françoise at the grocery store."

"Her ass is as soft as a Camembert."

"And smells like the feet of God!"

The beaters laughed and smoked and drank coffee, some adding Calvados from bottles that vanished as quickly as they appeared. The younger men shoved each other around and took long leaks down the side of barns.

Vincent went to the castle shortly before ten. The courtyard had been raked, the windows cleaned, and the dining room table set for eighteen. Two waiters hired for the occasion were moving appetizers and drinks into the living room. Long dark sedans slowly pulled up to the castle. François, dressed in a formal black coat with tails, greeted the guests at the door. After exchanging polite pleasantries he showed them to the living room, where Count Robert awaited.

Nicole went out to meet Vincent in the courtyard. She smiled and waved. Tall and lovely, she was wearing a green pleated kilt held together with a large gold safety pin. Her hair was tied at the back of her neck with a burgundy-colored velvet bow. Vincent took off his cap and, without looking at her, reached for her hand.

"Bonjour, Mademoiselle Nicole," he said, bowing his head.

Surprised, she frowned before turning to greet the chauffeurs—thin, dark figures dressed in either black or dark-blue corduroy suits. The men nodded and shook her hand and returned to their tasks: unloading the shells and shooting sticks, walking the Labradors, running felt cloth over their employers' matched pairs of shotguns. During the hunting season the chauffeurs also assumed the added duties of loaders. Though not formally stated, there was a specific pecking order predetermined by the social status of each employer and his ability to shoot. In the fall, fowling skills superseded lineage. The chauffeur/loaders were notorious snobs.

Having performed her hostess duties, Nicole turned to Vincent and, with a hand on his elbow, guided him to the brick wall overlooking the moat. "Why were you so formal?" she said. "Are you nervous?"

"A little," he admitted.

Vincent looked at the shadow of the castle on the water and thought about Eric and Nicole in Paris, laughing and carrying on as they had in the castle. "Where's your friend? I thought he'd be here," he said.

Nicole leaned over the top of the wall, where the moss grew green, and looked down at the red and yellow leaves drifting across the surface of the moat. "In Paris. You don't like him, do you?"

"I didn't say that."

"You don't have to. I can tell. But you should. Eric is nice and bright and comes from a good family." She reached up and brushed a twig off the lapel of his jacket.

"Not the bastard son of a maid, hey?" he said.

"What an awful thing to say!" Nicole exclaimed as she stepped back. "I didn't invite Eric because this was to be your day. I wanted you to do well, and I wanted to be here when you did. Now you've ruined it!" She spun around and went back to the castle. He stared at his reflection in the moat.

Inside the living room the men, who ranged in age from forty to seventy, wore three-piece tweed shooting suits and carried themselves in the unconstrained fashion of those confident of their rank and manner. Their wives, who were opinionated and witty, wore autumn-colored skirts with silk off-white blouses, and appeared to have gracefully accepted the transition from youth to elegance. Men and women alike were exceedingly polite, greeting the count and each other with wide smiles, open arms, and refined compliments. They sipped their drinks, listened attentively to each other, and laughed on cue whenever the situation arose.

At the end of the meal François brought Vincent to the dining room, where the lingering aroma of braised kidneys and Madeira sauce extended from the table. He stood at the head of the table, next to Count Robert, and every face except Nicole's turned toward him. The women smiled and winked at each other, but there was skepticism on the faces of some of the men. Henri Clackrul, a tall, blond man in his early forties whose parents had immigrated to France from Hungary, stared at Vincent with a look of bored resignation on his face. He was the best shot of the group and known for his cynicism.

"How old are you, young man?" he asked, stifling a yawn.

"Nineteen, Monsieur."

"I am very sorry for what happened to your uncle, and I am sure he taught you well, but even so, aren't you awfully young to be a gamekeeper?"

"I feel old today, Monsieur."

The guests laughed and Clackrul nodded.

Count Robert turned in his chair and asked his gamekeeper what the guests could expect. Vincent assured the shooting party that the birds were healthy, fully feathered, and that the weather should oblige a fine day of sport, adding with a smile that the ladies would undoubtedly find pleasure alongside their husbands. While the count commented on the summer's unusual breeding weather, its effects on the partridge broods, and ultimately his decision to postpone this first shoot of the year until October, Vincent, who was waiting to be formally dismissed from the room, looked discreetly around the table.

The Viscount de Loye, a thin, effeminate man wearing a silk ascot and English tweeds, burbled with enthusiasm from the end of the table and uttered small nothings to his wife, a woman with a long neck and a narrow, bony nose. The viscountess listened to her husband with one ear while staring at Vincent, darting her tongue from one corner of her mouth to the other. Her neighbor, the Baron de la Carriére, a bald man with heavy eyebrows, wiped his chin with the back of his hand, discovered a small piece of kidney, and made a production of cleaning himself with his napkin. M. Saint-Savin, the owner of an important trucking company puckered and unpuckered his lips each time he swallowed his food. Clackrul's pale blue eyes seemed blasé and unfocused. An older gentleman, a diminutive retired colonel wearing the medal of the Légion d'Honneur in his lapel, farted and then immediately readjusted his chair on the marble floor to cover the sound.

Clackrul lowered his eyes and, talking through his teeth, inquired, "And what do you intend to do about the smell, mon Colonel?" The room fell silent.

Vincent watched Nicole wedge a piece of napkin in her mouth to keep from laughing. When the Viscount de Loye, who had not heard the colonel's fart nor Clackrul's remark, asked if the record of 307 partridge bagged one blissful September day in 1951 could be broken, Vincent concentrated on the question and answered quickly before the laughter reached his lips.

"That depends, Monsieur le Vicomte," he said, "on how generous Monsieur le Comte has been with his claret."

The sedans followed the young gamekeeper's car to the Verdier farm and parked in the cobblestone courtyard. The guests were relaxed and joked among themselves while the chauffeurs unleashed the retrievers and removed the shotguns from their leather cases. Nicole had never loaded before and had difficulty putting her father's guns together. Vincent saw her struggling, walked over, and assembled the count's English Purdeys. Then he hung the shell bag over her shoulder. "I thought you hated this sort of thing," he said.

"I do," she replied, "but it will make him happy." She glanced at Count Robert and then turned to Vincent and smoothed the front of his jacket with her hand. "Let's forget about earlier." She looked at him and he agreed. She started to kiss him on the cheek but he turned and took her lips on his. She laughed, "For luck."

"You'd better wear gloves," he said. "If everything goes well the barrels of the guns will be too hot to handle."

"I feel like I'm in Africa!" she said, standing with a shotgun on each shoulder.

"Women go around naked in Africa," Vincent replied smiling.

"You have a short memory, gamekeeper." She grinned, her face bright from the sun.

"Your breasts are smaller than African women," he said. Nicole kicked at his shins and missed. "But don't worry. They're lovely. And you have a good French ass. Not like those American women, who are made like cows."

"You are demented," she whispered, but then paused. "How do you know that American women have big bottoms?"

"From magazines."

She rolled her eyes the way she used to when he would bring frogs into the castle. He glanced over her shoulder and caught the count looking at them. "I have to go," he said.

Robert de Costebelle led his guests on foot the short distance to the straw blinds that were planted like medieval shields across the width of the stubble field adjoining the farm. The count was particular about who stood next to whom during the shoots; he had offered each guest a numbered placement card corresponding to each drive. He manipulated the cards so that the weaker guns were flanked by good ones. Once he was satisfied that his guests were correctly positioned, he settled himself in the farthest upwind blind. It was the worst possible placement, but one that gave him the best view of the proceedings.

A kilometer away the beaters were waiting for Vincent next to a stand of yellow-leafed birch trees. The first drive would take them through three hundred meters of standing corn, an equally long alfalfa field, the stubble and, finally, to the guns. Vincent hung Serge's brass horn around his neck, loaded his shotgun, and went over last-minute details with Ragondin. Then, after silencing the beaters, he started down the hedgerow that bordered the cornfield. The men followed in single file holding their white flushing flags, wrapped around hardwood handles, low and parallel to the ground. Ragondin brought up the rear.

Vincent positioned a beater between every eighth row of corn and shaped the line like a horseshoe, with the wings cupping the extremities of the field. When the beaters were in place he took a deep breath, blew his horn to signal the guests that the drive had begun, and waved his men on. He knew that moving the partridge through the corn would be tricky. If a weakness occurred in the line the birds would crouch down in the undercover, wait until the beaters passed, and then flush behind their backs, just as Titi hopefully predicted. The men moved steadily through the shoulder-high field studiously whipping their flags against the dry cornstalks, waving them in the air, and calling out all the while,

"Oh, là! Oh, là!" Four large coveys flushed ahead and landed in the alfalfa. Three more got up and flew all the way to the stubble as the beaters emerged from the cornfield. Vincent marked them down and adjusted his wing accordingly, counting between twelve and fifteen partridge to a company. He looked up in the sky, where he knew Serge was watching. "Help me today if you can," he said under his breath.

The men fanned out across the calf-high alfalfa with the wind at their backs and the sunlight on their faces. They laughed and twirled their flags above their heads. The call of "perdreaux, perdreaux," rippled up and down the line each time birds lifted from inside the green hay. Vincent kept an eye on his man-made drag line and called out orders whenever he noticed the slightest hesitation take shape. To his relief, the men obeyed his commands promptly. A few coveys cackled and flew low, landing quickly in a whirl of brown wings. Others flew higher, canting from one side to the other indecisively, exposing cinnamon-colored breasts. The hares that ran out of the alfalfa dropped their ears and flattened themselves on the ground before striking off across the wheat field in low, hard drives.

Partridge rose out of the white stubble like small dust storms, momentarily eclipsing the sun with their wings, sailing across the deep blue sky to guns hidden behind yellow straw butts. The shadow of a high-flying cloud passed over Vincent, a single intrusion in an otherwise empty sky that stretched endlessly over the valley. Two coveys joined and then split twenty meters in front of the line of shooters before spreading right and left. The gunfire dropped a dozen birds to the ground, the reports a joy to Vincent's ears. As the beaters grew closer, the sound of gunshot rose in intensity, finally culminating in one long, drawn-out roar.

He blew his horn when the beaters were a hundred and fifty meters from the blinds, cautioning the guests to restrict the remainder of their shots to those birds that had crossed the line. Another covey flushed, veered to the right, and flew parallel to the guns out of range. The partridges gained altitude and curled back toward Vincent. He raised his gun too early, fired once, and missed. The birds flared, gained altitude, and canted back in the direction of the guests. He dropped a straggler with his second barrel. The partridge fell out of the sky in a wide graceful arch and bounced once on the ground, crippled. One of the beaters hit it over the head with his flag-stick and a final salvo of shots proclaimed the end of the first drive.

The beaters walked to the waiting tractors and the

guests released their Labrador retrievers, both sides of the line exchanging compliments to each other. The wives, who had been sitting next to the loaders during the shooting, helped with the pickup. Vincent went straight to Count Robert, who stood with one of his shotguns broken over his forearm. Nicole handed him three partridge and smiled with pride.

"How was it, Monsieur le Comte?"

"Good. The birds flew well and, except for the colonel who shoots like he farts, the rest of the line responded accordingly."

The pickup produced thirty-seven partridge and five hares. When it was time to move, the count slapped Vincent on the back and said, "Good shot on a long bird!" Nicole blew him a kiss.

Rows of wine bottles and pitchers of water stood on a long oak table in the courtyard of the Verdier farm. Duck pâté baked in pastry crusts, two legs of lamb, lentils, scalloped potatoes, salad, cheese, and plum tarts with fresh cream were served by women from the village wearing black skirts and white blouses. Étienne sat with the guests, most of whom he had known for years. No one acknowledged the shadow of the whore pacing behind the shutters of his sons' apartment.

Nicole took her role as hostess seriously and didn't find time to talk to Vincent, though the wife of the colonel did, at length, on topics as banal as the dilemma of poorly trained help, the expense of broken-down race horses, and the frustration of luxurious cars in need of repair. Vincent stood and fidgeted until she took her woes to a fresher and more sympathetic ear.

He slipped away to the hay barn where beer, wine, and sandwiches were set out on tables for the beaters. Vincent and Ragondin ate their lunch with their backs against a bale of hay and went over the morning drives. "Any problems on your side of the line?" asked Vincent.

"One of the boys threw a clod of earth at his friend. There was a rock in it and they started to fight. I split them up and it was all right after that."

Titi sauntered over.

"Oh, shit," Vincent muttered under his breath.

"Feeling good about yourself, gamekeeper?"

"Screw you, Titi," Ragondin said.

"Shut up, donkey face. I wasn't talking to you!"

"Save it, Titi," said Vincent. "I will fight you, but not today."

"You're wrong. I came over to say that I didn't mean what I said yesterday. I was hung over. I'm sorry." He put out his hand. "You're doing a good job. Serge would be proud of you."

"Thanks," said Vincent, standing to shake hands. He watched Titi walk away, unnerved by his sudden change of attitude.

In the afternoon, the weather held and the birds reeled over the line as if magnetized. The only difficult moment came when the colonel accused the Viscount de Loye of stealing one of his partridge during the pickup. The high-pitched dispute was eventually settled when Count Robert suggested plucking the bird. The guests formed a circle around the two men, joking and teasing, while the colonel's loader stripped the partridge of its feathers and pretended to fly it between the two butts. It was determined that the pellet holes that killed the bird originated from Loye's gun, which did little to calm the colonel.

At the end of the day Vincent formally presented the bag in the courtyard of the castle in rows of ten. The total was 275 partridge, twelve hare, eleven pigeons, and two woodcock. He packed a brace of partridge for each guest to take home. Ragondin helped him move the rest of the game to a room next to the kitchen, ready for shipping to Les Halles in Paris for sale the next morning. Vincent accepted the congratulations of the guests and gave Ragondin his share of the gratuities. Before leaving, the shooting party was offered drinks and Étienne played the French horn, his notes adding melodic finality to the close of a fine day.

Robert de Costebelle, Nicole, François, Vincent, and Ragondin had a drink in the pantry after the guests had left. The count remarked on the pleasant stillness of the evening. Nicole commented on how Loye's wife had berated him when he'd missed. Count Robert didn't respond, but he knew that it was because she came from a better family than the viscount, a fact she would remind him of to his grave.

"What was Henri Clackrul saying to you between the fifth and six drives?" Nicole asked Ragondin.

"That my side of the line was loose and because of it a covey of birds flew out of the range of his gun."

"That must explain why I saw you piss down the side of his car when Étienne was playing the horn," said François.

"That wasn't me," Ragondin said, red faced.

"Jesus Christ," said the count looking at Vincent.

"At least he didn't do it in the gas tank."

The count laughed and shrugged. "After today's success," he said, "I wouldn't be surprised if one of my guests tries to hire you out from under me, Vincent."

"And rest assured that his wife will sport designs to put you under her as well," said Nicole darting her tongue back and forth in her mouth in imitation of the viscount's long-necked wife.

They all stared at Nicole in disbelief. She blushed and said, "So what? I just finished reading *Lady Chatterley's Lover.*"

Chapter 15

The next morning, at Vincent's request, Ragondin rode his bicycle to the castle where he handpicked two woodcock and four partridge from the storage room next to the kitchen. He unruffled the birds' breast feathers into place, hung them back in the shade of the cellar for Count Robert's table, and then packed the remains of the bag into slat boxes and delivered them to the train station in Dreux. The stationmaster said he would store the game in a cool place and load them on the ten o'clock train to Paris. Ragondin thanked the official in the name of Count Robert and handed him a hare. He felt important for the first time in his life. The stationmaster beamed. "Fricasseed with sour cream is my favorite dish," he exclaimed, and invited Ragondin next door for a drink. Picking the hare up by its ears, the official flung it over his shoulder and marched into the bistro.

Vincent slept late Monday morning, waking only when the angle of sunlight shining through the dormer window moved across his face. He shaved in the kitchen sink, made coffee, and poached two eggs, breaking them on slices of toasted farm bread before carrying them to the table in front of the fireplace. Maurice Genevoix's book *Raboliot* was open on the table next to his uncle's bed. It had been one of Serge's favorites: the story of a poacher whose destiny was to take the life of a corrupt policeman. The pages were redolent with the shadowy inhabitants of hardwood forests, the durability of men carrying the weight of poverty on their shoulders, and the authority of despair. Vincent picked up the book and started to read. He drank his coffee but forgot about his breakfast on the table, and after a few chapters dozed off with the paperback open on his chest.

He fell deeper and deeper into sleep until he was inside the river Eure, holding his breath and looking up at the clouds sailing above his head, each cloud a thought, a memory of his swim with Nicole. When he couldn't hold his breath any longer he felt a presence, and woke with a start, confused to find her sitting on the arm of the chair next to him.

She touched his cheek with her hand. He looked up at the sun streaming through the window and sparkling inside a curl in her ponytail. A cream-colored sweater outlined the shape of her breasts. Half asleep, he wanted to pull her onto his lap and kiss her mouth.

"What are you doing here? I was dreaming about you," he said rubbing his eyes.

She sat up on the armrest, her brown eyes wide. "Tell me," she said.

"We were together at the island swimming but in my dream, you and I were children." Vincent blushed because there was much more to it than that.

She smiled down on him.

He wanted to bury his face in her hair and move his hands over her breasts but she placed a hand on his chest. "Up on your feet," she said laughing. "I'm taking us to lunch. Those eggs look awful."

Nicole drove her Sunbeam hard over the narrow back roads to Dreux. The shortcuts led them though freshly harrowed beet fields, pastures filled with beautiful tri-colored Norman cattle, and ripe apple orchards. They laughed each time her car skidded through a corner. On the straightaways Vincent urged her to go faster.

The smell of incense and cooked oil greeted them at the door of the Moroccan restaurant she had chosen for lunch. The dining room was dark and filled with Oriental rugs. They sat next to each other on a cushioned bench below ceiling fans that moved like the wings of giant dragonflies. While they waited for couscous they drank beer and he inquired about the countess. Nicole told him that her mother spoke often about her life as a Costebelle, about what a true gentleman the count was, but in every other respect she had blocked

Merlecourt out of her mind. Vincent asked if that included him as well.

Nicole nodded. "You remind her too much of Roland."

She told stories of her school, of New York, and of things he had only read about, such as yellow taxi cabs and buildings as tall as the Eiffel Tower, contests to see who could dance under broom sticks, and food called hot dogs. The excitement in her voice reminded Vincent of the wide-eyed wonder on the faces of young farmhands the day they returned from their first visit to Paris.

The waiter served a steaming bowl of yellow semolina, followed by broth in a tureen, Moroccan sausages, chicken, and vegetables. A stain of red grease floated on the surface of the broth, but underneath, the soup was clean and strong. In the middle of the table a covered glass bowl was filled with *harissa*, a hot North African pepper paste.

A familiar, faraway look came into Nicole's eyes when he talked about the estate. He recognized it from having seen the same look in mirrors at boarding school on days when his whole being yearned to be home. Nicole put her hand on his and said, "I've been back less than a week but already I know that as much as I love

New York and Paris, my world starts and ends inside the gates of Merlecourt."

"Your father says that light first fell through the trees in the park at Merlecourt three hundred years ago," said Vincent. Nicole nodded dreamily.

"I remember times," Vincent continued, "when the gardeners would push wheelbarrows full of flowers to the castle and François would spread swaths of newspapers on the floor and stand a dozen or more vases in the front hall. The countess and you, wearing long dresses, and gloves to protect your hands, would pluck and cut and fill the vases and sing English ballads. I would watch you through the window. The scene was like a Monet painting."

"It was only yesterday, you know," she said.

They walked to the square next to the belfry after lunch and sat on wooden chairs to listen to the town orchestra play a medley of songs ranging from Bizet to the national anthem. The musicians wore black suits and flat-topped caps with gold sequins on their brims, which reminded Nicole of the hats worn by seafaring officers. The large crowd in the square was made up mostly of mothers with children wearing bonnets and patent leather shoes. Sounds of crying were heard whenever a helium-filled balloon was accidentally released to the clouds. Sparrows bickered over pastry crumbs on the cobblestones next to the dais. Nicole laughed each time the fat man blew into the trombone.

They drove home by way of the departmental forest. The morning frosts had leached the green from the leaves and altered the dimensions of the landscape. The hardwood trees, rich in autumn colors, stood in contrast to the stark, plowed fields that stretched to the limits of distance. The storm of the previous week had leaned on the forest and opened great wind holes in the canopy, through which the sun found refuge on waves of golden ferns. When Nicole asked about the investigation into Serge's murder, Vincent told her about the great red stag and his theory.

"I hate to think we know murderers," she said.

"I'm going to find them, and kill them," Vincent replied, and in that instant he realized he had said the same thing to Ragondin and later in the bar and that his words carried only the weight of his bravado.

She parked the car in the forest and they walked some of the same paths they had walked as children. "I remember coming here with wicker baskets to hunt for *girolle* mushrooms," she said.

"I recall several of your nannies leaving us and slipping off into the bushes with Serge."

"Those soft yellow omelets Chef Gaston used to fold the mushrooms into would melt in my mouth." Nicole closed her eyes for a moment, and licked her lips.

"I'll make that dish for you, if you're still here next summer."

She put her hand in his and pulled him down a long corridor of trees, prompting clusters of rabbits to scatter into the brambles ahead of them. Shadows formed at the base of the trees where the earth was soft. They ambled past a pine stand, in which the perfectly aligned trunks stood at attention like toy soldiers, and they stopped next to a bomb crater—a reminder of the summer of 1944, when the American infantry shelled a division of Germans who were bivouacked in the forest. The crater was filled with water and the surface was black.

"Come and visit me in Paris," she said.

"No."

"Why not? I want you to see my apartment. I'll meet you at the Gare Montparnasse."

Vincent didn't want to go to Paris. Each time he had been to the capital he had hated it. To him the city was a jangle of nerves and irritations—too many cars, too much noise, his senses assaulted from all directions. A place of ill-mannered, condescending posers. The thought of going back made him sick.

"Come to the mill. I'll cook something special," he suggested.

"I'm going to Brittany on Wednesday and won't return until late Saturday. I'll wait for you in Paris."

"No one goes to Brittany in October," he said, looking at her.

She hesitated. "Eric has never been, and he starts work next week. I want to show him where we spent our summers."

When Vincent didn't say anything Nicole turned and blocked his path. "Come on," she said. "Don't be angry with me for taking a friend on a sightseeing tour. I know you don't like Paris, but I'll be there. I'll buy dinner if you take me dancing afterward."

"Does Count Robert know you're going to Brittany with Eric?"

"No, but that's not important."

"It will be when he finds out."

"Don't worry about it. Come to Paris, you can sleep on the couch and catch the early train to Dreux."

Vincent didn't want to admit that he had never eaten in a restaurant in Paris, much less gone out dancing. His only trips to the city had been to the zoo at Vincennes, a soccer game at the Parc des Princes, and two bus rides to the Louvre. He thought again about the streets crawling with people, the traffic, and the filth of the metros. He remembered the sounds, the glaring eyes, the impatience of the locals, and he loathed every bit of it. Nicole taking Eric to Brittany only added insult to injury.

"I have too much work."

"Sunday is your day off."

"Not until I catch Serge's killers," said Vincent full of self-righteousness.

Nicole looked at him and he could see the irritation in her eyes. She jabbed him in the chest and said, "Take one night off, Vincent."

He hated being poked that way. He stepped to one side but she followed him, holding on to his jacket, and he saw the irritation in her eyes disappear and dissolve into a look of hope.

"Come on," she said. "Please."

"It wouldn't look right," he said, knowing he was running out of excuses.

She dropped her forehead on his shirt. "I don't see anything wrong with you sleeping on the couch." She pulled at a button on his shirt.

Even though Nicole was smiling there was something in her eyes that embarrassed him. He had seen that look in Adorée's eyes whenever he'd rejected her offers to find him a girl. Vincent gave in. He would meet her in Paris; he would sleep on the couch.

"Bravo! Take the four o'clock train from Dreux, which arrives at Montparnasse at 5:10. We'll walk to my apartment on rue St. Jacques and have a drink. I know a good brasserie. After dinner we'll go dancing." She kissed him quickly on the cheek.

Chapter 16

The next morning, Ragondin left Dreux in the dark and, after hiding his bicycle on the edge of the Forest of Crothais, began a search for Monsieur and his harem of does. He walked the alleys, the footpaths, and the game trails, listening carefully for the deep, guttural sounds of stags in rut. But the vast forest of birch trees and oaks was quiet and the limbs above him immobile, waiting for the autumn sun to rise and wake the citizenry.

Ragondin proceeded in silence over an extended carpet of leaves. At the bottom of his coat pocket Suzette lay curled on her back nipping at the finger tickling her belly. Ragondin's exemplary behavior of the past week had to a degree dulled his natural instincts, so when his aunt had mentioned rabbit for supper he'd paused, but only for a moment, before dropping his ferret, Suzette, and a handful of mesh pouches, into his pocket.

Ragondin covered kilometers of alleys and lanes in the predawn hours without hearing a single stag bell and when the sun finally transformed his shadow into light he was no closer to finding the great stag. Disappointed, he gave up the search and headed home. At the crest of a hill overlooking the river Eure he spotted the mound of a warren crisscrossed with rabbit trails and fresh droppings. Ragondin envisioned shallots, small red potatoes, salt pork, and carrots slowly simmering in a dark wine reduction. He trusted that once the meat had cooked and the wildness of the rabbit had infused itself into the wine, the heady aroma emanating from the cast-iron pot would dissuade his aunt Tantine from adding her favorite mulled wine to the dish.

The underbrush was heavy with leaves and brambles and it took Ragondin time to find and block the escape corridors of the warren with his pouches. When he was satisfied he unfolded Suzette out of his pocket from a sound sleep and placed her on the ground next to the only open burrow. He watched as she fanned her whiskers in recognition of the fragrance of rabbit, flicked her tail at the prospect of a kill, and then, uninvited, darted into the hole. Moments later a commotion of terrorized feet rose from the arteries of the earth, and a large female rabbit hurled herself head first into one of his pouches. Raising the doe by her hind legs, he brought the edge of his hand sharply down behind the rabbit's ears and broke her neck. He pissed the rabbit by pressing on its belly, and waited for his ferret.

Suzette didn't follow the hind out of the burrow, which told Ragondin that she had made a kill of her own, and that after gorging herself on blood, would sleep. With no other choice than to wait for his hunting companion, Ragondin hid the doe in a fork of a tree, curled up on a mound of fallen leaves, and took a nap. An hour later Suzette poked her head out of the warren, ran to him, and wrapped herself in a ball under his chin. The bitter odor of her coat washed over Ragondin's face and woke him up. Drunk on blood, his huntress remained limp when he slipped her into his pocket.

Jacques drove the tractor to the mill after lunch and told Vincent that he was wanted at the castle. He went to the larder and picked up two bottles of beer. "You don't mind?" he said, once they were safely inside his jacket. Vincent didn't care one bit. He worried that something was wrong, that Ragondin had angered the count.

François was polishing silver in the pantry, his eyes watering and his hands stained green from solvent. He handed Vincent a letter. It was from Nicole and it read: Dear Vincent. Every gamekeeper should have one. Love, Nicole.

Vincent stood at the library door and waited for Count Robert to invite him in. He looked closely at the old man for a sign that would reveal his mood. "A present from Nicole," the count said, pointing his cane at a crate in a corner of the room.

Vincent went to the wooden box. Behind a wire mesh opening a black Labrador with white teeth and soft brown eyes stared back at him. He opened the door and the dog came out shyly, short-coupled and low to the ground, her tail tucked between her legs. The count stood next to Vincent.

"Her name is Ode," he said. "She's one year old and she belonged to a gamekeeper in Sologne. He trained her to sit, to heel, and to fetch. The rest is up to you."

Vincent got down on his knees and stroked the bitch's head. When she closed her eyes, he opened her mouth and spat down her throat. "Now you're mine," he said, and looked at the count. "Good looking, isn't she?" Ode licked his face.

"Good tail, a little narrow in the head, but she will square up. Take good care of her. Dogs, like women, thrive on affection. And Vincent, don't thank me, Nicole has been looking for this dog since before the shoot."

Count Robert patted Ode on the head and then placed a hand on the young man's shoulder. "I'm glad she did. You deserve a friend like Ode." Count Robert nodded his encouragement and returned to his desk.

Vincent hesitated and said, "Monsieur, you should have her. To keep you company . . ."

"No, Vincent. I look at dogs and trees as calendars of years passing. They help me to understand the concept of mortality. Owning a dog at this stage of my life wouldn't be fair. If by some miracle I survived Ode, for example, watching her grow old and die before me would break my heart. I would rather plant a tree."

On the way back to the mill the bitch was nervous and wet the seat. It wasn't until Vincent took her to the stubble wheat field in front of the mill and allowed her to chase thrush that she settled down.

When Ragondin returned from work he reported the details of his unproductive morning in the forest, without mentioning Suzette or the rabbit warren. He played with Ode on the floor in front of the fireplace while they talked, finally agreeing that Monsieur was farther east, in the area of Greenhead Lake.

"Her ears," said Ragondin, bewitched by Vincent's dog. "Have you ever touched anything so soft?" He touched them with his lips. "They're like the inside of a woman's thighs."

Vincent moved his belongings to Serge's bed after Ragondin left for Dreux. He wanted to be close to Ode. She was meant to sleep on the floor, but he woke during the night to a second head on the pillow and a cold busy nose sniffing his eyes.

Chapter 17

After the sun set the next day, Vincent rowed across the river in the plank boat that Serge had kept anchored in an eddy next to the island. Ode sat on the bow, invisible in the darkness. When they reached the far bank Vincent hung his shotgun over his shoulder by a leather strap and ordered his dog to heel. Together they crossed the pasture and climbed the moonlit hill into the forest, hiking north until they were opposite the castle. Vincent stopped next to a grove of pine trees and looked back.

He watched the river split on either side of the island, loosing and regaining its shape, unfolding past the mill on its way south to Rebours. He knew its every turn, the pools and runs, the eddies and backwaters favored by water fowl, the boulders behind which trout took command of the current, and the gravel bars where herons walked hesitantly in the shallows.

"This is where we live,"Vincent whispered to Ode, who looked up at him. "This is our home." He turned up his collar, gathered an armful of pine branches into a pile, and sat down. The dog moved to him, wagging her tail at their closeness. Vincent opened the breach of his shotgun and loaded it with buckshot before resting it across his thighs. The precise sound of the action pleased him. He looked down the hill and across the river into the middle of the valley where the castle stood as a pale shadow on a black moat. A lamp flickered in the count's library.

In June the sky holds its memory of the sun until midnight, but it was fall now. By ten o'clock only one light remained lit in the village and Vincent knew it to brighten the house of Mme Béton. He had studied geography with her in that small, whitewashed room with the blue imitation delftware plates on the walls and a kitchen table with two chairs in the center. At this time of night she would be reading from her Bible.

He looked beyond the village into the darkness of the next valley. There, Adorée, alone under a down comforter, would be grieving for the company of her dead lover. Vincent remembered how they had held each other and how her stomach felt scared and soft against his. It had reminded him of his mother's stomach and he wondered if that particular softness wasn't the essence of all womanhood. He thought about Nicole and the feel of her body against his, and he hated Eric for being alone with her in Brittany.

Vincent sat on top of the hill for a long time, settling into the rhythm of the forest. The temperature dropped, mist formed on the river, and a banner of stars brightened the sky. He adjusted the collar of his jacket, stretched out on the pine bough cushion next to Ode, and closed his eyes. The cold had worked its way up through his makeshift mattress and reminded him of a story about his uncle, that had it ended differently would have altered the course of the lives of those close to him.

Serge had been repatriated from the front after the armistice, but in 1942 he was still under orders from the French government. He knew that it was only a matter of time before he would be deported to a German labor camp. François had already been sent to Czechoslovakia, and other villagers were being transported daily to Germany and Poland. Serge was convinced he would not return alive if he were shipped to a labor camp, and when the time came he fled the department. Armed with false papers issued by the mayor of Chartres, a famous member of the Résistance, he spent the next four years roaming the forests ofVendée, bartering game for food, working the black market, and gathering intelligence for the Maquis. He avoided Merlecourt, returning only twice a year to see his family and visit Count Robert.

Just before the onset of war, the count had sent his wife and infant son to England and then traveled to the command post in Paris with the intention of enlisting. For a week he had tried to persuade his superiors, but from the beginning it was clear that his crippled leg would keep him out of combat. His next concern had been Merlecourt, the village, the valley, and the estate. Hoping to mitigate some of the negative impact of the German military, he remained in a wing of the castle during the Occupation, sharing his home with a colonel from the Luftwaffe and his staff. The officers knew Robert de Costebelle as an ace fighter pilot in the First World War, and treated him with respect.

In December 1943, Serge spent a night in the Forest of Crothais and camped on a knoll overlooking the river, with a clear view of the castle. It was a cold, cloudless night, and from under the branches he had cut for warmth Serge watched successive showers of German flak light up the skies over Dreux. Around midnight he heard and then caught a glimpse of a British Halifax flying low over the trees, the chafing noise of its Rolls-Royce engines loud and threatening. The next morning he discovered a container of small arms and supplies attached to a torn parachute in a thicket. He buried the container with the parachute, turned the arms over to the head of the local Résistance, and kept a pack of English cigarettes for himself.

Later, in Rebours, he stopped at the bistro for a drink and handed out half a dozen of the blond cigarettes to the patrons. He might as well have handed out scones and clotted cream. An hour later, on his way out of the bar Serge Lebuison was arrested by a captain in the Abwehr, the German counterespionage services attached to the Luftwaffe, and was brought to the castle for questioning. Hearing of the incident, Count Robert forced his way past the guard and confronted the captain in the boiler room where Serge, manacled by his wrists to the hot water pipes, was being interrogated.

The count inquired as to the problem, and the officer explained about the English cigarettes and said that it was his obligation to inform the Gestapo. Count Robert laughed and told the captain that he was relieved, that he had been under the impression that Lebuison was in trouble.

"He is, Monsieur le Comte," said the officer with authority.

"Captain, the cigarettes in question belong to me, from before the war. We saw each other in the village and I gave him some of mine."

"I am sorry, but I don't believe you, Monsieur."

The count removed a hard-cover pack of Dunhills from his pocket. "Would these give you pleasure?" he asked, handing the officer the cigarettes.

The captain accepted the gift and set Serge free.

Six months before the war ended, the man who had denounced Serge disappeared from Merlecourt. The story most commonly told by the villagers was that the gamekeeper had trapped a large Russian boar and turned it loose in one of the chalk caves cut into the hills overlooking Dreux. How he got the man into the cave was not known, but years later the informer's wristwatch, the skeleton of the boar, and a few slivers of bones were discovered in the grotto by a troop of Boy Scouts camping.

With Ode at his side, Vincent woke shortly after five in the morning, stiff and wet with dew. During the night the wind had circled to the south, and the mist that had formed above the river while he slept was spread into a thin, almost transparent cloud of fog that rose from the valley. He walked through the pine grove into mixed hardwood trees, following the puzzle of moonlight falling through the branches, faintly illuminating his path. He was aware of the sound his boots made on the leaves, and stopped often to listen for signs of life. At first he heard only a tentative silence. Then came the almost imperceptible scratching sounds of field mice, of rabbits feeding, of badgers backing into burrows, of crows yawning. The sounds, each one a note, grew into a melody that Vincent was familiar with.

He walked for half an hour until he reached the house of Labrissé, the whipper-in for M. Dutertre, owner of the deer-hunting rights to the Forest of Crothais. On one side of the house was the pavilion, an octagonal, two-story, brick building with tall, arched windows overlooking eight arterial alleys and a web of smaller footpaths and horse trails. It was here that the members of the stag-hunting party assembled to change and socialize before and after the hunt. On the other side of Labrissé's house were the kennels, now filled with five dozen sleeping hounds, among the best in France. Labrissé was a difficult man, and Vincent stayed clear of the house for fear of waking his dogs.

He made his way east, to the ruins of La Rotule, a ninth-century monastery that had once been inhabited by Templar priests and was now a favorite meeting place for his cousin Lisette and her friends on weekends. The ruins rested above a maze of secret underground passageways, one of which once led to the castle library two kilometers away. All that was left of La Rotule was a handful of rocks, a piece of standing wall, shallow holes dug by amateur archaeologists, and a legend that the monastery was built on the ground where St. Hubert had stood when God appeared to him as a stag. The locals were convinced that La Rotule was a sacrosanct haven for deer, and to support this claim they would point to the fact that over the centuries there had never been a story, verified or anecdotal, of a stag being taken on or near its grounds.

The sun rose as Vincent walked to the far end of the forest. The warm front that had passed over the valley during the night had spawned a wet wind. Dew on the foliage loosened beads of water on his young Labrador. The smell of wizened ferns and rotting leaves reminded him of all the times he had stalked Serge through the woods at Merlecourt only to have his uncle lose him at will.

He reached Greenhead Lake when the sun was halfway up the trees, and stopped next to a poplar stand favored by woodcock in winter. Ode had followed him silently for more than an hour and when he roughed her coat she rose on her hind legs and pawed at him with joy. Vincent propped his shotgun against a log and sat down with his dog at his feet.

Greenhead Lake was a small, shallow, pear-shaped body of water that in summer filled with frogs and lily pads. He and Roland would hike there in August and, using cane poles and strips of red cloth attached to hooks, entice frogs to jump at the lure. It was up to Vincent to separate the bodies from the legs, a messy affair that Roland considered beneath his surgical skills. Later, Chef Gaston would fry their catch in butter, garlic, and parsley. Roland would eat a dozen legs, Vincent half that many, and Nicole none at all.

When the surface of the water reflected the trunks of the surrounding birch trees, Vincent stood and explored the soft earth along its shore. He found signs that a herd of deer had been watering, and a day-old piece of torn ground with Monsieur's unmistakable spoor. Ode dropped her nose on the leaves and was introduced to the scent of a stag in rut. Vincent let out a sigh of relief. He had worried about not finding Monsieur. Now he and Ragondin could make plans for laying an ambush for the killers.

He turned to head home when a figure wielding a hickory cane jumped out from behind a tree. It was Labrissé, the whipper-in. "What are you doing here?" the man shouted. Ode ran behind Vincent and barked.

"Answer me!" Labrissé commanded, in the same deep voice he used on his hounds. "Who are you and what are you doing here?"

The dog man had the thin, bowed legs of a rider, and the sloped shoulders of a woodsman. His round face was punctuated by a short, turned-up nose and his coal-black hair was cropped close to his head. He took two steps and his cane was suddenly very near. Too near, Vincent realized, for him to get his gun off his shoulder before getting his head caved in. "My name is Vincent Lebuison."

"What is the gun for?"

"Nothing. I am taking a walk in the woods."

"Liar! No one carries a gun unless he's planning to kill. You're after deer. Admit it or I'll break you in two!" His cheeks were red and wrinkled and his eyes were dark and blue, the penetrating eyes of a forest dweller.

"Stop it, Labrissé! You know me. I am Serge Lebuison's nephew. He was murdered last month by poachers hunting Monsieur. There's a price on the stag's head. The gun is for protection, nothing more."

"A price on Monsieur's head?" Labrissé focused his eyes and lowered the cane. "Where did you hear that?"

"Serge told me. But everyone knows."

Labrissé shook his head. "I don't believe it," he said and hit the ground with his cane. A divot sailed toward Ode, who cowered. "You have no right to carry a gun in the forest. This is federal land and my employer,

M. Dutertre, pays for the right to stag hunt. Monsieur belongs to me. We'll hunt him next Wednesday."

"You want to hunt Monsieur on the first day of the season—with dogs that haven't been run in seven months?" Vincent said with a mocking laugh. "They won't last the morning. You'll wind up with egg on your face, again."

"Get out of here, you little bastard," Labrissé raised his cane once more. "I know all about you. Your mother slept with a German and that's why you have queer-colored eyes. Get out of my forest and don't return!"

Vincent stepped back, pulled his shotgun off his shoulder, and aimed it at the ground in front of Labrissé's feet. His neck was filled with blood and everything was going too fast and bending at the edges. He raised the barrel until it was aimed at the whipper-in's head. Ode growled.

Labrissé swung the cane back and forth in front of Vincent's face. "I'll tell you something," he shouted. "You're uncle was a know-it-all. I was happy when I heard that he was killed! I'll do the same to you if I ever see you or your dog in the forest again!"

"Get back!" Vincent yelled at the man, hating him and frightened because something dreadful in him wanted to pull the trigger; something he didn't understand wanted the man to die for being so stupid and rude and wrong.

"Shoot me? Hah, you don't have the balls," Labrissé said. "But I do, and I'm going to prove it before this is all over." He sneered and shook his cane. Then he turned and disappeared behind the trees.

Vincent sat on the ground and put his shotgun down beside him. Ode stood with her head next to his. He breathed deeply to calm his heart, but he could not stop himself from wondering what it would have felt like to pull the trigger.

Back at the mill, Ragondin was fixing breakfast. Vincent reminded him that he didn't live there. Ragondin immediately knew that something out of the ordinary had happened, and wished that he had stayed home. He cracked eggs into a skillet without looking up. Outside the wind had come up and now it leaned against the mill. Vincent sat in front of the fireplace, and when he glanced up at the boar's head he recognized Labrissé's nose.

Ragondin petted Ode and waited for his friend to say something. "I found Monsieur at Greenhead Lake," Vincent volunteered after awhile.

"Bravo!" Ragondin said, and he danced around the room. "You would make a fine poacher."

"Cut it out!" Vincent said. "It's been a bad morning."

Ragondin stopped dancing and stood in front of Vincent, suddenly angry. "What day of the week is it that you have fun?" he asked. "When do you get drunk and laugh and do what I did when I was nineteen?"

"Oh, shut up. I don't need a lecture right now."

"I heard you the other night," Ragondin said sitting down. "You were twisting the sheets into knots and cursing your mother and your aunt, even Count Robert. You're acting like an old man, castle boy."

With his hands on his knees, Vincent looked down at his shoes, hating Ragondin's perception. It was true that he felt different from everyone else in the village, and he had chastised himself for the shyness he displayed around his peers, conscious that it was, in fact, a form of snobbery.

A moment later, Ragondin tapped him on the knee. "Hell, don't mind me," he said. "I've trapped and killed for so long I don't react like other people. Death is as normal to me as taking a crap is to you." He interlaced both hands over his head and looked for the right words. "I think that all that fancy living in the castle when you were young, and then being sent to a Jesuit school in Rouen, and now working for the old man, has confused you. You were born poor and brought up rich.

Now that you're poor again, you're angry. You don't know who you are or who you're meant to be, do you?"

Before Vincent could answer they heard a car drive up the road and stop under the kitchen window. A moment later, Count Robert opened the front door without knocking and strode in. His herringbone jacket was open and he wasn't wearing a tie. Ragondin put his glass down and they both scrambled out of their chairs. Count Robert walked up to Vincent and stood inches from his face.

"I was rudely awakened this morning by Pierre Labrissé. He said you aimed a gun at his face. Is that true?" Vincent could barely see the blue in the count's eyes. "Answer me," he said.

"I was looking for Monsieur . . ."

"Goddamn it!" said the count interrupting him. "I don't care who you were looking for. You have no jurisdiction in Crothais and you know perfectly well that it's illegal to carry a gun in the forest, especially at night. What is the matter with you? Not only do you carry a weapon but you use it to threaten a good man doing his job."

"I'm sorry, Monsieur le Comte," Vincent said. "I meant Labrissé no harm, but he jumped me and called me a bastard and accused me of poaching." Count

Robert looked at Vincent for a moment as if he was trying to read something in his face. Then he turned and confronted Ragondin.

"My Baudelaire is back in the library. It was you who stole it, wasn't it? That story was a fabrication! You had it all along." Ragondin stepped back and for a moment Vincent thought the count was going to cane him.

"I swear," Ragondin said. "I swear I didn't have it! Please, let me explain . . ."

"Quiet, both of you!" Count Robert turned back and faced Vincent. "I am not interested in your criminal activities." Ode got up and yawned. The count took a breath and ran his hands through his hair. "I cannot believe that I am employing a thief and a potential murderer." He shook his finger in Vincent's face. "Do you take me for an imbecile?"

"No, sir."

"You have been under my care for almost fifteen years. You hired someone who steals other people's property, and now you threaten a man I have known all my life." He walked to the open door and stood outlined in the morning sun. "I'm warning you. If I hear so much as a rumor about either one of you involved in the smallest indiscretion—of any sort, anything at all—I'll fire you both inside the hour."

"So, does that explain your bad mood?" Ragondin asked Vincent after the count had left.

Vincent nodded and sat down. "When did you steal the book back?"

"Last night, before going home, and now you've ruined it. The count would have been pleased if he hadn't been so pissed at you for shooting the dog man."

"I didn't shoot him!"

"You might as well have."

Vincent closed his eyes to squeeze the morning's events out of his head. He gave his breakfast to Ode and thought about the count's anger. At least when he and Roland were boys a caning had cleaned the slate. Now, with Ragondin as his partner he viewed the reprimand as a sword precariously balanced over his head.

"How did you get into the Dufossé house?" he asked when Ragondin had finished cleaning the kitchen.

"Through the back door. They were in bed. The wife sounded like she was fermenting. Never heard anything like it."

"You went into the bedroom?" Vincent was incredulous.

"I already had the book by then, so I thought I'd take a look."

"Jesus Christ! I'm going to bed,"Vincent said shaking his head and taking his shirt off. "You'd better go meet with Jacques. He wants us to help him prune back the fruit trees next to the swimming pool."

"Fine, but before I go, do you mind cooking a hare for dinner?"

"You didn't?"

"Just kidding!" said Ragondin, laughing. Then he stood up a little taller and cleared his throat. "How about a pheasant?" he said caricaturing the face of a clown.

Vincent closed his eyes. "Where is it?"

"Hanging in the larder."

"Merde, Ragondin. What if Count Robert had gone back there?"

"I know, but it wasn't my fault. A fox was getting into the aviary. I hung a noose last night, but instead of finding Maître Renard this morning I discovered, much to her misfortune, Mme Oiseau!"

"Oh, stop it. You hang a noose three fists off the ground for a fox, two for a pheasant, and you know it!"

"Is that it? I couldn't remember."

"She'll need to hang for a few days," said Vincent with a sigh. "But the next time you're in Dreux bring back a bag of chestnuts for the stuffing." Exasperated, he pushed Ode off his bed.

Chapter 18

Clouds settled over the valley during the day and by afternoon the landscape stretched in dour uniformity. The Lombardy poplars across from the mill stood naked in the field, forgotten now that the wind had stripped them of leaves. Ducks migrating south from the coastal marshes of northern Europe stopped over in the backwaters of the river Eure, and chattered through the night.

Late in the afternoon Ragondin climbed the hill into the forest carrying sandwiches, a liter of beer, and a rainproof tarp for cover. It was his intention to spend the night at Greenhead Lake. The men who had killed Serge would be looking for Monsieur. He planned to stalk them and find out who they were.

Meanwhile, Vincent, eager for trout, assembled Serge's spinning rod, and led Ode to the island. The low sun hid behind dark clouds. Black earth stuck to the soles of his hip boots. The river, swollen by rainstorms that had fallen to the north of Merlecourt, now spilled into the estate pastures where blue herons walked hesitantly in their own images flicking steel-colored beaks at misguided minnows. Seagulls, driven inland by coastal winds, shrilled over the worms and snails, moles and field mice, which had drowned in the riparian surge.

Vincent pulled the barrel trap out of the water and turned it on its side. The carcass of the rat that had jumped into it after his swim with Nicole was partly decomposed. He crossed the bridge onto the island, remembering her standing there in her underwear, and followed a game path to the gravel bar, where the water ran quick and clean.

He told Ode to sit and pulled his hip boots up over his knees. A dozen mallards flew upstream toward the island, their wings mirrored on the surface. The Mitchell reel was stiff from lack of use. He pulled a few meters of frayed line off the spool, bit the worn monofilament off with his teeth, and threaded clean line through the rod's guides. Then, he retied the gold spinner and set the drag.

The gravel bar fell into a long and widening pool that was deep and slow enough at the tail to hold carp. The trout lay farther upstream, with their heads facing the current.

Vincent waded into the water until he felt the strength of the river against his legs. Ode watched him from the bank. He studied the flow of water over the gravel bar and, when he was satisfied with his position, cast upstream into the shallows, allowing the current to carry the lure downstream into the pool. When the line was at an angle below him, he closed the bail, retrieved the spinner, and felt the strike.

Vincent raised the rod and the fish rose out of water. It angled to one side in midair, bending, falling, and then ran below the surface across the river. The big trout spawned commotion in its wake and leapt again, golden against the backdrop of trees. Vincent felt every muscle of the fish from the tip of the rod down to his wrist. He watched the monofilament feed off the reel downstream and stop in an eddy fifty meters below the island. There the fish fought the treble hooks with short, hard strokes of anger. Then it sulked close to the bottom before shaking its head and running back upstream in an attempt to dislodge the hook from its mouth. The wind came up and blew against the current, throwing small whitecaps against Vincent's waders. Ode stood on the edge of the gravel bar with her ears perked while the fish swam from one bank to the other in a desperate search for freedom. Finally the trout gave in to the bow of the rod and when Vincent backed out of the shallows it followed him across the smooth golden rocks until its flank broke the surface. As he had expected, the trout was a native brown with a small half-moon head and a thick, spotted body. Except for the gold spinner in the corner of its mouth, the male fish looked like a shadow in the river.

Ode placed her nose on the tail of the trout and nipped at its body until Vincent picked it up, turned it upside down, and broke its back by applying pressure on the roof of its mouth. The teeth left small abrasions on his thumb.

He threaded a branch through the trout's gills and then sat on the bank. Night clouds surged across the valley toward him and he recalled the times he would stand in this same spot with Roland, wrap a mutton head in a net, secure it to the bank with a rope, and drop it into the water. A few days later they would pull up the net and discover hundreds of finger-long crawfish embedded in the mesh. In winter, during the hard freezes, they would ambush ducks on the island, taking turns shooting them when they landed on the gravel spit. The heavily downed drakes wore dazzling green neck pieces and purple-black tail feathers. Roland would pluck the cowlicks at the base of their backs and give them to Jacques and Hubert, who wore them proudly in the folds of their caps.

From his seat on the bank next to Ode he observed the river as it rushed past a clutter of overhanging branches, balked at eddies, and made obscene noises while passing in and out of rat holes burrowed into the bank. The wind swirled across the river, pushing the willows in one direction and then bullying them into another. Vincent hated wind. The dry, moisture-stealing *sirocco* from Africa gave him headaches, and the cold, hungry gales from the North Sea took him back through time to the damp corridors of his boarding school in winter.

Carrying the brown trout on the branch, Vincent started for the mill, remembering how much Serge had loved to eat trout. In the past days his uncle's face had lost definition, and his voice had fallen out of reach. As he walked, Vincent watched the low-hanging yellow branches of a willow tree inclining toward the river. The rain didn't come until he was halfway home.

Water washed down his face; but instead of feeling cold he felt lonely, longing for laughter and music and, most of all, for Nicole. Ragondin had accused him of not knowing who he was, a statement that upset him. He was nineteen years old, in love with a beautiful girl, and trying to make sense out of a bad dream in which his uncle was murdered. Who else was he supposed to be? A German bastard? The almost-adopted son of a French count? Why had God, that imperious deity with the unfettered ability to impart good and evil, chosen to make his life one of loss and uncertainty?

Vincent stopped, opened the sluice gates, and watched a backup of water from one river pour into the other. The rain fell at an angle on his head. He stood holding the rod and the branch with the trout and felt an urge to dance. He closed his eyes, raised his left foot and then his right knee to his chest, lifting his legs slowly at first and then faster.

He set down the rod and fish and danced to a waltz by Chopin that the countess had practiced the summer Roland had died, for a family concert she never gave. It sounded Polish and finished fast. He sang and danced and clapped his hands, pulled by the wind and pushed by the rain, fighting, spinning, and aware of his body inside his clothes. Ode looked at him with a puzzled expression on her face, and then joined in on the fun, running circles around his feet, leaping into the air, and barking. Vincent jumped up and down, knelt and twisted his hips like the gypsies at the village fair. No one disturbed him, nothing slowed him; the only thing in the world that mattered was the music. And when the waltz in his head came to an end he stopped singing and danced in earnest to the music of the wind. He danced without thought or feeling or memory, blind to his surroundings, and alone outside of himself. Ode looked at him, panting, her tongue hanging to one side of her mouth.

A billow of smoke rumbled out of a thatch-roof house across the clearing. He stared, his chest tight from the exertion. Something was happening there, something terrible. Terror gripped him. His house was burning down.

Chapter 19

Vincent ran to the mill and through the front door with Ode at his heels, expecting the room to be engulfed in flames. Instead there was a wood fire in the chimney and, curled up in an armchair beside it, Adorée looking warm and comfortable. Ode ran across the room and smelled her feet and her dress and then licked her hand. Vincent leaned against the door jamb, his heart pounding from the dancing and running, and the fear of fire. Adorée laughed at the startled expression on his face.

"Jesus. You scared me," he said, feeling weak.

"You dance like a goat," she said, reaching out to Ode. "Who's your friend?"

"A present from Nicole. What are you doing here? Where's your car?"

"Parked under the trees in back. Come in, you're wet. The fire will thaw you out." She cupped Ode's head between her hands and cooed.

Vincent looked at the water seeping out of his rolled-down boots and remembered his fishing tackle and the trout. He went out to retrieve them and returned to find that Ode had settled at the woman's feet.

"Want a drink?" he asked, dropping the trout into the sink.

"Not just yet."

The white underside of the fish had yellowed and the red markings on its back were tarnished like old blood. It was a broad trout, weighing a kilo, fleshed out and dense to the touch. He turned on the cold water and washed the grass off of its flanks. For a moment the fish felt alive in his hands.

"Do you mind that I'm here?" asked Adorée.

"Of course not," he said wiping his hands on a kitchen towel. "Join me for dinner?"

She nodded and Vincent opened the fish, inserted two fingers in the gills, and pulled downward. Hundreds of tiny gray shrimp spilled out of the milky stomach cavity into the enamel sink, where they seemed to dance in the water. He ran his thumbnail up under the dark band next to the backbone and the water turned red. The flesh beneath the translucent bones was salmon colored.

Adorée sat in the armchair and watched him clean the trout, a red scarf wrapped around her shoulders, her legs tucked up underneath her. Her hair was pulled back from her forehead by a gold band.

"I brought you a loaf of bread and some pastries." She looked around the room. "I've missed this place."

Her voice was low and her brown eyes were gentle and he knew why she had been Serge's favorite. He kissed the top of her head.

"I worry about you being here all by yourself," she said.

"Ragondin is with me during the day and Ode keeps me company at night. I'll see how winter goes."

"Winter?"

"My memories turn into nightmares at night, and winter is a long night." He emptied the remains of an opened bottle of red wine into two glasses and sat in front of her on the hearth.

"You should ask Count Robert for your old room back at the castle. I'm sure he wouldn't mind," said Adorée.

Vincent explained that his relationship with the count had changed in the years since he had moved to the mill. The estate was under his charge now, and he wanted to do his best to fulfill the duties that had been Serge's.

Adorée smiled at the serious tone in his voice as he went on about his responsibility to the count and his obligations as the new gamekeeper. "And do your duties include dancing in the rain?" she teased.

Vincent shrugged and felt the fire on his shoulders. He stood and paced in front of the hearth, imagining steam rising from his wet clothes. After a while he told her about Monsieur and the reward from the syndicate in Paris, and how he and Ragondin were looking for the murderers. She listened with her hands in her lap, the fire reflected in her eyes. She told Vincent that Maurice Corneille had stopped by her shop the day before. The police had found nothing.

"They never do."

"Maurice told me that if it hadn't rained that day the murderers would be in jail now."

"Acts of God make for good excuses. But, to be honest I'm not doing any better than they are. All I've managed to accomplish is to get in trouble with Father Ménardeau, Labrissé, and Auverpois, not to mention Count Robert." Vincent picked a log out of the wicker basket next to the hearth and dropped it on the fire. Flames rose into the chimney. He felt the heat through his wet trousers and sneezed.

"I'll cook dinner," said Adorée, standing.

"No. I will," Vincent said, walking with her to the kitchen.

"Not this time. I want you to take a bath before you catch your death."

Vincent made a face behind her back. Those were the same words his mother had used when he was a child. "You want me to take a bath while you cook? Not a chance!"

"And why not?"

"Because that's the bathtub." He pointed at the enamel tub, which sat beside the counter where Adorée would be working.

"I know that," she said with a slow smile.

"I'll just towel off and change."

"No bath, no food." She connected the hose to the hot water faucet.

"It's my fish."

"Not if I leave and take it with me." She dropped the hose in the tub and turned on the water. "What's the matter? What do you think I am going to do?" She put her hands on her hips. "You spent the night in my bed. Did you lose something there?"

"There was nothing to lose," he said indignant, his face red. "I'm not a virgin!" He went out in the rain to the larder and brought back a bunch of parsley and some lemons, cream, and a handful of red potatoes.

"It's almost ready," she said, tossing a bar of soap in the tub. "Go ahead. I won't look." She scrubbed the potatoes and dropped them in a pot of boiling water.

Vincent knew she would keep pestering him until he gave in. And he was cold; a hot bath would feel good. He turned his back to her, pulled off his boots and then his clothes. The water was hot and he stood for a moment in the tub, bent over and facing the opposite wall.

"What's the matter?" asked Adorée.

"I'm being scorched," he answered over his shoulder.

She laughed. "The back of your neck needs a scrubbing."

"Jesus Christ," he said, and sat down. He rubbed the soap in his hands between his legs until the water was cloudy and he couldn't see the bottom. He felt the heat rise up his chest and watched steam paint the window panes above Adorée's head. She chopped parsley until a dark mound glistened in front of her fingers. She swept it to one corner—staining the cutting board green—rinsed the fish and placed it on its belly between rows of the small parboiled red potatoes and a heap of butter. She laid thin lemon slices along the trout's flanks, then studied the cutting board like a painter might his palette. "I'm ready," she said.

There was a fullness below her waist that contradicted the speed of her fingers. Vincent held his nose and went under water, rinsed his hair and surfaced. "I'm going to soap myself," he said, "so please don't watch."

Adorée turned toward the stove. He stood and lathered himself while she playfully sang a song about plucking daisies until he sat back down. She went to the larder to get a bottle of white wine and Vincent stepped out of the tub, toweled himself, walked to the dresser next to his bed, and changed clothes. Outside the wind had picked up and was throwing hard rain against the house. Vincent turned the fire over and sat in an armchair. Heat washed over him and he fell asleep.

A sweet smell of white wine and cooked cream woke him half an hour later. His head felt congested and the side of his body closest to the fire was in a sweat, the other half was cold. He got up and followed a draft of air to the kitchen, where Adorée had cracked a window. To his dismay he realized that in the time it had taken to bake the trout he had caught a cold. "Don't overcook it," he said, standing next to her while she checked the fish. He chased a potato with his knife.

"I know my men and my fish," she said, lightly slapping his hand. "I like them strong, firm, and fresh." Vincent made a face that she wasn't supposed to see but did. She turned and looked into his eyes while the fish sizzled in the oven.

"You little puritan," she said, and pinched his leg above the knee.

"Please," he laughed, doubling over. But she did it again and so he held her against the counter with his leg between hers to make her stop. She relaxed and Vincent looked over her head into the black window, strongly aware of how different Nicole had felt in the river. Where Nicole had been taut and lively, Adorée was soft and vulnerable.

Something warm touched the front of his neck; Vincent looked down and saw the tip of Adorée's tongue disappear into her mouth. He felt himself getting hard. Adorée laughed. "You are a goat," she said, and moved out of the way.

She picked up a wooden spoon and opened the oven. The trout rested in a puddle of butter and cream. She tasted it, pursed her lips in his direction, and transferred the fish to a serving plate. The lemon slices had caramelized around the edges. Adorée brought the trout to the table and made incisions on either side of its backbone, peeled off the metal-colored skin, drew a fillet, and served it with potatoes and parsley. She told him to start, lifted the backbone away from the pink flesh, and served herself. The sound of the wind and the smell of hot cream, along with her presence, made the room feel smaller than it was. Vincent ached and felt the fever in his head. Chills raced up and down his back. He soaked the bread in the juice in the pan, added it to the fish already in his mouth, and washed everything down with long swallows of wine.

"Tell me about Nicole," she said.

"She wants me to see her in Paris, but she just took her American boyfriend to Brittany. I don't understand."

"Maybe she loves you and doesn't want you to know," Adorée said, shaking her head. "Or maybe she loves you and doesn't know it herself. It would feel the same. On the other hand, she may think that you worry too much to have any fun. That would feel different. Finish your fish."

He didn't think he worried too much, and he knew that Nicole couldn't really care for him and still be with Eric. He was certain of that.

"Do you love her?" Adorée's voice sounded like it was coming out of a tin box.

"No," he lied. He felt the fever climb over the cold and settle in his head.

"Do you love me?"

"Of course."

"That's right. I forgot," she said in a mischievous voice. She got up and sat in his lap and wiped his forehead with her napkin. "You're making yourself sick by being so serious all the time!"

He tried to push her off but she wrapped her arms around his neck. When he stopped resisting her he realized how nice she felt against him.

"All right, I take it back," Adorée said smiling at him. "You aren't serious, you're feverish." She kissed him on the mouth and her lips tasted like buttered potatoes. "You smell like the river," she said, and she brought the bottle of wine to his mouth. "Drink!"

"No more," he said moving his head to one side. "I'll be sick."

"No you won't. Drink, it will make you sweat," she said from behind the bottle. He tipped his head back and let the wine fall straight into his stomach. The room started to spin.

She held his face between her hands and kissed him again. The room grew smaller and smaller and the noise of the wind and rain on the roof slipped away until there was only Adorée. When it felt like her heart was beating into his, she asked, "Have you really been with a woman, Vincent?"

"No," he answered, resting his cheek on her shoulder, too tired to lie. He imagined his breath falling down her blouse to her breasts.

"I didn't think so. Come," she said, getting up and taking him by the wrist. "I'll take care of you and the dishes and the fire and everything else. But first I have to get you into bed." She pulled and he followed without resisting.

She helped him undress and then sat down next to him. Vincent closed his eyes and let his body sink into the mattress. Adorée toweled the sweat off his chest and sang songs under her breath that were difficult for him to understand. He drifted off, and when he opened his eyes again he was between the sheets, naked and cold, and she was still sitting beside him. He listened for the wind and rain against the mill, but it was quiet and he knew the worst of the storm was over.

"The fever broke," she said stroking his forehead. "How do you feel?"

"Cold." He reached for a blanket at the foot of the mattress. "What happened?"

"You caught a chill and I put you to bed. You fell asleep and the wine did the rest." She rubbed his chest and Vincent remembered her hands undressing him. "Would you like me to get under the covers with you?" she asked, looking down at him. "To warm you, of course."

He nodded. Her face was blurred, as if it had been painted on water.

"I suppose you would like me to take my clothes off

as well," she said, unbuttoning her blouse. "And perhaps I should make love to you?"

When she was undressed Adorée slipped under the covers and moved close to him. He turned on his side to face her and felt her soft and warm and naked against the length of his body. She kissed him and gently pushed him over onto his back and ran her hand down his chest and stomach until he thought he might never catch his breath again. Then she covered his body with hers, and with her hands on either side of his chest she rose and straddled his thighs. Vincent cupped her breasts, feeling a weight he had only imagined before. Adorée removed the gold band from her hair and leaned over to kiss him, taking him in one hand and guiding him while lowering herself onto him.

"Now that you are inside a woman," she said from behind a curtain of warm, brown hair, "I am going to teach you how to make love to one."

In the long silence that followed their lovemaking Vincent listened to the blood flooding through his veins. He listened to his body and he listened to Adorée's breathing and he touched her with his fingers and smelled her skin and kissed her. They made love again, and again, and each time Vincent grew bolder and more assured until, laying back on the bed with beads of sweat moistening her upper lip, she begged, "Please. That's enough." He smiled.

"You're a good student, Vincent," Adorée admitted at dawn, when he finally let her go. He pulled the blanket over his shoulders and felt her warmth in every muscle of his body.

She let Ode out, dressed, made coffee, and carried two cups back to bed. "I won't be back, you know?" she said, standing next to the bed.

"What do you mean?" He sat up and looked at her in disbelief.

"I wanted to sleep with you so that you would know how it should be. Now we are friends who share more secrets than most, that's all, and I want to keep it that way. It's not possible for us to be both friends and lovers."

Adorée adjusted her hair and Vincent saw pencil marks in the corners of her eyes and wrinkles that fell from the sides of her mouth. Then he looked away and felt guilty. He stood up, kissed her, jumped back in bed and pulled the covers up under his chin. "I'll come to your apartment on Monday and we'll talk about it."

Adorée nodded, put on her coat, and walked to the door.

"You made me happy, Vincent," she said, leaving. A wave of cold air rolled across the floor and Vincent buried himself under the covers.

When Ragondin returned from Greenhead Lake the sun was high and Vincent was asleep with his face under the pillow. Ode greeted him at the door. Ragondin looked into the kitchen and noticed the extra plate and wine glass in the sink. He smacked his lips and said, "I smell woman! Lots of woman."

Walking over to Vincent's bed he put his head under the covers. "I know that smell. Don't give it a name. Let me guess."

"Jesus Christ, Ragondin, leave me alone," Vincent said, sitting up and pushing his friend away.

Ragondin breathed in the air, slapped his forehead, and exclaimed, "Mme Béton! You plugged old Mme Béton!" He rolled around on the bed laughing.

"Imbecile!"

"Who then?"

"Not a chance."

"You think I don't know?" Ragondin put his hands under imaginary breasts. "And so does your uncle Serge, but you won't have to deal with that problem for some time. A good thing, hey?"

Vincent wondered if cuckolding a dead person was a sin, but knew that his uncle would have laughed at his concern. Realizing his cold was over he got up, pulled his pants on, and invited his friend to go to work.

"Not me. I spent the night at Greenhead Lake." Ragondin stretched out on Vincent's bed and crossed his hands behind his neck. "And I have news."

"Go on, tell me," Vincent said, looking for his shoes.

"I saw a car."

"Labrissé?"

"No. Take another guess."

Many years later, Vincent admitted that at that moment he felt that something disagreeable and unreachable, like a black spider, was crawling down the back of his neck. He sat on the bed and looked at Ragondin without blinking.

"Tell me," he said uneasily.

"We should have known," Ragondin said. "The car belongs to Gros-Louis. Titi was with him. They had a gun."

Vincent's face filled with rage, but he did not say or do anything for several minutes. Ode, sensing something, went to the kitchen and lay down under the table. "How close did you get to them?" he finally asked.

Ragondin joined Ode in the kitchen and poured himself a shot of Calvados. He explained how he had circled the Verdier brothers' car and then crept on all fours in the ditch until he was even with the front door. He'd seen the barrels of a shotgun through the window when Gros-Louis lit a cigarette. Titi was fantasizing out loud about using his half of the bounty to buy whores in Paris.

Vincent walked out of the mill to the water's edge to be alone. Sitting with his head between his hands, he relived the episode with Titi at the bar. He recalled how embarrassed he had felt wearing the gamekeeper's uniform he had so proudly picked out that morning. He shuddered when he realized that the laughter of the brothers mocking him outside the bistro must have been what Serge had heard while he was being dragged to his death. Ragondin was right. He should have kicked the shit out of Titi when he had him down.

Vincent went back to the mill and sat down in front of the fireplace. His hands shook. Ragondin offered him a glass of Calvados and Vincent swallowed it the wrong way, coughing the liquor out his mouth and nose. "I'll see them in hell," he promised as soon as he found his voice again.

He got up and stared out the kitchen window at the river, his river, and was lost in thought again until he felt

Ode sit down next to him. Slowly, irrational anger turned into determination, and Vincent thought again about Serge's gun, a twelve-gauge Darne that had been dropped and was chipped in the bottom corner of the stock. To avenge his uncle he would have to find it, and then he would have to fight the brothers, and kill them. He didn't know how he was going to do that.

Ragondin said that he would search the Verdier farm for Serge's shotgun while Vincent was in Paris with Nicole and then go back to the mill and wait for his return. He was sure the brothers would try and ambush the stag again after dark. If Serge's shotgun was in their quarters, he would find it.

"What about Étienne?" asked Vincent.

"Titi and Gros-Louis have their own rooms."

"What about the woman? She'll tell them."

"I don't have a choice. She never leaves the place."

"What if she doesn't let you in?"

"She's a whore, isn't she?"

The Calvados and the long night at Greenhead Lake finally caught up with Ragondin, who fell asleep in the armchair. Vincent paced from the kitchen to Serge's bed for half an hour, until Ode started to whimper. So many bad memories, so many nightmares, he thought. And now the Verdier brothers, the most feared men in the department, were characters in his latest drama.

With no one to talk to, Vincent left Ode behind and drove the Citroën to Dreux to be with someone he trusted, but at the bakery he was told that Adorée had gone out to lunch with Dr. Jobard. He drove to the castle.

Though it was past noon, Robert de Costebelle was reading in bed with the lights on and the curtains drawn. He looked frail in his silk pajamas, his skin as pale as the light he was reading by. Taken aback by his condition, Vincent stood at the end of the bed and fought the urge to report the news about the Verdier brothers.

"Chateaubriand was correct, you know, when he wrote late in life that every day is a good-bye," the count said, oblivious to Vincent's discomfort. "However, contrary to popular belief, enduring to old age—with all the joys and regrets the years impose—is a long proposition. Breaking down the numbers from decades to minutes, a life is a marvel of time. I feel as if I have been around for centuries." For the first time since he had known him, Vincent observed a tone of resignation in the count's voice.

Nicole called at that moment and, after talking to her for a few minutes, Count Robert handed him the phone. Without taking his eyes off Vincent's face, he lit a cigarette. Aware of being in the count's bedroom, Vincent's speech was stiff and formal. Sensing his awkwardness in front of her father, Nicole teased and cajoled him until he reassured her that he would not miss the four o'clock train.

Vincent told Count Robert that he was going to have dinner with Nicole in Paris and take her to a movie afterward. He certainly wasn't going to mention nightclubs or dancing. Something odd had crept into the old man's eyes, a disdainful look that Vincent recognized, having seen him use it on others. You're not good enough to take my daughter out, it said. He decided to keep the information about Serge's killers to himself.

Vincent took his leave. When he turned back at the door to say that he would stop by Monday, after his trip to the city, he saw that the count had closed his book and was watching him through the smoke of his cigarette. Vincent lowered his eyes and walked away.

Chapter 20

The men who shared Vincent's compartment in the third-class section of the train to Paris were dressed in similar shades of gray and brown. They either read newspapers or, resigned to the banality of the commute, studied the backs of each other's heads. The women conferred in hushed voices about the hardships of rearing children and the constant anxiety of unpaid bills.

Vincent nodded and blinked and nodded again, remembering an incident at boarding school. It had taken place on a Sunday while he was working for allowance money at a neighboring farm. That morning, the headmaster's son and two of his friends found him shoveling manure while the farmer and his wife were at church. The three boys, all from respectable bourgeois families of the region, surrounded Vincent. Taking turns, they tormented him into a state of rage. Eventually, the headmaster's son poked him in the chest and called him *sauerkraut*. Vincent hit him just as he had hit Titi, and when his friends ran away Vincent picked the boy off the ground and shoved him into a wire-mesh chicken coop.

At first the headmaster's son shouted insults and threats, but when he realized Vincent was not going free him, he begged and then cried to be released. Vincent shoveled manure on top of the cage to keep him quiet. When the farmer's wife returned from church she found that one of her capons had suffocated in the coop, where the boy was still imprisoned. The woman wanted to call the police but the son of the headmaster pleaded with her not to, and paid for the dead bird. Vincent had threatened to skin him like a rabbit.

The abrupt roar of a train rushing by in the opposite direction startled him upright. The jolt to his senses, the unpleasant boarding school memory, and his sleepless night with Adorée conspired to remind him of the metallic hell that his mother surely must have heard before dying.

Half the passengers disembarked at the station in Versailles, allowing a gust of raw air to rush through the compartment. The branches of plane trees growing on either side of the track had been pruned back for winter, and the château was visible from the window. The next stop was Paris. Vincent went to the bathroom, removed his corduroy jacket, and splashed water on his face. He adjusted his gray trousers and black tie, checked to make sure his heavy-soled shoes were clean, and that his gamekeeper's badge was pinned to the inside of his wallet. When he looked in the mirror he saw that his face was drawn and his eyes had lost what Serge called the spirit of Pan. Nicole will change that, he thought, we will dance in Paris tonight.

Vincent saw her waving on the station platform and as he jumped off the train she ran up to him and put her arms around his neck. A wall of passengers opened and closed behind them; the station was filled with commuters waiting to be shuttled to the suburbs. They followed the crowd down a broad stone staircase and into a brightly lit hall, which split and disappeared through heavy brass doors.

Nicole wore jeans and leather boots that raised her nearly to his height. She held his hand as they walked up the Boulevard Montparnasse and he felt the bowels of the city under his feet. Crowds made him uncomfortable and Vincent avoided eye contact with the faces advancing on him. Nicole pointed out stores and restaurants and old buildings branded with official dates. Schoolchildren, joyful to be out of their uniforms for the day, skipped along the wide boulevard, bumping into pedestrians, laughing and lingering in front of corner bakeries. Thin young men wearing beards and blue jeans sat knee over knee on the terraces of bistros reading the evening papers, arguing politics. Middle-aged men stood pressed one against the other at zinc bars sharing drinks, making horse bets, and talking about wine, women, and more politics. Dark shapes carrying groceries and warm baguettes hurried by, hunched over the pavement, bound for the underground subway and home. A yellow-gray sky journeyed over the city.

Nicole suggested that they have a drink in the café on the corner of rue St. Jacques. They sat at a small round table and Vincent peeled a hard-boiled egg to eat with his beer. The waiter wore a white apron tied around his waist. The shadows on his face looked green under the fluorescent lights. He left the bill in a saucer next to the plastic egg holder. The lights reminded Vincent of the hospital in Dreux.

"This is all I have to wear," he said, fingering his corduroy jacket while looking at the other customers, some of whom were clothed in dark suits and long coats with elegant scarves nonchalantly knotted around their necks.

"You look fine," she said, looking at him. "But if you like, Eric left a jacket for you at the apartment."

The concierge of Nicole's building inspected Vincent through a crack in the door and he felt her suspicions follow them up the stairs. White curtains and a blue carpet brightened the small, single-bedroom apartment, as did a jardinière of yellow mums on the table in front of the couch. The cream-colored walls were a century old.

Nicole spoke excitedly about living in Paris, independent and alone for the first time in her life. She told him about the neighborhood, the students who lived in the building, and the inexpensive Vietnamese restaurants where one could buy lunch for a thousand francs. She poured him a glass of Cinzano and walked back and forth, straightening things that didn't need straightening, showing off pictures of her mother, the count, and herself in New York. There was a framed photograph of President Kennedy sitting at his desk in the Oval Office.

Vincent sat on the couch, grateful to be off the street. He hadn't intended to bring up the Verdier business until after dinner, but when Nicole was changing for the restaurant she walked by him in a white cotton robe. He wondered what she had on underneath.

"I know who killed Serge," he blurted out.

Nicole sat on the couch next to him. When he was finished telling her about the Verdier brothers and Greenhead Lake she asked him if he had alerted the police. When he said he hadn't she wanted to know if he had told her father.

"I was going to but I changed my mind."

"But you have no right to keep this from him," she said raising her hands above her head in exasperation.

"When I said I was coming to Paris and that we were going out together he looked at me like I was a peasant."

"So what!" she said louder. "You should have told him." Her robe slipped, exposing a breast perfectly encased in black lace. Vincent moved to the far end of the couch.

"I don't have to say anything to anybody!" he said. "Serge was my uncle. His murder is my responsibility."

"Goddamn you, Vincent. After everything my family and Papa have done . . ." Nicole looked down and hit the couch with her hand. Her hair fell across her face, hiding her anger. Vincent stood up.

"Why is it that everyone wants to remind me of the favors they've done for me? What I am supposed to do? Kiss my aunt's ass for having fed me for three months after my mother was killed? Or kiss your family's crest for the years that I worked at the castle? And I suppose you expect me to grovel at your feet for the honor of being here?" His hands started to shake.

"Damn it!" he continued, pushing his fists in his pant's pockets. "Years ago, after your mother gave my pony to that woman in Paris, François warned me that your family lords its generosity like Ménardeau wields his piousness. You give so that you can take away."

Nicole sat looking at him until tears formed in her

eyes. Then she ran into the bathroom and closed the door. The apartment fell silent. Outside, Paris went on about its business, the streets talking to each other in a language Vincent would never understand. He stood up and looked out the window overlooking the rue St. Jacques. The city was alive with lights and sounds, laughter and tears, but all he could think about was how each time he started to feel as if he were a part of the Costebelle household, someone in that family relegated him to the role of servant.

She returned so quietly that he didn't hear her until she was next to him. When he turned she was in his arms.

"I'm sorry," she said. "I didn't mean to ruin our evening together." He put his arms around her shoulders. "It's just that you keep scaring me. It used to be my brother, now it's you. All this talk of killing reminds me of Roland and those terrible experiments he used to perform." She looked up and he saw gold flecks floating behind her tears. "Ever since I've returned to Merlecourt, you and I fight. I hate it."

Her bottom lip was filled with worry. Vincent opened his hands on the small of her back and held her close. "I didn't mean it," he said. "Your father is the father I never had."

Nicole stood against him, tall and silky, like a cattail. "I love you," she said. "We are family."

He desperately wanted to kiss her mouth and carry her to bed, but he didn't dare.

They went to La Coupole, a brasserie on the Left Bank, and dined in a high-ceilinged room surrounded by the portraits of famous personalities. The silverware, chrome table legs, and tight plastic bench covers all sparkled. The noise of giddy laughter, clattering plates, and the insistent tapping of steel-toed shoes overcame the background clamor of a hundred eager voices.

Their waiter delivered a round platter filled with seaweed and chipped ice, on top of which Belon oysters, shrimp, clams, tiny brown periwinkles, purple sea urchins, and spiny langoustines were neatly displayed. He moved their glasses out of the way and set the tray down with a cheerful, "Bon appétit, les amoureux." Quartered lemon wedges, a basket of sliced country bread, and a crock of sweet yellow butter rested on a small round table to one side.

Vincent and Nicole drank a bottle of Muscadet quickly to erase any lingering ill feelings and ordered a second one to toast the arrival of the poached turbot in cream sauce. By dessert Vincent talked as if he had rediscovered his tongue after five years of silence.

He told her stories about the night raids that Roland and he had made on the village, stories about boarding school, stories that made him appear foolish, and still others that were funny. He even admitted to spying through a keyhole while she was taking baths, though he'd been too young to know what he was looking at; he didn't think about what he said, his heart fed his words. She laughed and her cheeks were flushed. When he insisted on paying for the meal, the bill with a tip almost emptied his wallet.

It had rained while they were eating and the macadam under the cars gleamed. They walked with their arms around each other, their long legs quickly overtaking other strolling couples. Oblivious to the rest of the city, neither noticed the policemen in dark blue uniforms, the old men hugging bottles of cheap wine, the students lingering in front of movie theaters, not even the lovers embracing in doorways. The rain had washed the sidewalks and the sky spawned a shoal of blinking stars. The streets of the capital were blue.

It was a private club but when Nicole waved through a peephole in the door a blond man wearing a tuxedo hustled them inside. She pointed out to Vincent the restaurant on the first floor, the bar and lounge beyond the lobby, and then led him down a revolving staircase to a second bar where the music was loud, the lights were dimmed, and the tables were set in shadows around a small circular dance floor.

Although Nicole had been at the club the night before, her friends greeted her as if she had just returned from a long voyage. Vincent felt out of place but she was gay and went from table to table introducing him, exchanging compliments, laughing, and running her fingers through her hair. The men stood; some pecked the back of her fingers and others kissed her cheeks. They all shook Vincent's hand with amused expressions on their faces. A thin, black-haired Italian with a silk handkerchief in his breast pocket spoke foreign words into her neck. She blushed and Vincent suppressed the urge to slap his face.

Vincent felt the stares on his back as they moved from table to table and desperately wished he had exchanged his corduroy jacket for Eric's blazer. When she had finished greeting the room they sat at an empty table next to a wall and were joined by four of Nicole's friends, a young woman and three short, very well-dressed men whose names Vincent immediately forgot. Self-conscious, he slumped into the soft bench cushions to keep from towering over them.

"Nicky tells us you're very good at your job," declared one young man with slick-backed hair and wire spectacles. Nicole was in deep conversation with the girl. The three men looked at Vincent expectantly. He looked back, not knowing what to say.

"What exactly do you do?" inquired the most energetic of the three, a dark-haired man with sharp features and a long nose.

"My job," replied Vincent with a straight face, "is to protect Count Robert's estate from Parisians." He smiled into three blank faces.

Sobered by their inability to appreciate his wit he continued, "I tend to the game birds, look out for poachers, make sure . . ." He realized they weren't listening and so he reached for his drink. He hated who he was almost as much as where he was.

"Come on," Nicole said, taking him by the hand during a lull in the conversation. "Let's dance."

Vincent stood to follow her through a maze of tables and animated faces. As he pushed a chair to one side he overheard one of the men at the table. "We employ two keepers in Sologne. That way when one steals, the other turns him in."

Then he heard the girl say, "Nicky is slumming tonight." Vincent turned and looked at her. Red faced, she averted her eyes.

Vincent stopped at the edge of the small hardwood dance floor and looked at the dancers who moved in circles and twisted their hips and punched the air with their fists—their feet carrying on like tiny windshield wipers. Pinpoints of lights fell from the ceiling. The music was so loud no one bothered to talk.

"Wait a minute,"Vincent said as Nicole tried to pull him onto the floor. "I don't know how to do this."

"Watch me. It's easy," she said.

"Merde de merde!" he said under his breath. Nicole pulled him deeper into the crowd. He tried with all his might to imitate her.

The dancers were singing "Be Bop a Lula" in French and acting as if they were on a serious mission. He tried to smile at Nicole but immediately forgot his feet and had to start all over. His face burned, his stomach rumbled, and his jacket felt like a horse blanket. Nicole waved and Vincent saw that Eric had joined the table and was watching them. His felt his chest tighten.

Nicole whirled and reeled to the music. Sweat poured down his face. "That's enough," he called out to her before the song was finished and they made their way back to her friends.

After they shook hands Eric suggested that Vincent take off his jacket. "You're going to suffocate in that thing," he said as he removed his own blue blazer so that Vincent wouldn't feel uncomfortable.

Eric was jovial and charming and ordered a magnum of champagne. He engaged Vincent in conversation, asking him about the shoot and the estate, trying to make him feel relaxed and less out of place. Nicole continued her conversation with her girlfriend and every so often looked across the table at them. Eric danced with her twice and made crazy gestures with his arms, scattering the other dancers across the floor. Vincent's heart sank. Nicole was having the best of times, and he realized that she hadn't said more than a few words to him since they arrived.

When Nicole went to the bathroom Vincent was left alone with the others. Eric immediately turned around and started talking to one of the men about banking, leaving Vincent to sit with his big hands between his knees, waiting for his date to return. He looked at the dancers, the waiters, a dozen tables filled with pretty women and well-dressed men. He pretended interest in conversations he didn't understand much less care about, and grinned when the others laughed. He nodded and smiled until he couldn't hold back the resentment that filled his heart. He felt that everyone at the table was making fun of him and he loathed them as he loathed the Verdier brothers. He wondered how Nicole could bring him to a place like this and then disappear.

Vincent waited for her until the waiting became so unbearable he knew he was going to do something he would later regret. He stood up all at once and walked away without looking back.

Vincent expected to run into her on the stairs or in the lobby, but she never materialized. Instead he found himself on the street alone, next to a drunk groping for his car keys. Damn her, he thought, and damn America for teaching her to be so rude. He studied the map of Paris outside the entrance to the metro, walked down a number of deserted side streets, and caught the midnight train to Dreux.

Chapter 21

Until that evening in Paris, Nicole had always sided with him against the rest of the world. Vincent's anger gave way to a deep sense of loss. For days he had been dreaming of her as she had appeared to him on the bridge, laughing and suntanned, lovely in every way. On the train home, looking out of the window at a black landscape of fields and forest, it became increasingly apparent to him that God didn't take unfettered fantasies into account. Perhaps He didn't take anything into account.

Vincent woke the next dawn in a sweat, having dreamed that Roland had surgically grafted Titi's face onto his. He got up, opened the front door, and watched Ode run to the river, prompting a brace of moorhen to race downstream and bury themselves under the eaves of the bank. He saw Ragondin's bicycle leaning against the side of the mill and took a deep breath to rid himself of the foul business of the city. The sky above him was powder blue.

When he came back inside he threw a log on the fire, called up to the loft, and told Ragondin to wake him in an hour. He climbed back into bed. The smell of Adorée and their lovemaking lingered on the sheets.

After his sortie at the Verdier farm the night before, Ragondin had returned to the mill. He loved sleeping in the loft and when Vincent called to him he turned toward the dormer window, looked out on the blue-gray colors of dawn, and pretended to be asleep. An hour later, when he went to the outhouse, Ode followed him back to the mill, covered with frost from playing in the river.

He fried two pieces of bacon and forked them onto bread. When he finished eating he leaned back in satisfaction and told Vincent what had happened.

"I showed up at Salomé's door around nine." He cleaned his plate with a piece of bread and smacked his lips.

"Salomé?"

"Don't interrupt," Ragondin said putting a hand up. "As I was saying, I got there a little before nine carrying two of bottles of cheap red wine. I knocked, she came to the door, spotted the wine, and pulled me inside. She charged me ten thousand francs."

"I couldn't have done it," Vincent said shaking his head and making a face.

Ragondin punched him in the arm. "Of course not," he held up his fists and let out a harsh laugh, looking through his arms, waiting for Vincent to hit him back.

"You're a nice boy who only sleeps with women who wear clean underwear, like Adorée. I get drunk, take what I can, and say 'thank you.' So what if Salomé doesn't look like Bardot? She's a woman. The important thing is that she passed out after the second bottle and I went exploring."

Ragondin explained how he had found Serge's shotgun in the cellar, behind a barrel of cider. It was just as Vincent had described it. He had then taped it to the bottom of Gros-Louis' bed. The only thing that bothered Ragondin was that Étienne had seen him going into the house. He told Vincent that he had the feeling the old man had been watching him the whole time.

"You know," Ragondin said about Salomé, "she's not a bad person. I think her mother rocked her too close to the wall when she was a baby. And no! In case you're interested, it wasn't much fun. She smelled like tripe. I want my money back."

Vincent reached for his wallet and gave him the last of his cash.

Vincent went to the castle before lunch and found the count leafing through Stendhal's *The Red and the Black* in the library.

"So, Vincent," he said putting the book on the desk. "How did you fare in Paris?"

"Not so well, Monsieur. I'm not comfortable in the city. The people there are too smart for me."

"Nonsense. Parisians are educated but they don't know how to do anything practical. How was Nicole? Did you go out after dinner?"

"For a short while, to Castel's, and I didn't make much of an impression there. Her friends are very up-to-date and wear nice clothes."

"The habit does not make the monk. These are people who, among other things, pout for effect. Do you know what I mean by pout?"

"Yes, Monsieur," Vincent said laughing. "Pouting is a disdainful pursing of the lips practiced by those who believe they are better than the rest of us. Most of the women on the dance floor at Castel's pouted. I can tell you Monsieur, I was happy to get home."

The count seemed pleased and Vincent was sure that it was related to his failed evening with Nicole, but he didn't care any more. Their aborted night together had silenced him. In his heart Vincent now understood the limitations of his birthright; he was on his own, and he would never escape the knowledge that he was inferior.

"Would Monsieur mind if I shot a few ducks on the river this evening? I'd like to work Ode," he said.

"Go ahead, and if you're successful give one to François. I'll share it with Nicole, who called and is coming out this evening."

"I'm happy she's back in France," Vincent said to please Count Robert, but secretly he wished that she had stayed in New York, where she belonged.

"Me, too," replied the count. "The sight of her face fills my heart with memories."

He lit a cigarette and continued, his eyes drifting into his past. "When I was young, all I thought about were girls. When I was a little older I was infatuated with money. But now that I am old my concern is about making one final transition with grace." The count frowned and moved some papers on his desk. "When you have finished your education, Vincent, and the military has taught you how to dig trenches, I want you to come home and help Nicole. Estates like this are meant to be passed on from one generation to the next, and Merlecourt only makes sense if it is filled with children and laughter and music." He paused and looked at the leather-bound books in the walls. "I don't know if she will marry that American fellow, but it makes no difference. It takes a man the village trusts to run Merlecourt."

"I'll do as you wish, Monsieur le Comte,"Vincent said, staring at the floor. He knew perfectly well that once Robert de Costebelle was gone his status as a German bastard would become an unconditional liability in the village.

"You don't seemed pleased at the prospect."

Vincent hesitated, not sure how to answer. "Oh no, Monsieur. It's just that ever since I can remember, my life has been filled with tragedy. First it was my mother, then Roland, and now Serge. When you talk about death and exits and legacies, and ask me to help Nicole run Merlecourt, I don't see your request as an opportunity but rather as an extension of another catastrophe."

"I'm sorry that you have lost so much so early in life, but your will to survive will benefit you in the future," the count said in an understanding voice.

"I beg your pardon, Monsieur. I don't mean to be insolent, but you're forgetting that the villagers regard me as a German. A bastard who survived thanks to your kindness and generosity. They'll never trust me."

"Stop looking for validation,Vincent. You underestimate your abilities. The villagers were impressed with the way you managed the shoot and so was I. If the beaters wanted you to fail, it never showed. What the village wants more than anything from the estate is a strong man who is capable of managing the affairs of the castle. The livelihood of the inhabitants of Merlecourt depends on such strength. And trust me, it is their livelihoods the villagers are interested in."

Vincent had decided before coming to see the count that he would not mention the Verdier brothers or the shotgun for fear his employer would call the police. He wanted his uncle's murderers for himself. He turned to leave.

"Vincent," said the count, putting out his cigarette, "about your uncle's killers. The police will get them, they always do. Live your life, not the lives of the dead."

Ragondin's eyes lit up at the prospect of eating mallard. Vincent told him that he was going to drive to the island and that Ragondin should take the path next to the river and walk toward him after he had settled into position. Vincent knew that any ducks his friend flushed between the mill and the island would circle the valley high and then fall into the backwater between the bridge and the mainland, where he and Ode would be waiting.

Ragondin rubbed his hands together and fantasized about dinner. He told Vincent he would give him twenty minutes to get situated. "And, for Christ's sake, don't miss!" he added with a hungry look on his face.

Vincent approached the island at a right angle from the pasture. The dead trees surrounding the field stood like the masts and riggings of abandoned ships. Ode, attentive to his every move, sensed something in the offing. The sun was hidden behind an orange haze and the duck chatter in the eddy above the bridge was loud. Vincent knew that once flushed the ducks would not return. He made up his mind to take what birds he could before Ragondin got started.

"Stay!" he whispered in Ode's ear before he ducked under the pasture fence.

Thickened by the cold, the ash-colored water moved slowly downriver, curling around boulders and obstructions too deep to see. Vincent had always imagined creeks as veins, rivers as arteries, and lakes as the planet's eyes. A wall of saplings shielded him from the birds in the water. He listened to the ducks until their chatter stopped. Then he stood up.

Five mallards—three hens and two drakes—swiveled their heads in unison to look at him. They hesitated for an instant, allowed themselves to slip downstream and then flushed, stretching their necks to the sky. Their calls were clamorous. Vincent swung and fired.

The first shot felled two birds, a hen that landed on its breast with its head anchored out of sight, and a drake, which fell on its back, groggily staring at the tops of its orange feet. He shot again, and the bird's dark green neck slowly unfolded into the river. The current caught the high floating bodies and they sailed swiftly under the bridge toward him.

The retrieves were straightforward, but because they were Ode's first attempts he made a fuss over her before moving to the head of the island. A skein of ducks painted a pattern on the darkening sky. He crouched between two young willow trees growing far enough apart to open a window over the river. Ode sat at his side. A single hen came skimming inches above the surface of the water, melting into her own reflection. Vincent was slow raising the gun and the bird flew out of range before he could pull the trigger.

Seven more mallards flew from the direction of the mill at tree level. They passed on the far side of the island, sailed momentarily out of sight, swung back over the pasture, and dropped sharply toward him. When the ducks reached the island they flew low over the water, in close formation, like a squadron of fighter planes. Vincent allowed himself to be mesmerized by the synchronized wing beat and suddenly the birds were upon him. He missed a hen flaring directly over the trees, but caught up with the last duck in the formation. It fell like a stone at the end of a long throw.

Ode jumped in the river at the sound of her name and swam hard across the current. She treaded water, lost sight of the duck, raised her head, and then pushed forward to correct the angle when she found it. Her tail creased the surface and a moment later Vincent saw an elbow of water build between her chest and the mallard. A swirl in the current told him Ode had the bird in her mouth, and he watched with pleasure as his Labrador retrieved dinner from the heaviest stretch of the river. It was then he realized that he hadn't thought of Serge, Nicole, or Count Robert for the first time since the shoot. He hadn't even thought of the Verdiers. All he looked forward to was roasting the duck, carving thin, pink slices of breast meat, and drinking the special claret Serge saved for such occasions.

He met an excited Ragondin on the path leading to the mill. "A feast for us tonight!" he exclaimed when he spotted the ducks hanging from Vincent's fist.

"Drive this one to the castle. I'll meet you back at the mill," said Vincent, handing him one of the two drakes.

"Do we have turnips?" Ragondin asked in anticipation of the meal.

"Mais oui, mon enfant!"

"Jesus, patron," he exclaimed as he started the car and smacked his lips. "I don't know what I love more, rare duck or girls."

When Ragondin returned from the castle Vincent was singeing pin feathers in the fireplace. He sat down at the kitchen table, poured himself a glass of wine, and handed Vincent a note.

He unfolded the thick, white stationery and read the message: "Meet me at the castle at nine o'clock tonight. Come to my room and don't make any noise." At the bottom of the page and off to one side was a drawing of a girl's face with long hair. The note was from Nicole.

"Damn!" Vincent said. "She wants to see me."

"Patience pays off my friend. Now, let's eat. Rare meat will give you energy. Stamina is what separates the men from the boys."

"I'm no longer hungry."

"How about me?" Ragondin was distraught over his friend's disconcerting change of heart. "I'm hungrier than hell."

"All right. I'll cook the ducks for you, but first I'm going to take a bath."

"Why?"

"Jesus, Ragondin. I stink."

"So?"

When Vincent had bathed and cooked the birds, he still had not recovered his appetite. "You must be out of your mind," Ragondin said. "No woman tastes as good as duck."

Vincent turned off the car lights, parked in the alley of oak trees leading to the courtyard, and walked to the darkened castle. He was dizzy at the thought of being alone with Nicole in her bedroom. He climbed the servants' staircase in the wing farthest from the count's quarters and at the third floor turned on the light. Silently, he walked down the narrow corridor to her room. He could feel his heart beating in his chest.

She stood waiting for him under a glass chandelier, barefoot on a thick powder-blue rug, wearing a cream-colored nightgown. Her hair was tied in a bun on the back of her head and she wore a thin pearl necklace around her neck. A dressing table with a skirt that hung to the floor faced the wall opposite the door. Stuffed animals were piled high on top of a low chest of drawers next to a full-length mirror. Her bed was in the alcove, below a brocaded canopy. Nothing in the room had changed since she had lived there as a child. Nicole walked over to him and stood so close that her toes touched his shoes.

"Please," she said looking into his eyes, "forgive me for the other night. I met some friends who had just flown in from America and I sat with them in the upstairs restaurant and lost track of time. When I came back you were gone and Eric said I had been away an hour. I didn't know. It was rude of me and I can't tell you how sorry I am."

Vincent didn't say anything and, pretending to be more put out than he was, stood inflexible with his arms at his sides. Her hair smelled of shampoo, and a dusting of talcum powder lay on her shoulders.

"I left because I was ready to leave. You had nothing to do with it," Vincent said with as much sincerity as he could muster.

She buried her head in his shirt and cried. It surprised him, and he relaxed and stroked the length of her back. She wrapped her arms around his neck and said, "I love you." She kissed him on the lips and he tasted the salt in her tears.

"Come," she said, pulling him to the alcove. The bedside lamp cast a cloud of light on the carpet. She sat down cross-legged on her pillow and he sat next to her. A stuffed bear stood in the corner between the headrest and the wall.

"When I returned to the table, Eric told me that you had left the club. I cried, and he didn't like it. He said some stupid things about your shoes and the way you held your glass, and I called him a boor." She looked at Vincent, hoping he was proud of her, and smiled.

"To hell with Eric and Paris," he said, wondering why she would bring up his shoes. "He's there and we are here, together."

They looked at each other and the silence grew around them. Vincent felt his breath shorten.

She reached over and touched his hand and said, "Let's play."

"What's the game?" he said smiling.

"How about doctor?"

"Sure," he answered in a voice he didn't recognize.

"The last time we said good-bye, we were too young and too shy to kiss, remember?"

She let her hair down. Then she opened her nightgown and the pale silk fabric fell to her waist. The glow of the bed lamp embraced the satin texture of her breasts. Vincent scrambled out of his clothes as fast as he could, pulling his pants over his shoes, tripping, and hopping on one foot trying to get them off. When he was naked he lay down next to her. She rolled on her back, giggling.

"I've never seen a boy like that before."

"You haven't?" he said, covering himself with the sheet.

"No," she said running her hand down his chest. "I've felt boys on the dance floor, and when they kissed me, but this is the first time this way."

"I thought . . ."

"What?" she said, gingerly picking the sheet up between her thumb and index finger. "You thought I was sleeping with Eric. Well, I wasn't, and neither will we tonight. Promise?" She looked under the sheet and then back at him.

"Yes. I promise." He didn't care. He would have agreed to anything at that moment.

They played and kissed and touched each other and he worried they were making so much noise that Count Robert, who slept below, would hear them. François's room was directly above, but Vincent knew he would never say anything. Nicole didn't seem to care, and the pearly quality of her laughter made him shiver. When they caressed each other too intimately she used the same laughter to hide other feelings, but the look in her eyes gave her away, and it was difficult for him to keep to his word.

At one point during the night she made Vincent stand on his head, and when it was his turn he asked her to dance for him on the powder-blue carpet while he sat and watched her from the bed. She laughed at his expression and made fun of the look of wonder on his face. Later she said flattering things that made him blush. During the long night Nicole uncovered a piece of the puzzle he had lost when death first entered his life, and lovingly returned it to his heart.

"In the morning, I will cut a rose from the garden to remember this night," she said.

He cupped the pleasing weight of her hair in his hands, turning it back and forth in the light so that he could see the colors change. Her body was long and supple and when she touched him she wasn't shy. "I have loved you ever since the day my mother and I moved into the castle," he said before dawn. "I was five years old and you and Roland were standing on the bridge and you stepped forward and kissed me."

She looked into his eyes and whispered in his ear, "Tonight I will come to the mill and you will feed me and hold me and . . ." Her voice trailed off and she turned her face away. He could see the blush on her neck and knew they would make love that evening.

Vincent caressed her face and ran his strong hands down the length of her body, touching her as lustfully as he had touched Adorée. Her breath quickened and her mouth opened with words he had not heard from her before. And, when he felt that she was on the verge of accepting him, he moved his hands away from the sheen of sweat that had formed between her breasts and said, "I have waited for you all my life. What's another day?"

They kissed then, and made plans for the afternoon, agreeing that he and Ragondin would follow the stag hunt on their bicycles until she met them for lunch with the Citroën.

"I love loving you, Vincent," she said to him while he was getting dressed.

"I'll drop off the car in the morning," he said, tying his shoes. Nicole stretched the sheet up over her nose so he kissed her eyelids. Hugging a pillow in her arms, she looked as though she were holding a swan. He walked to the door and left her room and the castle as silently as he had entered.

Chapter 22

The sun rose unseen by Vincent; his return to the mill was filled with images of Nicole and a night he had not allowed himself to wish for. He stopped inside the door to savor the aroma of coffee brewing, his imagination lending poetry to his senses. Noting the satisfied look on his friend's face, Ragondin muttered that he would sell his soul for a night with the young mistress of the castle. When he asked his friend for details Vincent merely smiled and poured himself a cup of coffee.

Envious and mildly offended to be excluded from the story of his friend's night of enchantment, Ragondin abruptly turned his attention to the Verdiers.

"By now they must have discovered that Serge's gun went missing the night I visited Salomé," he said. "I suppose it is just a matter of time before they come after me."

"If they do, it would give me an excuse to shoot them," Vincent said without the conviction of his earlier outbursts. He buttered a piece of bread and dunked it into his coffee. When he was finished eating he went to Serge's bed, sat down, and pulled off his boots. "As long as the gun is in their house we have the proof we need to have them arrested."

"They will say they found it in the Roberta Woods," Ragondin replied. "Or that they bought the gun off a gypsy."

"Perhaps, but the Napoleonic code proclaims them culpable if the authorities are convinced they committed a felony. They will then have to prove their innocence. With their record and Serge's gun in their possession, they will hang. Let's be there at daylight tomorrow morning. They will be tired after the hunt. I want them to wake up with my shotgun in their faces."

"A major accomplishment."

"Meanwhile, if they do come after us while I'm taking a nap . . ."

"What?"

"Blow their heads off!"

"Thank you," Ragondin said. "I'll look forward to that."

In the 1830s, during the final, tenuous reign of the Orléans dynasty, as many as five dozen hounds pursued by a legion of riders overwhelmed the valley of Merlecourt every day of the week in pursuit of boars and stags, roebuck and hare. The horsemen, known as devil hunters, butchered cattle for sport, caned peasants for entertainment, and raped farm girls for pleasure. Though manners and decorum had replaced such historical recklessness, it was evident that even in 1963, when the deerhounds were turned loose and the French horns signaled the onset of the hunt, the only matter of importance to those who lived in the valley was the chase.

By midmorning low clouds had moved over the forest, eclipsing the sun. On the grass between Labrissé's kennels and the pavilion a crowd of fifty men and women stood socializing. Some, such as Maurice Corneille and Étienne Verdier, had been honorary members for years. Others, including Gros-Louis and Titi, who drove the kennel relay truck and picked up stray hounds, were on salary.

Vincent and Ragondin walked through the trees surrounding the pavilion to the parking area, which was filled with trucks and trailers. The stable lads, who stood no taller than the horses' withers, were backing the animals out of their mobile stalls. The horses had been clipped and groomed for the occasion; their tack oiled and polished. Navy-blue and burgundy-red blankets, the hunt club's colors, each one embroidered with the initials and crests of the horse's owner, rested like small tents on the relay mounts.

"You boys should eat more horse meat, it will make you grow," Ragondin jeered.

"Up yours!"

"Careful now," Ragondin said in mock seriousness. "Your heads are just about even with your charges' oversized assholes."

When they reached the kennels Labrissé nodded at Ragondin but turned his back on Vincent. The whipper-in had separated the club's sixty liver-and-white hounds into two lots and, in their eagerness to hunt, the dogs, gangly and tall on their feet, strained at the wire mesh and trampled each other on forelegs as broad as ax handles. In April, by the end of the season, they would be pared down to little more than ears and bones.

The official name of the hunt club was Haute-Normandie, and its president and master was M. Dutertre, a dark wiry man of Mediterranean descent, cursed with a temper. At eleven o'clock the hunt club's seventeen members and their invited guests filed out of the pavilion and stood in a semicircle in the cobblestone courtyard, next to the kennels. The men wore long blue hunt jackets and polished knee-high riding boots. Daggers sheathed inside narrow scabbards hung from their elaborately embroidered belts. Clasps fashioned out of the eye teeth of vanquished stags pinned the folds of their white scarves. Half of the riders wore French horns draped across their chests like gold sashes. The members acknowledged the crowd of spectators and shook hands with the habitués.

Mme Dutertre, wearing cream-colored jodhpurs, black riding boots, a white blouse, and a colorful scarf under a blue hunt jacket made of the same material as the men, stood erect next to her husband in the middle of the semicircle, her blond hair pulled back and tucked inside a hairnet. Impatient for the hunt to begin, her gray eyes cut back and forth between her husband and the crowd.

With Sebastien Moulin standing next to him, Étienne was sitting in a chair entertaining the head of the local grain cooperative and a group from the bistro on the principles of training young hounds by pairing them with older broken-in dogs during the summer practice runs. Corneille and three neighboring gamekeepers stood to one side and made plans to dispose of a herd of boar that had been rooting up beet fields on the farmlands adjoining the forest. The courtyard was the center of ceremonies and the reunion place of long-standing devotees; hats were flourished at distant recognitions and titles were either extended in homage or bandied about in spirited jest. The men from the village wore corduroy or canvas jackets and brown rubber boots. The women were dressed in loose-fitting loden coats, knitted sweaters, and wool bonnets.

The common ground for all in attendance, rich or poor, was to pay homage to the rituals of the hunt, the chase, and the putting to death of the stag with a blade. The feeding of the hunted animal's entrails to the dogs, referred to as the fleshing of the hounds, and the formal presentation of one of the stag's hooves and forelegs to a follower of merit, was as important a ceremony to all present as the hunt itself. Those historical rites, born out of religious beliefs, sanctified the proceedings.

Labrissé and his helpers, volunteers and men who worked the kennels, stood facing the crowd with their backs to the hounds, waiting to deliver their findings. At daybreak the men, each with a tracking dog on a short leash, had fanned out from the pavilion and walked the perimeter of the forest looking for the fresh spoor of stags with antlers. As Labrissé and his trackers gathered, the crowd grew quiet.

Dutertre made a formal welcome to the members of the club, the guests, and followers. He wished them all a good and safe season of hunting, and then turned to Labrissé. One by one, each tracker stepped forward, removed his hat, and delivered his findings.

"I have knowledge of a six-pointer on the north side of the Village Woods," said one man proudly.

"Nothing for me," admitted a second, shuffling his feet.

"A big, heavy-bodied spike on the hillside above the castle," said a third.

Finally Labrissé gave credence to the rumor that had been spreading among the spectators. "Monsieur is holding court at Greenhead Lake," he said. "The stag has been fighting. I counted nine does with him." Labrissé stood rigid, his face intense and engaged.

Dutertre thanked the men and turned to face the gallery. "It has come to my attention," he said, his face darkening, "that a group of men who dare to call themselves sportsmen have put a bounty on Monsieur's head. These men are Parisians, of course, and I would say to them that if such rumors are true, and I discover their identity, I will personally thrash each one of these cowards to within an inch of his life. I tell you this to officially put them on notice."

M. Dutertre then reminded his audience that the hounds were not yet in shape and, with a look of one slightly put upon, announced they would attack at Greenhead Lake, adding, "Monsieur will be just as surprised that we found him on the first day of the season as I will be."

Everyone there knew that Dutertre would go after the royal stag. The animal had been his bête noire for years. This time the unseasoned dogs gave him an airtight excuse for failing. The crowd dispersed and headed toward the lake, two kilometers away. The Verdier brothers, dressed in riding clothes and wearing the small brass buttons of the hunt club in their lapels, gathered half the hounds and hustled them into the back of a high-sided relay truck.

Labrissé led the starters out of the kennel and shouted them into a pack; Dutertre rallied the dogs and cantered down a narrow alley off-limits to cars. The hounds fanned and regrouped behind him to the crack of his whip. Three longtime members sitting in the saddle, and Étienne, standing, faced each other, raised their horns, and played "The Departure to the Hunt."

A stream of cars slipped by on the dirt road that was rutted hard from three cold nights. Adorée and Dr. Jobard waved as they passed. Excited at the prospect of the chase, Ragondin beat his bicycle with his cap to make it go faster, and in a show of audacity, knelt on the seat, followed a rut into the underbrush, and pitched over a tree stump.

Greenhead Lake was centered between four narrow dirt roads running east and west, north and south. When the motorcade reached each of the four corners the spectators filed out of their vehicles in silence. Dutertre rode into view, sitting straight in the saddle, his eyes focused on the ground ahead. He absentmindedly tipped his riding toque at his supporters as the hounds jostled for position behind him.

A small bundle of branches made up of ferns and pine and oak tree limbs that Labrissé had left that morning on the side of the road marked Monsieur's tracks. The whipper-in stood holding his horse, and when the hounds neared he removed his toque and waved them to the scent. The pack responded by spreading out into the forest, followed by Dutertre. The rest of the riders took position in the roads and trails surrounding the woodlot. A hound bayed, then another, and then there was silence. The gallery stood huddled together, waiting for Monsieur to jump into view.

"You came to the store on Sunday?" Adorée asked Vincent, who was standing by himself. She was wearing a brown leather coat and black boots.

"Yes, and then I went to Paris," Vincent said. He remembered her straddling him.

"So, did you see her?" she asked with mischief.

He nodded. "I love her."

They walked down a side alley carpeted in golden leaves. Adorée reached up and ruffled his hair. "Have you told her?"

"Yes."

"And what does she say?"

"She feels the same about me."

"You're kidding," she said, sounding surprised. "She told you that?"

"Of course she did. More than once."

"Have you been with her?"

"None of your business."

"Come on," she insisted, "you can tell me."

"But I won't."

"I see," she said bending over to pick up a copper-colored leaf. "Does Count Robert know?"

"What, that we love each other? I doubt it. But he will."

"He's not going to like it."

"I don't care."

From deep inside the woods the baying erupted all at once and a shiver rippled up Vincent's spine. Holding Adorée's hand he ran back to the crossroads. Ragondin, who had been talking to the Verdier brothers, started back toward his bicycle.

The insistent sounds of a brass horn signaled visual contact. Four grown does pushed off their hindquarters and jumped the alley, their necks stretched forward. A second, more distant horn sounded on the far side of the enclosure, proclaiming a stag with twelve or more tines, a royal stag. The gallery ran to their bicycles and cars and headed in every direction, each driver trying to anticipate Monsieur's first run. Ragondin stopped at Jobard's car and gallantly opened Adorée's door with a flourish.

Vincent and Ragondin followed the Verdier brothers as they drove down an alley and Ragondin pointed out the spot where he had found them parked the night Vincent went to Paris. A white sun tried to work itself through the overcast.

"Titi wants me to pay him for sleeping with Salomé," Ragondin said with a smirk.

"They should pay you."

"That's what I told him," Ragondin laughed. "Also, I heard this morning before the hunt that Gros-Louis publicly accused his father of trespassing in his apartment. Étienne denied knowing what his son was talking about, and when he started to walk away Gros-Louis shoved him in the back, pushing the old man down on the ground. Corneille saw it all and helped get Étienne to Dr. Jobard, who warned him that he had a cracked rib and should stay home. If this weren't the opening day, he wouldn't be here. Corneille told me that when Étienne was down he threatened to whip his sons to the bone and Titi just laughed at him."

If the followers were concerned about Monsieur's condition after a fortnight of courting, their concerns were unfounded. For more than two hours the stag dragged forty dogs, twenty-five horsemen, and fifty spectators from one end of the forest to the other, eventually returning into the very woodlot from which he had originally been flushed. On a hunch, Ragondin suggested they leave their bicycles on the side of the road and follow an obscure game trail to a clearing a few hundred meters into the underbrush. A magpie screeched and they hid behind an oak tree moments before the huge red stag cantered toward them. Silver light poured down into the clearing, cut out of a stand of birch trees. Monsieur stepped into the opening, stopped, and faced the wind, his swollen neck jutting sharply out of his chest. His magnificent rack rose to heaven like the hands of God. Steam escaped from his coat and his flanks were black with sweat, but his eyes reflected neither fatigue nor fear.

The lonely bay of a single deerhound separated from the pack reached them through the trees. The stag's scent had been revealed. Indifferent to any implication of danger, Monsieur slipped quietly into the woods, almost immediately backtracked, and then stopped at the exact place where Vincent and Ragondin had first seen him. A moment later, without warning or visible effort, the stag leapt clear to the far side of the opening, three meters away, and vanished.

The two friends looked at each other.

The hound came loping along a minute later with its nose on the ground. It stopped where Monsieur had stood, followed his tracks into the woods, reappeared a moment later, let out a long frustrated howl, and ambled back in the direction it had come from. Vincent and Ragondin walked out of the woods to their bicycles in silence.

Labrissé and Dutertre had circled the lake and were now working the pack deeper in the woods. The spectators had spread out over several kilometers of roads and alleys, settling down under the trees on blankets, and dedicating themselves to lunch. Wealthy bourgeois unloaded wicker baskets in which carefully wrapped goose pâtés, Camembert cheeses, sugar cookies, and champagne lay next to silver tumblers and porcelain plates. The working class produced unmarked bottles of red wine, local cider, pickles, hard cheese, and thick ham sandwiches. The long chase and cold weather had stimulated a variety of appetites. With a grin Ragondin pointed out a couple of seemingly abandoned cars bouncing on their springs.

The excitement of the morning eventually faded into lassitude. The stag had evaporated. Some of the less ardent riders and most of the followers abandoned their fervor for the hunt and instead chose to pursue social pleasantries and backseat naps. The roads leading to Greenhead Lake were lined with parked cars, bicycles, and tree-tied horses. The women handed out cups of coffee, sugar cookies, and shot glasses of Calvados.

Vincent knew that one day a black sun would rise and cast a lasting shadow over Monsieur. One cold winter afternoon the hounds would hold him at bay long enough for Labrissé or Dutertre to slip a dagger into his heart. The word would spread throughout the valley and there would be rejoicing in the hunt club, but later, after the hide had been pulled off Monsieur's carcass and after the hounds had fed on his entrails, even the most avid hunter would mourn the loss of the great red stag. Some believed that, having outwitted man and dog for so many years, the stag had stolen the soul of those who hunted him. Others believed that whoever killed Monsieur would subliminally inherit his powers. A few, such as Étienne and Corneille, fervently hoped that Monsieur would never be brought to bay, and die instead of old age.

Titi and Gros-Louis had refreshed the pack with new

hounds and picked up strays along the way. The hunt was into its fourth hour and the pack's lack of conditioning was evident. The brothers joined Corneille, Vincent, and Ragondin under a tree. Gros-Louis offered his flask and his opinions.

"He's long gone," he said, referring to Monsieur.

"The dogs are inside out," replied Corneille, wiping his mouth and handing Ragondin the flask.

A tan-and-white male, ears flapping and testicles swinging, trotted up the road. Titi called to it, wrapped his whip around the hound's neck, and dragged it into the back of the truck.

"I got twenty more out there," Gros-Louis said pointing to the forest in disgust. "The sons of bitches are lost from here to Rebours. It's going to take us all night to round them up."

The cold fall weather, lack of sleep, and a fierce desire to beat the brothers to death, left Vincent weak. He walked into the woods under the pretense of taking a leak, and sat on a stump, vaguely noticing the mushrooms that had sprouted at its base. He knew he had to finish the thing quickly, and then talk to the count about Nicole. He closed his eyes and saw Serge lying inside a wooden casket, fertilizing the lilies that bloomed in May.

Chapter 23

The cloud cover darkened the valley and gave way to a strong north wind that whistled down the alleys and pried open the sky. Satiated with food and wine, the spectators stood in small groups mingling, stomping their feet, and backhanding their noses. Some dozed in the warmth of their cars, oblivious to Mme Dutertre, who galloped excitedly up and down the alleys projecting an image that she alone admired.

Vincent and Ragondin sat on the side of an elm tree protected from the wind and watched the Verdier brothers hold court next to the relay truck. In the distance Vincent recognized the sound of the estate Citroën and stood up. The car came into view straining its springs, slipping in and out of ruts, and scattering bystanders into ditches.

"In the name of God," Ragondin said, "she's going to kill someone."

Vincent waved. The car stopped and the window flap on the driver's side opened. François poked his long bird face out into the gloomy light.

"Vincent, the count wants to see you right away," he said.

"Where's Nicole?" Vincent looked inside the car. "What's wrong, François?"

"Never mind. Just put your bike in the trunk and get in so we can leave." Ragondin picked it up and placed it into the back with the front wheel propping the trunk lid open.

"I'll catch up with you later. Stay with them." Vincent said, nodding in the direction of the Verdiers.

He watched the assembly of hunters and spectators recede in the side mirror. Ragondin tentatively lifted his left hand to his shoulder and waved. Vincent felt intuitively that he and Nicole were in trouble. Then, from within the forest, he heard Labrissé's voice boom through the trees.

"Taïaut! Taïaut!" The whipper-in had spotted Monsieur and was urging the hounds on. Vincent stuck his head out the window and looked back. People, horses, and cars were scattering in every direction. The clamor of the pack receded into the distance. A lost deerhound ambled across the road, headed toward the commotion. François braked hard to miss it. Vincent was tempted to jump out and run back to the chase.

"François. What's going on?" he asked.

"I'm not sure."

"What do you mean?" Vincent looked in the butler's face but recognized only sorrow.

"They had a terrible fight in the library an hour ago.

Nicole ran up to her room crying and a few minutes later Count Robert told me to find you." François turned in his seat and said, "I heard you last night."

"What you heard doesn't concern you," Vincent said more sharply than he intended. He imagined the upcoming encounter with Count Robert and wondered if Nicole would be present. What would she say if the count forbade her to see him? In his heart he knew the answer: she would never go against her father's wishes.

"She's gone!" Vincent exclaimed when they crossed the moat into the courtyard and Nicole's Sunbeam was no longer there. He turned toward François for an explanation but the butler shook his head, parked the car, and walked into the servant's quarters of the castle without saying a word.

The curtains in the study were drawn and shadows shared the room with the light from the desk lamp. Robert de Costebelle looked old and bent and gray behind his desk. His right hand rested on the manuscript of his memoirs, which lay open on the leather desktop in front of him. Vincent stood cap in hand, his pulse beating against his temples, waiting. The room was so quiet it felt like night, when the smallest sound proclaims its importance. The count picked up a page of the manuscript and looked at Vincent.

"I'm sure you know why I sent for you. What happened last night has made it necessary for me to discuss certain matters concerning your life." Count Robert spoke slowly, without taking his eyes off Vincent's face.

"First and foremost, I want you to understand that I cannot and will not give you and Nicole my blessing." He paused and removed his reading glasses. "Not now. Not ever."

"Monsieur, I just want to say . . ." said Vincent, stepping closer to the table.

"Listen to me first. Then you may speak."

Count Robert held up a stack of manuscript pages and continued. "This is the story of my life. I began writing it shortly after the First World War and I expect to complete it in the near future. Though the timing is not as I had hoped, I'm compelled to read to you certain passages from it now."

But Vincent had no interest in anything that didn't include Nicole. "I love her, Monsieur. I love Nicole." The words poured from him.

Count Robert leaned forward so that his eyes moved out of the shadows into the light. They were withdrawn, with dark semicircles underneath. He seemed as pale and exhausted as he had at the cemetery the day Serge was buried. "I believe you, Vincent. But your love for Nicole cannot be as you want it. Now sit down and listen."

"You don't understand. Nicole loves me, too," said Vincent, defiant. "We'll leave Merlecourt if we have to."

The count looked at Vincent and recognized his passion. It was sorrow, however, that filled his voice when he said, "I don't know if it is God's will, if it is fate, or if it is happenstance, but nature always follows its own path. If you two are meant to be together, you will. But not with my blessing. You cannot have that."

"Does Nicole care about your blessing?" Vincent knew it was wrong to question the count, but he couldn't stop himself.

"Nicole is angry and hurt, and said she was moving back to America, and that she never wants to see me or Merlecourt again. For now, I believe her. She is a strong-willed young woman, who we both know does exactly as she pleases. But I also believe that in time she will return. Merlecourt is her home. She belongs here."

Count Robert nodded toward the couch and Vincent sat down. He leaned forward with his elbows on his knees and his head in his hands. The count put on his glasses and pointed to the upper righthand corner of a page.

"I wrote this in London on September 1, 1943," he said.

Vincent wanted to tell the count that he didn't care about his life story, that only Nicole mattered.

"'Perhaps it was presumptuous of me to think that my presence could affect the lives of my people,'" the count read, "'but I hope that my daily visits to the citizens of the valley of Merlecourt were helpful. In these times of war, my duty was to my people and, in the beginning, I did what I felt was right. A benign sense of autocracy motivated my actions; I wanted the village to feel my presence, to know that I was there for them, if needed. I believe that in a small way I was successful. A year later, however, my motivation changed from a sense of responsibility to one of desire. I developed a private reason for my outings, and as a result will undoubtedly regret the consequences of my actions for the rest of my life.'"

Count Robert pushed his glasses down on the bridge of his nose and looked at Vincent from over the rims. "What I wrote back in 1943 is not correct, Vincent. I want you to remember this conversation and know that I have never been sorry for my behavior back then, and I have not ever regretted the outcome."

Vincent, who had not been listening but instead was thinking about what he was going to say after the reading was finished, was caught off guard when the count looked at him. "I will certainly remember this day for the rest of my life," he said under his breath.

The count nodded and pushed his glasses back into place and resumed reading. "'I don't know when she started following me, but suddenly the girl was behind every tree, in doorways, around corners . . . everywhere. I knew who she was, of course, but whenever I visited her parents' farm she was absent. The only time I'd spoken to her was ten years earlier, at her First Communion.

"'My wife and son were back in England and I was flattered and charmed by this lovely girl of seventeen whose wide brown eyes followed me wherever I went. She was brighter than all the other girls in the valley and delicate in her movements, like a fawn. I should have approached her then and ended it quickly, but I didn't, and without a word uttered on either part our game of hide-and-seek went on for days. As the Occupation of France and the castle dragged on, so did my infatuation. Her presence became more important than the visits to my people—visits that I curtailed to be alone with my elusive shadow.

"'One afternoon, after following me back from Rebours at her customary distance, she vanished.

Without hesitating, I turned back and went looking for her. I found her picking flowers on the edge of an immense alfalfa field. When she saw me she waved and walked to where the grass was high and swallows dipped out of a summer sky.

"'I sat next to this girl in the middle of a field that was the size of an ocean and held my breath while I waited for her to speak. In a voice that was as natural and beautiful as the flowers she held, she turned her back to me and said, "Brush my hair."

"'I fell in love that afternoon—in love with a girl who I learned was terrified by the odious presence of war and the uncertainty of her future. What this young woman wanted was to be cherished and reassured by a man she could trust. The consequences of the Occupation and what it had done to her world terrified her. She mistook my outings for bravery and my understanding with the Germans for power, and even though she never said so, my caresses calmed her and my words restored her confidence. She fell in love with the notion of gratitude, and I fell in love with her innocence.'"

The count fell silent and Vincent watched as he turned a dozen pages of the manuscript without looking up. He read silently to himself for a while and then pushed his glasses back down his nose and looked at Vincent again.

"Here we are. Are you listening to me, Vincent?"

"I am, Monsieur," replied Vincent, now torn between the story and his intent to defend his feelings for Nicole.

"'I should have been grateful and had the insight to realize that our paths would cross but briefly. The more demanding I became, the less favorably she responded. I suspect that having won me it didn't take her long to recognize the weakness in my character, and from there, the futility of our relationship. Had I been twenty I would have showered her with promises. But I wasn't twenty, or even thirty, and I have since learned that women, even young ones, recognize these elemental weaknesses better than men. So it was that I lost her as I found her. One day she simply wasn't there, and forty-eight hours later I left for England.'"

Count Robert put the pages down on the desk, removed his glasses, and looked up. "Vincent," he said in a low, deliberate voice, "the girl I loved that summer was your mother."

Vincent looked at the count without flinching, determined not to avert his eyes. The clock on the mantle struck four o'clock, and through the carillon of bells he heard the count say, "Vincent, you are my son."

Vincent stared at the man in front of him until he vanished and was replaced by a long afternoon shadow passing over a green ocean, in the middle of which a tall man was brushing his mother's hair. She was so young then, two years younger than he was now, and so beautiful. He saw them together in love in the woods, in the fields, in the castle, in the very room he was sitting in now.

Suddenly, the years of being publicly and privately condemned as a German bastard were lifted from him, and for an instant Vincent's heart swelled with joy. He felt weightless and free of burdens and shame. But when he closed his eyes he remembered the count sitting in the castle nursery with Nicole on his knees. Then came the images of what he and Nicole had almost done the night before, and the promise of what was to happen between them that night.

Later Vincent would realize that his passion for her had begun to erode the moment the man in front of him uttered the word "father." Nothing anyone could ever do or say would carry enough weight to dismiss the fact that Nicole was his sister. "I ask you, Monsieur," said Vincent as he stood up. "Would you have told me all this if what you think happened last night had not?"

Count Robert closed the manuscript and placed it

on the side of the desk. "No. I would not have told you until your twenty-first birthday."

Vincent walked to the bookshelf and fingered the spine of the medical volumes that triggered the latch to the underground passageway. "So this secret, this lie that has cost me the respect of everyone in the valley, not to mention my self-esteem, for all these years, didn't really bother you until now—until you thought I was sleeping with my sister? That must explain why you stood by and watched me being treated as a bastard without once coming to my defense. It explains how you could send me back to my mother's family, where I almost died of grief. And later, to boarding school, where I endured the insults and loathing of my schoolmates. Did you assume I would take it like a man because I am your son?"

"Think what you want, Vincent," said the count, lighting a cigarette. "But you would not have known Roland or Nicole, or the fine surroundings you grew up with, had you not been my blood. You have had a good life and are assured a better future. I did what I thought was best, and I certainly didn't foresee what happened between you and Nicole. Had I guessed, I would have told you sooner. Perhaps it is my fault and certainly I am sorry, but I cannot reshape history. I can only explain it and hope you accept it."

The count sat back in the chair and his face receded into the shadows. The glow of his cigarette grew brighter. It struck Vincent as odd that Count Robert's voice was not that of a guilty man, a man asking for forgiveness. Where was the remorse, the sorrow? It seemed that, on the contrary, the count's tone had grown stronger, as though by telling Vincent the truth of his birth he was absolving himself from the guilt associated with a difficult episode from his past.

Vincent turned from the books and looked at the count's frail shape in the chair. He thought about Roland's death, and the rumors of the count and countess adopting him, and the nights he had spent dreaming of being a part of the Costebelle family. How different his life would have been had the man in front of him told him the truth then.

"You often say that honor is all you have left," Vincent said, standing in front of the desk. "Was it honorable to let me grow up believing I was the son of a German, a *boche*, the pigs who stole our country, occupied your home? Is honor a commodity to be harvested by some and not by others?" A surge of self-righteousness rose in Vincent's throat. "The man who really taught me about honor died clean, like the earth he gave his life to protect."

"Sit down, Vincent," said Count Robert leaning forward in his chair and stubbing out his cigarette in an ashtray. Vincent obeyed in the same manner he had obeyed his Jesuit teachers at school.

"This memoir tells of the choices I made and expresses the feelings I had for those people who were and are important to me. When I die you and Nicole will read it and, I hope, understand why I chose not to tell you about your mother until now." He paused and then continued. "I have remembered you in my will, Vincent. A legacy awaits that will assure you a comfortable life." The count sat back in his chair and the darkness swallowed him once again.

Vincent felt the anger rise in his chest. Did he think that a legacy would heal the past? Did he believe that money would make things right?

"Tell me," said Vincent standing to leave. "How did you feel about my mother working as your maid? Was it your conscience that hired her? Did you ever talk to her about your son? Did the countess know?"

"That's enough, Vincent," Count Robert said. "I won't be questioned by you or by anyone else who uses that tone of voice. I have apologized for withholding facts about your life. For that I am grievously sorry. But I do not regret my actions and I will not apologize to anyone for them. I love you and I loved your mother and she loved me for one brief summer a long time ago. I don't have to justify that memory to anyone. In fact, I celebrate it."

Vincent turned to leave but the count raised a hand. "Wait," the count's voice softened as his eyes searched Vincent's. "Of course your mother and I talked. She knew that I would take care of you, as did Serge. They knew what I was giving you and when you would receive it. And they agreed with me that it shouldn't happen until either I was dead or you were twenty-one." He stopped talking then and placed his hands on the manuscript.

"I want you to listen very carefully to what I am going to say next," said the count. "I love Nicole with all my heart. She is my daughter, but in many ways she takes after her mother, who is headstrong and spoiled. She is also fickle and as such would have eventually discarded you like one of her stuffed animals. As difficult as it is for you to understand it now, when this is over you will have gained a sister. And rest assured that the love of a sister is worth all the lovers in the world."

Vincent didn't want to gain a sister. He wanted Nicole as he had wanted her the night before.

"What does she say about all of this?"

"That she hates me."

Vincent turned and walked to the library door. Baudelaire stood next to Villon, Rimbaud next to Chateaubriand. Vincent asked the man in the shadows, "Who am I?"

"You are Vincent Lebuison," the count said.

"That's what I thought." Vincent closed the door behind him.

Chapter 24

Vincent gripped the steering wheel of the Citroën with one hand and wiped the tears streaming down his face with the sleeve of his shirt. "Damn him! I don't want to be his son," he yelled, beating his free fist against the dash. "What have I done to you, God, to treat me like this?" he screamed out the window.

He passed the water garden and Jules's grave, the weathered *solitaire*, and a few minutes later crossed the bridge leading to the mill. Nicole's Sunbeam was parked under the plane tree. Then she was running out of the mill toward him, calling his name. Vincent got out and took her in his arms. When their bodies touched she shivered and stepped away.

"No," she said. "We can't." But then she stepped back to him. He stroked the hair away from her damp face with his fingers.

"Nicole, Nicole," he said softly and tried to kiss her. She turned her face.

"Please, Vincent, we cannot be together that way again. It isn't right." She leaned away from him and looked into his eyes. "How do I to go from being in love with you to being your sister?" She buried her face in his chest. "I feel that half of you is being torn from my body."

"I don't want a sister," he said holding her tight against him. "I want to kiss your stomach and touch your breasts."

"Oh, Jesus! Vincent, that's incest!" Nicole pushed him away again and looked at his face, frowning.

He gazed at the loveliness of her features and for the first time recognized in the shape of her face his own. The resemblance astonished him and he wondered how they could have known each other for so many years without seeing themselves in each other's eyes.

"Stay here with me," Vincent said reaching for her hand. "Just for a while."

"I can't be alone with you right now," she said, tears forming in her eyes. "Just the thought of last night feels queer. You are my brother."

Vincent knew then that she would never change her mind. Her love for him had changed and was even now exploring new dimensions. He could feel her drifting, embracing the inevitable relationship that would govern the rest of their lives.

"How could Count Robert do this to us?" he asked.

"You mean our father, Vincent," she said forcefully. "Robert de Costebelle is our father."

They stood holding each other for a time, trying to sort out the mystery of their existence while a quiet despondency sailed over them, dragging the last vestiges of their physical desires into the grayness of reality.

"Vincent," she finally said. "I know I'm not supposed to say this, but I will remember us together as we were last night all my life, and when I want to think of something beautiful, I will think of you." She looked at him, wanting to be reassured of their innocence.

"I remember us together right now," he said, his eyes searching hers. "I don't know how else to think of you."

Vincent watched her expression slowly change from one of confusion to one of control. From his weakness she was gathering courage, and leaving him behind.

She put her arms around his neck and kissed his cheek. "We will learn to accept each other as brother and sister. We have a long life to live together." He held her but didn't resist when she moved away and walked to the Sunbeam. She started the engine and leaned out the window. Her eyes overflowed with tears.

"Maybe what our father did wasn't so terrible after all. We are finally the family you always wanted us to be."

Vincent watched her car until it disappeared behind the trees and then he kicked the door of the Citroën shut. Then he kicked it again, harder, and screamed until his face turned red and his throat ached. Ode barked from inside the mill and he went to her.

He sat down on the floor next to his dog, feeling the comfort and warmth of her uncomplicated love. He listened to the familiar sounds of the river and the wind passing through the trees, and then he looked at the boar's head over the mantle, the worn armchairs, the books on the shelf above Serge's bed, and his own shotgun standing in a corner of the fireplace.

"My legacy!" he said.

Ode moved away from him and stood at the door with her ears perked.

"What is it, girl?" He got up and opened the door. Ode ran toward the sluice gates and he heard the sound of a French horn. He tracked the melody up the hill to the forest and recognized Dutertre's horn ordering the hounds back to the kennel. Monsieur had once again eluded him.

Dizzy and confused, Vincent felt a wave of nausea rise in his throat. He ran to the kitchen sink and cradled his head in his arms and watched, with a certain detachment, as images of his past swirled down the drain. He saw Serge stiff and naked on a marble slab, the countess cradling Roland's head next to the fountain, his mother glowing under the cycloptic eye of a steel monster. He felt lightheaded. When he looked out the kitchen window he thought he saw Serge and Jules. He ran cold water, washed the sickness from his mouth, and looked again. Ode and Ragondin were running toward him.

"Monsieur's in the Roberta Woods!" Ragondin yelled as he ran into the mill. "Come quick!"

"What for?" said Vincent, who only wanted to be left alone.

"What the hell's the matter with you?" Ragondin said in disbelief. "Didn't you hear me? Monsieur's on the property!"

Ragondin reached for the bottle of wine on the kitchen table and drank a third of it without taking a breath. A gust of wind carried the distant sound of a gunshot through the door. They looked at each other.

Vincent grabbed his shotgun and they ran out the door. "I heard the horns signaling the end of the hunt. Who's shooting? Labrissé? Dutertre?" The wind filled his jacket. The cold found his skin.

"I told you! Monsieur tricked the pack." Ragondin turned and faced Vincent at the car. "The dogs lost him in the hills above the river. But Titi and Gros-Louis knew he would head to the Roberta Woods. They must have shot him. Or tried to."

Ragondin got into the passenger seat, cursing and flailing his arms. Ode jumped in the back. Vincent worked the gears and drove as fast as the Citroën allowed.

"Where have you been?" Ragondin asked, looking at him. "Jesus, what's the matter? You look like you're ready to puke."

"I've already done that. Nicole's gone."

"Ah, shit. I knew something was wrong when François drove you away. I'm sorry."

"Me, too," Vincent said suddenly resigned. "What happened in the forest after I left?"

"The hounds flushed Monsieur along with four does and a spike. They jumped out of a bog next to the lake. Monsieur ran alongside the young buck for twenty minutes and when the pack had the scent of both stags firmly in their noses, he slipped away. The dogs picked the wrong trail but Titi and Louis figured it out and waited for him on the hilltop. I could see the brothers when Monsieur swam the river and crossed the fields to the Roberta Woods. The Verdiers came in through the front gates, so I took the shortcut through Rebours to the mill. They must have waited until Dutertre called the dogs off and then used the shotgun that Labrissé keeps in the relay truck."

"Goddamn! I should have been with you."

Vincent drove down the dirt road that led to the fallen oak tree overlooking the field where Serge had been murdered. Dusk was falling under the cloud layer and the woods had turned gray. He parked the Citroën short of the trees and they got out.

"Wait! Wait a minute," Ragondin said, grabbing Vincent's arm. "What are we going to do? You just can't run up to them and start shooting."

"I will if they've killed Monsieur." Vincent loaded the shotgun and walked quickly, with Ode at heel, to the verge of the woods.

"At least let me lead," Ragondin said, catching up and holding on to his coat.

Vincent stopped and turned. "All right. I'll cover you."

The wind swirled in the high branches and covered the sound of their boots on the leaves. In the fading light the underbrush took on the color of the shotgun barrel. A cock pheasant crowed from inside the aviary, the shrill call provoking a flutter of fear in the pit of Vincent's stomach.

They heard the brothers' voices before they saw the truck parked in the middle of the roundabout. The Verdiers stood off to one side, swearing at each other. The hounds locked in the cab of the truck paced and growled and jumped up on the truck's panels, enflamed by the sweet, cloying smell of innards and blood. Vincent looked over the hood and saw the deer's head on the ground next to a sapling two meters inside the woods. The stag's tremendous antlers were lost in the branches. His tongue hung large and pink and grotesque out of the corner of his mouth. Monsieur was dead.

Ragondin imagined the stag's legs buckling when the shotgun slug found its mark. He visualized Titi sticking the knife into his neck, laughing and carrying on, working the blade between the vertebrae until Monsieur's head fell off, slowly, like a rotten limb.

The brothers bent over the carcass, their arms bloodied to the elbows from butchering Monsieur. One of the hounds howled and Vincent reached for Ode, but he was too late and she growled. An explosion of noise erupted from the truck and the Verdiers turned toward the commotion. Gros-Louis reached for his whip and stepped forward, his left hand wrapped around Monsieur's heart.

Crazed from imagining the death of the great red stag, Ragondin jumped out from behind the truck, screaming at the top of his lungs. "You sons of bitches. What have you done?"

Vincent remained hidden behind the truck, waiting his turn, his heart pounding.

"Well, well, little man, did you enjoy the hunt?" said Gros-Louis, grinning. He pointed to the mound of guts lying on top of the hide next to the carcass. "Just think, after all these years, after all those hunters came from all over France, me and Titi got him. How do you like that?"

Gros-Louis snaked the dog whip so that it lay in front of him and laughed as he raised Monsieur's heart above his head. "I have something for you," he said to Ragondin. "Something that will give you strength, so the next time you screw my woman she won't complain."

"Wait!" said Titi. He sidestepped his brother, thrusting his knife up and down in his right hand, his eyes open and wild. "Let me have him, Louis. I want to bleed him."

"No," growled Gros-Louis, pushing him away. "He's mine!" He stared at Ragondin and squeezed Monsieur's heart until his fingers met and blood dripped on his head and ran down his face. "See what I am going to do to you, you deformed little monkey." He threw the heart on the ground.

"Please, Louis, let me do it," Titi stammered. He grimaced with painful longing.

"Quiet! You can carve him up afterward. Blood is what gets your prick hard. What do you care if he's dead? The blood will still be in him." Gros-Louis stepped forward and cracked the whip. The sound ran like a rifle shot through the woods.

"Okay, but do it slowly," said Titi licking his lips in anticipation.

Vincent stepped out from behind the truck, raised the gun, and thumbed the safety. Gros-Louis hunched his shoulders and Titi fell into a crouch behind him. The hounds ceased howling and silence fell over the clearing as though a lid had been dropped over the woods. Ode sat and watched.

Twilight tumbled quickly from branch to branch until it reached the earth and died. Monsieur's eyes, visible one moment, disappeared the next. The only proof of his whereabouts was the steam rising from his carcass.

"Drop the knife, Titi, and lie face down in front of your brother," said Vincent. When Titi hesitated he aimed the shotgun at his head. "Believe me, I'd be happy to shoot your fucking face off if you don't do as I say." Titi cursed, sat on the ground, and tossed his knife on the leaves in front of him. Ragondin went over and picked it up, and then went to find a flashlight in the truck.

"What are you going to do?" asked Titi.

"Never mind. Lay on your stomach and put your hands behind your back."

Ragondin returned with the light and stood to one side, shining it from one brother's face to the other.

"Your turn, Louis," said Vincent. "Get down on your knees and tie Titi's wrists with your whip."

Gros-Louis did as he was told and then turned and stared at Vincent, a grimace on his face. Vincent stepped closer and lowered the gun barrel so that it grazed his forehead. "Turn over," he said.

"Screw you."

"You tell him, brother," yelled Titi.

Ragondin knelt next to Gros-Louis and rested the knife on his cheek so that the tip of the blade lay on the side of Gros-Louis's nose. "Do what he says."

Gros-Louis growled and spat in his face. Ragondin drew the blade back and blood followed. The big man cursed and turned over. Ragondin tied him with his belt and knotted his shoelaces to his brother's.

They sat in the truck with Ode between them. Where the sky fell through the hole in the trees to the roundabout there was a memory of light. Beyond that, where Monsieur's head lay on a carpet of leaves, it was pitch black. Vincent rolled down the window and listened to the brothers grunting and swearing, twisting their bindings and rolling over onto their backs, struggling to get free.

"Now what?" Ragondin asked, shaping and licking a corn-paper cigarette.

"Go home," said Vincent.

"What do you mean? You expect me to leave after I've come this far? I don't think so." Ragondin lit the cigarette, turned in the seat, and faced his friend.

Vincent didn't have a plan, because as often as he had dreamed about avenging his uncle, he had never really seen himself pull the trigger. "I have to kill them, Ragondin. But I don't want you here. Go back to the mill."

"Are you out of your goddamn mind? It's over! There's nothing more to do except turn them in." The cigarette in Ragondin's mouth shook as he spoke.

Vincent didn't answer. Under the circumstances he wasn't sure how honor worked. All he knew was that Count Robert had not lived up to his rank, and he didn't want to be like him. Was killing his uncle's murderers more honorable than turning them in? In Serge's eyes it would be. But would his uncle want him to kill his murderers and go to jail for it? Vincent moved and fidgeted in the seat of the truck.

With the brothers bound and lying on the ground, shooting them was going to be impossible. He should have shot them earlier, when they had been about to kill

Ragondin. Merde de merde, he thought, I can't do it. He hated his limitations, his weaknesses. He wanted to be Serge.

Ragondin put out the cigarette and rested his chin on his chest. Steam formed on the windowpanes of the cab. He was silent for awhile, and then he turned to Vincent.

"I've helped you from the start. I tracked Monsieur to Greenhead Lake, I went to the Verdier farm and found the gun, I followed Monsieur here while you were puking in the sink. Tell me. Don't you owe me something?"

"Trust me, Ragondin."

"Come on. Let's call Corneille."

"I'm staying here. You go call him."

"If I do, will you swear not to kill them?"

Vincent looked out the side window, away from the Verdiers and Monsieur, away from everything that had happened to him since he and Nicole had been together in her bedroom, and he knew that what he wanted most was to be alone. He wanted to call a truce with his past and the events of the present. He was tired of talking and tired of listening. All he wanted was to be with Ode.

"All right. I swear." Vincent looked at the brothers on the ground and knew that if he killed them Nicole would never forgive him.

Ragondin walked to the tree line and stopped when he heard Vincent get out of the truck. Gros-Louis's voice rose from the ground.

"We've been lying here for an hour," he said, making himself sound friendly. "It's cold, Vincent, and we're hurting. Come on, man. We all went to school together, for God's sake! I'm sorry about Monsieur. He's worth a lot of money. You can have it all but you have to untie us."

"Tell me about Serge," said Vincent, turning the flashlight on and pointing it at the brothers.

Gros-Louis didn't answer. The blood from Monsieur's heart had congealed in his hair but the blood from Ragondin's knife cut was still running. Vincent kicked him in the head, just as he had kicked Ragondin years before, except a lot harder. This time it was done without shame. Gros-Louis grunted. Titi rolled on his side and stared, wide eyed, into the light.

"Just wait," he screamed. "I swear on my mother's grave that the next time I see you I'm going to carve your eyes out."

Vincent went and picked up Monsieur's head by the antlers and propped it on the hood of the truck. He angled it so that the dead, opaque eyes looked down on the brothers. Then he rested the palm of his hand on Monsieur's forehead and made a small sign of the cross with his thumb between the stag's eyes.

He jumped when he heard the door of the truck open. Someone turned the headlights on, shining them on the brothers and lighting up the roundabout. Étienne Verdier eased himself away from the driver's door and stood holding Labrissé's shotgun in one hand and his French horn in the other.

"Papa! Get us out of here," Titi cried out.

Étienne looked at his sons without expression. He turned from one to the other and slowly shook his head. "What you don't know," he said without emotion, "is that I was working late the night you killed Serge, and for weeks now I've lived with the sounds of your crime. I can still see you driving across the stubble field with Serge's hand trapped in the door. Every minute I'm alive I hear your laughter above his screams and I pray for the police to arrest you." He turned to Vincent.

"I'm sorry I didn't tell you or the authorities," Étienne said. "I couldn't bring myself to inform on my own sons, but I was wrong. Terribly wrong. Forgive me. Now that they've killed Monsieur, I am responsible for his death as well."

"What are you doing here?" Vincent said.

"I have obligations," said Étienne in a weighted voice.

"You insane old bastard," said Titi.

"I heard what you said earlier, Vincent," said Étienne. "I want you to know that I wouldn't have let you kill them and ruin your life." He put his big, callused hand on Vincent's shoulder. "It'd be better if you left now." The moon found an opening in the clouds and a splinter of light pinpointed the clearing.

Étienne carefully put his French horn and the gun on the ground and then walked over to the remains of Monsieur. Stiff, and grimacing with pain, he stretched out the skinned hide and placed the mound of guts on top. Then he rolled the entrails up in the pelt and, with great effort, carried it to where his sons lay. The bundle was awkward to handle and just as he reached them it slipped from his arms and fell. The old man followed it right down to his knees and plunged his hands into the stag's intestines.

Vincent looked on, fascinated by Étienne's actions. The innards looked warm, almost reassuring. Vincent closed his eyes. He felt strange and a little excited. The stench of excrement pulled him out of his trance. Gros-Louis stared in horror as his father picked up Monsieur's stomach and threw it on Titi's face.

"Stop it, old man!" yelled Gros-Louis.

"Leave me with my sons, Vincent. Go to Ragondin," said Étienne without taking his eyes off his boys.

The stag's stomach wrapped itself around Titi's face then slipped off and lay huge and quivering next to his head. Titi screamed and tried to pull away, his breathing coming in short, hard bursts. The brothers tangled in each other, rolled apart, and reared away from the wet, gray stomach, ending up on top of each other. Étienne picked up the rest of the offal and threw it on his sons, piece by piece. When he was finished, he covered them with Monsieur's hide, up to their necks.

Vincent walked beyond the range of the headlights into the darkness of the trees. Ragondin joined him and Ode sat between them. They watched from the woods. Suddenly Étienne's action made sense. This was the prelude to the fleshing of the hounds. Verdier was going to feed his boys and Monsieur's guts to the dogs. The hounds that ran the stag would devour the men who killed it.

"Papa, why are you doing this?" asked Gros-Louis, his voice pleading.

"Because you revolt me. You hastened your mother's death and disgraced her memory by bringing a street whore to live in her home. You are of less value to me than the shit I throw on your faces."

Titi shook his head back and forth, spitting and choking. "All right! I'm sorry, father, but stop . . . I'm begging you." Gros-Louis rolled over and inadvertently pushed his brother back into the stag's guts. Titi started screaming and didn't stop.

Étienne fetched Titi's whip from the cab and went to the back of the truck. He slipped the latch and the dogs leapt out of the cargo hold in a single, purposeful wave of brown-and-white bodies.

The hounds moved toward the hide and Étienne cracked his whip to stop them. A quiver ran from their noses to their tails. Over Titi's screams he shouted the pack to attention and shaped them into a semicircle behind him. Monsieur's scent, which had been in their heads since morning, maddened them. The bolder ones took to baying. Étienne led the dogs around the truck and stopped them on the far side of his sons. Gros-Louis begged while the pack snarled and fought and edged forward.

When the sound of the pleading was replaced by the furor of the dogs, and when the resonance of death filled the woods so completely that there was room for nothing else, Étienne closed his eyes, raised his horn, and blew the first bars of "Requiem for the Dead." Then he slowly pulled back Monsieur's hide, stepped aside to release the hounds, and returned to the music.

Vincent and Ragondin stood close together and observed the frenzy. They looked at Monsieur's head and antlers outlined in the moonlight and listened as the sounds of the screams faded and the woods filled with the noise of feeding hounds. When it was over, Vincent called Ode. But she wouldn't come, and instead cowered and howled. The two friends turned and walked away though the woods, waiting for the sound of the shot that would end Étienne's life. When it came, Vincent sensed Ode behind him, and felt a cold nose nudge his hand.

Epilogue

On a cold February morning in the year 2002 a tall middle-aged woman wearing a green loden coat walked across a wooden bridge that led to an old paper mill. The freezing temperatures of the previous night had raised patches of ice on the oak planks. Sheets of fog lifted off the river and she emerged through them as an apparition. The church bells in the village summoned parishioners to Sunday Mass.

He met her at the front door and she touched her cold cheek to his, explaining as she stepped inside that she had heard him shooting in the woods next to the farm and decided to come early. He helped with her coat and she glanced up at his weathered face, raising her hands to the bun of auburn-colored hair on the back of her neck.

She walked to the hearth and savored the warmth of the fire. He followed the faintness of her perfume, and admired the fullness of her hips. The woman was unhappy with the way her body had changed over the years, but he didn't mind, in fact he treasured the progress of her womanhood.

"You are a fine wine," he said.

"What wine am I?" she smiled conspiratorially.

"Champagne, of course: La Grande Dame."

"And you?"

"A knotty old Cahors."

He left her in front of the fire and went to the kitchen, where he had been peeling shallots.

"Would you like coffee?"

She nodded, and then joined him at the sink where she picked up one of the wood pigeons he had shot that morning behind the Verdier farm. She studied the bird and smoothed the down on its breast with the tips of her fingers.

"Last night I dreamt about Roland digging up my dog to dissect it," she said. "That was over forty years ago . . . but it feels like yesterday." The pigeon's head slipped through her fingers and a kernel of corn trapped inside a bubble of blood fell from its bill.

"Oh, merde," she said, and dropped the bird.

He handed her a towel and picked the pigeon up off the floor, adjusting its crop with his thumb. A thick pouch of grain moved from one side of its craw to the other. The bird had fed that morning in advance of its long flight to the wintering grounds of Morocco. She searched her clothes for stains but there were none, and she relaxed while he filled the kettle with water and lit the stove.

Though she had been in the mill hundreds of times, she always made a tour of the rooms, to touch with her eyes those things that brought back memories of their years together. She looked at the moth-eaten mount of the head of a royal red stag hanging over the fireplace, the cardboard picture book of Merlecourt in his library, his reading glasses on a sideboard next to an open copy of Guy de Maupassant's *Les Contes de la Bécasse*. On the wall above the table were framed photographs of his uncle, their father, and Ragondin Artaban. From habit her eyes went to a black-and-white photograph of two young men with their arms around each other. She placed a finger on the tack holding the picture and smiled. The faces, laughing into the camera, validated the uncomplicated eagerness of youth, oblivious to the fact that the ears on either side of their faces stuck out like artichoke leaves.

"Have you heard from him?" she asked.

"His letters are still postmarked from the Pyrénées, but he says that by spring he'll be home."

He poured the coffee and added milk and sugar to hers, his hands concealing for a moment the porcelain cup he saved for her visits.

"Ragondin's in love with the mountains," she said looking surprised.

"He says that in December the sun paints the snow blue but that the winters are too cold, a little like you."

"He's always felt that way," she said.

"Not really. He wrote that he misses you and me and Normandy."

"I didn't sleep well last night," she said, not wanting to discuss Ragondin. "Do you mind if I rest before we have lunch?"

"No, of course not. I like watching you sleep."

He added Calvados to his coffee and thought about the hunting that morning. How the pigeons had flown in low, skimming the tree tops above the ground fog on their return to roost. He had been waiting for them in a stand built high in the canopy of an oak tree, and on separate occasions aimed at their eyes, dropping four.

"They feel like gravestones," she said, poking one of the birds.

"They won't after I braise them with shallots. Go to sleep. I'll wake you when lunch is ready."

She went to his bed and lay down on top of the covers, her face a cameo against the white pillow. He turned from her and looked out the window to where the Eure ran under the bridge. For centuries the river had carried the clean dark earth of plowed fields; added to it now were the grass trimmings from putting greens and the excavated debris of future fairways.

Three years had passed since she had sold the castle and seven hundred hectares to an international conglomerate. The sale had paid off the debts she'd incurred over twenty years of Socialism and high taxes. All that remained of the original estate were the renovated Verdier farm, where she lived, and the mill, which had been bequeathed to him.

The first floor of the castle now served as a clubhouse and restaurant, and the upper floors had been transformed into corporate offices. During the week the sound of bulldozers and trucks in the valley was loud.

On his last visit Ragondin had begged them to follow him to the mountains. "There," he said, "the wind blows cleanly through the trees and on summer nights young girls dance in the meadows with their hands in the air." But the woman would not leave the land she had lived on for half a century, and when she refused to move, as they both knew she would, Ragondin's resolve weakened.

The man plucked a brace of birds and looked at her fondly on his bed. She was breathing peacefully. He smiled at her sleeping face, seeing after all those years a girl as young and dreamy as ever.

When the woman woke she said that she had dreamt about their father and their brother and the island where they played as children.

They ate lunch and the pigeons were as tender as he'd promised they would be. She raised her glass as a compliment to his cooking and her smile was elegant in its enigmatic secrecy. They drank coffee. Afterward he walked her as far as the sluice gates, where he kissed her cheeks and watched her cross the bridge and walk away.